FORGIVING MaXIMO ROTHMAN

by A J Sidransky

Berwick Court Publishing
Chicago, IL

Berwick Court Publishing Company
Chicago, Illinois
http://www.berwickcourt.com

Cover design by Beth Zagoria

Sidransky, A. J.
  Forgiving Maximo Rothman / by A.J. Sidransky.

  p. ; cm.

  ISBN: 978-0-9889540-0-7

  1. Jewish refugees--Dominican Republic--Fiction. 2. Jewish refugees--New York (State)—New York--Fiction. 3. Murder--New York (State)--New York--Fiction. 4. Jews--Fiction. 5. Fathers and sons--Fiction. 6. Detective and mystery stories. I. Title.

PS3619.I37 F67 2013
813/.6   2013932360

To my father, you were better at it than I ever knew.
To my son, I hope I was as good at it as I thought.

Acknowledgments

First and foremost, I want to thank my wife for providing me the opportunity to write this book. It is the culmination of a dream that began more than forty years ago. Your patience, love and understanding helped bring it to reality.

This book is the result of my interactions with many people over many years. In particular I want to mention my uncle and aunt, Max and Helen Grunfeld, who in their moment of terror stood up to be counted. Their life in Europe was turned upside down by people and events well beyond their control.

Alone and adrift in Italy, they became agricultural settlers in Sosúa, a tiny settlement on the north coast of the Dominican Republic. Ultimately, approximately 850 refugees from Nazism were saved by the generosity of the Dominican Republic. The story told here of Sosúa is fictional in terms of its characters, but I hope a bit of the life of the settlers, and of the debt they owed the Dominican natives who helped them survive, comes through.

I would like to extend a special thanks to my Dominican friends. You've taken me into your lives and your culture in a way I never thought possible. When you whisper to me "tú eres un morenito como nosotros," it touches my heart very deeply. For you there is no color and there is no distinction by religion. Americans could learn much from you. I particularly want to thank my dear friend, "mi hermano de alma," William Cruz. You don't realize how much you've changed my life. You make me a better man every day. You're in here,

"Pa," on just about every page.

A special thanks to the Rodriguez family of El Condé Steak House. I wrote much of this book sitting in your restaurant after eating lunch. Your Dominican home cooking and music, and your good humor and encouragement, nurtured this book. Good luck with your new restaurant. I will be a regular. I expect to write my next book there.

Much thanks and a deeply felt indebtedness to my Publisher and Editor, Matt and Dave Balson. You made my book a much better book and that's because you "got it." Thank you for recognizing my work and believing in me enough to take a chance on publishing my work. A special thanks to Jeffrey Maduro for helping to edit the Spanish phrases and ensuring they are "pura Dominicana." Thanks to Miriam Edelstein for contributing your keen eyes and broad knowledge base to our final proof. Much thanks to Beth Zagoria, my friend of more than 30 years who designed the cover. It meant a great deal to me that you did this.

Additional thanks to the many people who have read all or part of this work throughout its development but in particular my cousin, Fred Miller for his support and encouragement. Also to Michelle Roberts, Doug Robbins and Anthony Bloomfield and to Gotham Writers' Workshop of Manhattan without whom I never would have realized my dream of becoming a writer.

I would also like to mention a woman I met some years ago through my synagogue. Her name is Larissa Perchevsky. She and I are of the same vintage. She came to this country as a refugee from the Soviet Union. I was fortunate enough to be born here. One day we got to chatting and I told her how I had been actively involved as a teenager in the fight to free Soviet Jewry, as were many of my peers. Her eyes lit up and she smiled. I asked her why and she responded with a question: Did I know how much good we had done and how much pressure we had put on the Soviet authorities? I answered her honestly that I didn't, and that my friends and I at the time didn't really think we had accomplished much at all. She told me we wouldn't be standing there together that day if we, my generation of Jews so affected by the Holocaust hadn't fought for them to prevent a second, cultural Holocaust.

I would also like to thank a man and his son whom I've never met. They live in my neighborhood. I've watched them together for the many years I've lived here from the time the son was a toddler. The man is a traditional orthodox Jew and is raising his son in a community that has been here since the 1930's, when his predecessors arrived here as refugees from Germany. The son has Down's Syndrome. I am and have been moved by the way this man, whose community which prizes nothing higher than intellectual prowess (except perhaps its children), values and loves this child. That fatherly love, pride and caring, is evident from blocks away to someone they have never known. To this man, I say thank you. You made me a better father.

This book is about fathers and sons and what we do to each other. I hope men will read it and think more about their fathers and their sons and the kind of fathers and sons they are, have been and can be.

A. J. Sidransky
Washington Heights, New York

1

María Leguenza walked briskly down Bennett Avenue, wrapping her brown cloth coat a little tighter against the chill in the autumn air. At 65, she was not as spry as she had been when she arrived in New York twenty years earlier. Men and women in somber dress rushed past her on either side. Tassels dangling from the men's clothing flew in their wake. The women, holding onto their wigs, dragged their straggling children while trying to keep up with the men.

She pulled the keys out of her bag at 105 Bennett Ave. The shiny new security doors proved difficult to maneuver. Juggling her pocketbook and her shopping bags, she opened the interior door to the lobby, nearly dropping the special treats she had brought for Señor Max: ripe plantains for maduros, pork chuletas and peppers, and a big slice of tres leches cake. She held the cake's plastic container tightly so the creamy liquid inside wouldn't spill.

Exhausted from the awkwardness of her arrival, she placed her packages on Señor Max's welcome mat and inserted her key into the top lock. She left her packages by the door and flicked a switch to light the hallway in front of her. "Señor Max," she called out. "Buenos tardes, estoy aquí."

There was no answer.

"Señor Max, dónde estás?" María called out a second time. Still no answer. "Señor Max?" She felt a tightness in the pit of her stomach. Her heart began to race. He was old, very old.

She walked down the hallway toward the dark bedroom. The rubber soles of her shoes squeaked against the wood floor. Perhaps he was sleeping? She turned on the light. He wasn't in the bed. It was unmade. Her heart now pounded in her chest. Turning back toward the bathroom, she noticed the light under the door. As she opened the door, the bright light from the fixture over the sink bounced off the white tile walls, momentarily blinding her. She blinked. Then saw him.

In the brightly lit vestibule of the synagogue on Bennett Avenue, Rachel Rothman's deft hands attempted to help her son remove his coat. "Baruch, my darling, help me help you," she said as he fought her attempts. Though he was 17, he was as difficult as a small child.

"Zay," Baruch kept repeating, struggling with the Yiddish word for grandfather. He pointed toward the heavy wooden doors of the synagogue each time they opened, making Rachel's efforts all the more difficult and nearly knocking her over, her slight frame no match for his long arms. She had to stop and respond to each "Good *yom tov**" she received from arriving congregants. "Yes, Zayde lives across the street," she replied with infinite patience acquired over years of disappointment.

"Zay," he repeated again, "Zay."

"Perhaps later, darling. Right now it's *yom tov*, we need to daven." She felt a hand on her shoulder and turned her head.

"Rachel," said Shalom from behind her, "he isn't ready yet? The service has begun, I have to go in."

"Just one more minute," she said, tugging at the black material, struggling

---

* *Yom tov*: Holiday (Hebrew)

to free up Baruch's extended arm.

"Then you take him upstairs with you," Shalom said, turning toward the sanctuary doors.

"You know I can't do that anymore," Rachel said, finally pulling the arm of Baruch's coat free. "He's too old to sit with the women. You have to wait a moment."

"HaShem doesn't wait," Shalom replied, adjusting the wide brim of his hat.

"Yes, He does." She straightened her dress, the gray flannel fabric smooth under her fingers.

Shalom took Baruch by the hand and led him into the sanctuary. He found two empty seats in the middle of a pew a few rows up from the back of the room. The service was in full swing, the congregants deeply focused on their prayers.

Shalom chanted with the congregation in near ecstasy. He loved the sound of the prayers: the timeless phrases floating up to HaShem, a supplication from his people, a plea for attention, for connection. Baruch stood to his left, nearly as tall, his beard finally growing in, though still scraggly in spots. He swayed along with his father, mimicking as Shalom had shown him. Shalom searched Baruch's face as he prayed. He saw the same blank expression as always. He wondered if the words had meaning to Baruch. Did his son know HaShem?

The voice of the congregation swelled as the men began dancing with the Torahs. They carried them down the aisle — the blue-, red- and green-velvet covers brilliant and shiny — out through the doors and into the street to dance with them in celebration. Shalom took Baruch's hand and led him out into the street to watch. As the men chanted and whirled, their fringes flying wildly in the cold night air, a scream came from the building across the street.

María grabbed the towel rack with one hand and muffled another shriek with the other. She saw the blood from Señor Max's head pooling slowly on the white tile floor. She backed out of the bathroom and began to cry. After a long moment, she steadied herself and looked back into the bathroom. She thought she saw Señor Max's body move slightly, as if he might still be breathing. She ran into the bedroom and grabbed the phone.

"911. What's your emergency?"

"Señor Max, he is on the floor in the bathroom…" She peaked into the bathroom, glimpsed blood and turned away.

"Is he breathing, ma'am?"

"I don't know." Her heart beat hard in her chest. "Dios mío, ayudame."

"Ma'am, can you go over to him and see if he's breathing?"

"No, no, I can't to go back in there. You just send the doctor, please. Hurry please, ay dios."

"OK ma'am, calm down. What unit are you in?"

"105 Bennett, 6C. Please, hurry, please."

Detective Anatoly Kurchenko stepped out of the elevator onto the sixth floor of 105 Bennett Ave. He looked around. He had been in this building many times over the years. His family moved to Washington Heights in the late 1970s. He'd had a girlfriend who lived on the third floor. The walls were still painted that same shade of beige. The insufficient lighting made the hallway appear even dingier than he remembered. He saw the stretcher at the end of the hall.

"You don't have a sheet over him so I'll assume he's alive," he said to the paramedic. Whenever he was nervous his slight Russian accent peeked through his otherwise solid New Yorkese. And he was always a little nervous at the start of a case.

"Yeah, he's alive, but barely," the paramedic said.

He looked down at the old man. An oxygen mask covered the lower part of his face; the rest of his face was bloodied and raw. "Anybody see anything?" he asked.

"I dunno, Tolya. The old woman inside called it in," the paramedic answered. "Ask her."

"The wife?"

"No. Might be the maid," he said, pushing the stretcher toward the elevator. "She found him."

Tolya opened the door slowly. He noticed the mezuzah on the doorpost. He scanned the foyer for any telltale signs of forced entry or struggle.

In the living room sat two uniformed officers with an older Hispanic woman on a high-backed, aging velvet couch. "Evening officers," Kurchenko said, taking the two steps into the sunken living room in one stride.

"Evening detective," both uniforms said.

"Is the evidence team here yet?"

One of the detectives pointed to the bathroom. Tolya saw a leg jutting out of the doorway, the strobe from the camera flash pulsating every few seconds. "Looks tight in there," he said. "Let me speak with the nice señora." He sat down on the sofa. "May I ask you some questions, Señora…?"

"Leguenza, but you just call me María, everybody just call me María." She looked up at him.

"Thank you María."

"I find him just laying there, the señor," she said before Tolya could get his first question out of his mouth. "Just laying there. Is terrible."

"Yes, I'm sure it was terrible," he replied, "but I need to ask you a few…"

"Dios mío," she continued. "Who would do such a thing to Señor Redmond? He is a fine man."

"Yes, I'm sure," Tolya said. "That's why we need your help, so please let me ask you some questions."

"OK, OK, sorry," she said, beginning to cry.

Tolya looked around the room while María composed herself. It was a study in drab. Faded furniture and yellowed curtains. "Was the door locked when you arrived?" Tolya asked.

"Yes, like I tell the woman policeman, the door is locked. Everything is like normal, except Señor Redmond is on the floor in the bathroom."

"What time did you arrive?"

"A qué hora llegué?" María mumbled, touching her fingers to her forehead. "I think about 6:10. I supposed to be here at 6:00, but I want to buy Señor Redmond something special because it is their holiday tonight."

"Yes, I know," Tolya said. "We couldn't get through the crowd."

"So I go to the bakery first to buy tres leches, he love tres leches," María said.

Tolya stifled a smile. The idea of an old Jewish guy who likes tres leches cake was sweet to him.

"Ay dios," cried María. The crying returned to weeping.

Tolya knew there was no benefit in continuing the questioning at this point. The woman was too upset. "María," he said, "I need to ask you one more thing right now."

"I so sorry sir," she said through her sobs. "I too upset to talk."

"I need to know who to contact. Does Señor Redmond have any family?"

"Yes, yes," she said, her crying subsiding momentarily. "He have one son. His name is Steven Redmond. I get you his information."

María rose from the sofa and went to the drawer in the center of the large mahogany desk against the back wall of the living room. She wiped her face with a lace handkerchief she took from her pocket, then absentmindedly slipped into the cuff of her sleeve at her wrist. She took an envelope from the desk and handed it to Tolya.

He examined the envelope, "emergency" written in neat script across the front. Inside was a single sheet of white paper. "This is his son's name and number?" he asked.

"Yes," María said. "But he no answer the phone now because of the holiday. He very religious."

Tolya smiled. Another victim of superstition caught in a time warp.

"But if you go downstairs to la sinagoga and ask for him, you find him now," María said, interrupting his thought.

"Steven Redmond, right?" Tolya said looking at the name on the piece of paper again, turning it over in his hands as if expecting something else to magically appear.

"Yes, but at la sinagoga, ask for Shalom Rothman."

2

Tolya pushed his way through the crowd on Bennett Avenue. On either side of the sawhorse barrier, women dressed in dark, dull tones huddled together gossiping as the men whirled in ecstasy with their holy books. They began clapping their hands spontaneously, chanting along with the men. As Tolya pushed his way through the throng, a woman swinging her arms elbowed him. "Sorry," she said.

He continued walking forward without acknowledging her. He never felt comfortable among them. They looked like pictures from his childhood textbooks. What was the caption? His mind switched back and forth between Russian and English. "The Jews are oppressed by their religion and the capitalist system. Communism will liberate them!"

He wedged his way between men packed into the street in front of the synagogue. Not able to move further, he flashed his badge at a middle-aged, overweight man wiping beads of sweat from his brow with a stained handkerchief despite the cold night air.

"Are you Jewish, officer?" asked the fat man.

"Detective, and yes," Tolya answered him.

"Would you like to dance with the Torah?"

"Perhaps later."

Scanning the crowd impatiently, not knowing who or what exactly he was searching for, he said to the fat man, "I'm looking for Shalom Rothman."

"Shalom? Oh, of course, he's right there," the fat man said, pointing toward a tall, thin man dancing with a Torah. "Nothing wrong I hope, Baruch HaShem?"

"No, nothing," Tolya said, flashing a smile. He hated that expression. "I just need to speak with him."

"Please wait here, I'll get him for you."

Tolya watched the fat man push his way through the crowd toward the dancers; the tinny sound of the music coming through the antique speakers reverberated against the walls of the apartment buildings on all sides of the street. The fat man tapped the tall, thin man in a regulation black suit and wide-brimmed hat on the shoulder from behind. The man turned and handed him the holy scroll. Taking it, the fat man whispered something in his ear. The thin man's gaze followed the fat man's outstretched arm to the waiting detective and he walked over.

Tolya extended his badge toward the man. "Are you Shalom Rothman?" he asked.

"Yes," Shalom answered.

"I'm Detective Anatoly Kurchenko. I'm looking for Steven Redmond."

Rachel stood among the women, observing her husband and their son. She rubbed her elbow where it had collided with the stranger, watching Baruch with relief. She thanked HaShem for all the progress Baruch had made in the past year. Now he could at least stand with the men and participate in the celebration, even if they wouldn't let him touch the Torah. They couldn't chance him dropping it. But she knew he was closer to HaShem now.

She felt someone tap her shoulder from behind. It was Miriam.

"Look there, look what's going on," Miriam said, pointing toward the stretcher being rolled out of 105 Bennett.

"I see," Rachel said. "Baruch HaShem it's not one of us."

"I am Steven Redmond," Rothman answered.

"I thought you said you're Shalom Rothman," Tolya spoke loudly over the noise.

"I'm both," he replied. "My given name is Steven Redmond, but I go by Shalom Rothman. It's rather involved."

"If you don't mind, I need to speak to you privately."

"Certainly," said Shalom.

They walked down West 186th Street toward Broadway, the din from the music fading as they gained distance from the crowd. When they reached the corner of Broadway, Shalom turned to Tolya and asked, "How can I help you officer?"

"You are Steven Redmond?" Tolya asked again.

"Yes, I told you, I am," said Shalom, leaning forward and putting his hands in his coat pockets.

"Mr. Redmond." Tolya paused. "Or should I call you…your other name?"

"I prefer Rothman, but Redmond is fine, officer," Shalom replied.

"Detective," Tolya said. He watched Shalom's gaze shift back toward the crowd.

"Sorry," Shalom said, looking toward Tolya again.

"Is Max Redmond your father?" he asked.

"Yes," Shalom replied.

"I'm sorry to have to tell you like this but he was just taken to the hospital."

"My father?" Shalom asked.

"Yes, his maid found him assaulted in his apartment. I'm afraid I have to ask you to come with me. Again, I'm sorry."

"Now?" Shalom said, turning his head back toward the crowd again.

Tolya wasn't sure what or who Rothman was looking for. "Yes now," he said. "We can take you to the hospital to see him but we'll need to speak with you first."

"Officer, um, I mean detective, I'm sorry but..." Shalom stammered.

Tolya watched his gaze shift back and forth between him and the crowd. "But Mr. Rothman?"

Shalom turned back to Tolya. "I can't do that, I can't travel by car. It's a holy day."

"I see," said Tolya, almost speechless.

Rachel was enraptured by the rhythm of the chanting and clapping. She loved the *nigunnim*, the wordless repetitive chants that brought them closer to HaShem. She closed her eyes and let the music sweep over her. When she opened them again, the scene had changed. Shalom wasn't dancing, he was gone. She searched for him and for Baruch.

"Miriam," she said, her heart racing, "where is Shalom? Do you see him? I don't see him."

"He's there," Miriam said, pointing toward the nearer barricade.

"And Baruch?"

"There, with Shimmy Eisenstein. Relax, Rachel. He's fine."

"Thank you Miriam," Rachel said, still unsure of the situation. It was never good to leave Baruch with strangers, even if they were strangers he knew. Her eyes moved back to where Shalom was standing. He was gone. He'd been speaking with the strange man who had banged into her arm.

"I'm sorry," Tolya said. "Did I just hear you right? You can't attend to your father because it's a holy day and you can't travel by car?"

"Yes, I did say that," Shalom replied, taking a step back.

Tolya thought Rothman was insane. The memory of his own father lying dead in a hospital room swept through his mind. He would have given anything to have gotten there just a few minutes earlier, anything to have said his goodbye. He took a deep breath. "Well, you are then a man of principles, I suppose." He stopped and paced side to side in small steps, his hands clasped behind his back. "So I have some good news and some bad news for you," he said. He sensed his accent thickening again.

"Excuse me?" replied Shalom.

"Good news and bad news," Tolya repeated. "The good news is you won't need to ride in a car. You can walk. Your father was taken to Columbia Presbyterian, that's only about twenty blocks. The bad news is you'll be coming with us now to the station house around the corner and then you can proceed on foot to Columbia at your earliest convenience."

"But it's *yom tov*…"

"Mr. Redmond," Tolya said, using Shalom's father's name to intimidate him just a little bit more. "I don't care what day it is, you will be coming with me now."

Tolya smiled as he watched Shalom deflate, his shoulders and back hunched in defeat. "All right. Let me collect my wife and son. I will meet you back here in five minutes."

"No, we'll go together."

3

Rachel had never seen the inside of a police station. The dark-blue uniforms and the other people in the waiting room, all of them speaking Spanish, made her nervous. She sat at the end of the row of black vinyl seats nearest to the door and put her sweater on the seat next to her so that no one else, especially a man, could sit there.

Miriam had taken Baruch. Rachel didn't know how he would react or if she could control him inside a police station. Afterward, they would have to walk to the hospital to see her father-in-law. She didn't want to drag Baruch twenty blocks.

Baruch was very attached to her father-in-law, a fact she would just as soon forget. She didn't want Baruch to see him in the hospital. That, too, could set off a meltdown. Baruch liked Miriam. She knew how to handle him. He would be fine with her, Rachel convinced herself, gazing at her hands in her lap.

"Excuse me," said a woman police officer, startling Rachel.

"Yes?" Rachel answered. "Can I see my husband now?".

"Oh, I'm sorry ma'am," said the officer, kneeling in front of Rachel and touching her arm. "I don't know,"

Rachel stared at her long, bright-red fingernails. She wanted to pull her arm back from the stranger but didn't want to insult her.

"I was just going to ask if you'd like something to drink," the policewoman continued. "I thought you might be thirsty."

"Oh." Rachel smiled weakly. "No, no thank you, I mean. I can't, no I don't want anything to drink." She hesitated then looked up at the policewoman. She noticed the woman's eyes, a deep, dark black set against the honey color of her skin. "But could you find out how much longer my husband will be?" she asked, her voice faltering.

"Sure," said the policewoman. "I'll see what I can do."

Tolya entered the interrogation room. It was a tight fit, with the table and chairs taking up most of the space. He stood in front of the door, puffing out his chest in hopes of intimidating Rothman. He flashed him a big, toothy smile, pulled out the chair opposite Shalom, sat down and opened his case folder.

"Do you prefer Mr. Rothman or may I address you as Shalom," Tolya said.

"Shalom will be fine, detective," Rothman said.

He liked that Rothman addressed him as detective. "Good, then let's keep this light," he said. "You may call me Tolya."

"Thank you," replied Shalom, shifting in the hard metal chair.

"Shalom, is there anyone you can think of who would have done this to your father?"

"No." Shalom shook his head. "I can't imagine who would have done this."

Tolya searched Shalom's face for some sort of emotion. He saw only the same clinical disinterest he had seen earlier on the street.

"Someone must have broken into the apartment," Shalom said.

"But the caregiver..."

"Who?" Shalom said, his brow crinkling.

"The caregiver," Tolya repeated. "Her name is María Leguenza."

"Yes, you mean the maid," Shalom said, a weak smile appearing around the right side of his mouth. It was the first emotion Tolya had seen him display. "She fancies herself his nurse."

Tolya crossed his arms. "She reported that the door was locked when she arrived and found your father in the bathroom."

"I see," replied Shalom, averting his gaze from Tolya.

"Mr. Rothman," Tolya said, "forgive me, but you don't seem very upset about this."

Shalom's expression tightened as he looked up. "Detective, I'm upset, very upset, and I find your remark to be offensive. My father and I have very different views on the world and a long, unpleasant history. But he is still my father."

"My apologies, I was out of line," said Tolya, uncrossing his arms. He was pleased with what had just happened. He wanted Rothman a little angry.

"We are somewhat estranged," Shalom continued, unprompted, "so what you misread as a lack of concern is really none of your business."

Tolya let Shalom's remark hang in the air. He looked down at his clipboard for a moment.

"Detective, will we be discussing this much longer?" Shalom asked. "My wife is outside, our son is with a friend and we still have to walk down to the hospital."

"No, no, Shalom. I have just a few more questions." Tolya smiled at him again.

"Please," Shalom said, looking at his watch.

"Do you see your father often?" Tolya asked.

"As of late, once a week."

Tolya nodded and noted Shalom's response on his pad. "Who has access to him?"

"What do you mean?" Shalom said.

"Who takes care of him? I assume he can't take care of himself."

"Mostly Mrs. Leguenza. She comes by in the morning to help him get up and dressed, and she leaves about noon. She comes back about 5 or 6 in the evening to make his dinner, then leaves after putting him in bed at about 8:00."

"Is he able to get around at all without help?"

"Some, not much. He's very frail."

"So Mrs. Leguenza is the sole caregiver?" Tolya continued.

"No, my wife helps out some as well."

"Your wife," Tolya mumbled straightening up in the chair and making a note in the file. "Does anyone else have keys to the apartment besides Mrs. Leguenza and your wife?"

"No. Wait, yes. There is a boy, a teenager, he comes to keep him company a couple times a week."

"His name?"

"Carlos, I think."

"Carlos what?"

"I'm not sure, he's Dominican."

Tolya was amazed. How was it possible that a kid, a stranger, would come to visit Rothman's 90-plus-year-old father regularly and he didn't know the kid's name? "How did he become involved with your father?"

"Through a community program to help the elderly."

"And you don't know his name?"

"Excuse me miss, follow me please," said the woman officer to Rachel.

Rachel grabbed her things from the chair next to her. The officer led her to a small, windowless room at the back of the station. It contained a slate gray table, three chairs and a phone set.

"Where is my husband?" Rachel asked the officer, scanning the empty room.

"I'll go and find out," she said. "You wait here, please."

Rachel felt reassured by the officer's quiet, soothing voice and sat down in the chair closest to the door. She crossed her legs and arms, pulling her sweater tightly around her small, thin frame. Several minutes later, the woman officer returned with a man.

"This is Detective Pete Gonzalves. He wants to ask you a few questions," she said, turning to leave.

"Wait, where is my husband?" Rachel asked again, standing and raising her voice, her arms still crossed.

The woman officer stopped and turned back. "He'll be along shortly. First, the detective needs to speak with you," she said, leaving the room and closing the door behind her.

Rachel's mind kicked into overdrive. She couldn't be alone in this room with a man. She immediately went to the door and grabbed the knob. "Unlock this, right now," she shouted at the detective.

"Whoa, ma'am, calm down," said the detective, reaching a hand in Rachel's direction.

"Don't touch me," Rachel shouted, slapping the detective's hand with her own. "Shalom," she shouted. "Shalom."

Shalom heard the ruckus from the other room. He recognized his wife's voice muffled though the walls.

"Tolya," he said, interrupting Kurchenko's questioning. "Right now I don't care what the boy's name is. Why is my wife screaming for me?" He rose and bolted toward the door. "Why is this locked?" he shouted. "Unlock this now."

Tolya jumped up from his chair and wedged his way between Rothman and the door. "Shalom, relax. Sorry," he said, sliding his key card through the reader and opening the door. "They lock automatically, security reasons."

Shalom burst out of the room into the hallway. By the time he got to the adjacent room, Rachel was in the hallway as well. She reached for him, nearly in tears, then released him as suddenly. Stepping behind him, she bowed her head and whispered something to him in Yiddish.

"Did he touch you?" Shalom asked her in English.

"No," she said, breathing heavily. "I was just…frightened."

Shalom took her hand and held it tightly. "Officer," he said to Tolya.

"That's detective."

"I don't care what you call yourself," Shalom growled, taking a step toward Tolya. "My wife is a pious woman. She cannot be alone in a room with a strange man. Your actions, the actions of your partner and of this precinct, have been disrespectful to us all evening and I plan on filing a complaint."

"Please, Mr. Rothman, please calm down," Tolya said. "We just wanted to speak with your wife."

"I should have been present," Shalom shouted.

"It's customary for us to interview sus…" Pete interjected. Tolya caught his eye and shook his head in the subtlest possible manner.

"…I mean people connected to the case separately."

"So now we're suspects?" said Shalom.

"No, no, not exactly," said Tolya.

"Detective," Shalom said, drawing out the last syllable of the word, "I am going to see my father in the hospital now. If you want to speak to us any further about my father's case, please let me know and I will have an attorney present. Otherwise, I trust the next time I hear from you it will be to update me on the progress you're making in finding the animal that did this to my father."

Shalom took Rachel's arm in his and walked down the hallway toward the front of the station. He had turned out to be tougher than Tolya expected. Shalom stopped and turned mid-stride. "Oh, and since I understand you're Jewish, detective," he added, "good *yom tov*."

4

Tolya slowly opened the door to his apartment and slipped off his shoes. He didn't want to wake Karin. Crossing the darkened foyer into the living room, he stepped on the point of Karin's pump. "Shit," he half-shouted. "Why the hell does she leave those in the middle of the floor?"

He had lived alone for years in this apartment, which he had inherited when his father died. He had renovated the apartment himself, room by room, restoring the wood floors to a hi-gloss finish. He repaired the cracked, chipping old plaster and recessed the lighting into the ceiling to diffuse its effect. He built the new kitchen cabinets himself. They were of dark mahogany with clean, straight simple lines and no handles. They opened by pressing them inward. The bathroom fixtures were white, in stark contrast to the black leather furniture and dark wood that populated the rest of the space. There was no clutter anywhere, no books or papers stacked or strewn about desks and countertops. Instead he kept his library in the drawers and shelves of the low mahogany cabinets that lined the walls of the living room, dining room and foyer. The few pieces of art on the walls were modern, abstract and enigmatic, the way he thought of himself. He was obsessively neat and it showed.

Karin teased him about it. She said the apartment was so spartan he could be one of the 300. "I like it that way," he told her. "The world I work in is chaos. This world is order."

Karin had moved in about six months earlier. They had already been dating for six months. He sometimes thought she created the mess just to mess with his head, to see how far she could push him, challenge him. But that's what he loved about her, despite his now aching heel.

Tolya sat down on the low, black leather couch. He crossed his leg over his knee and rubbed his heel where the point of the pump had dug into it. The pressure of his fingers soothed the lingering pain. He continued to massage the heel gently, sitting back against the couch and replaying the crime scene in his head.

No forced entry. The maid comes, the door is locked, she opens it, she calls out, no one answers, she goes to look for him in the bedroom, he's not there. She walks by the bathroom, the light is on but she doesn't check there first. Why? There is no apparent struggle. Nothing is missing, at least not that we know of.

Tolya laid his head against the back of the couch. The cool leather felt good against the skin at the back of his neck. He let go of his heel and massaged his temples instead, his large hands spanning his head from one side to the other. He was too tired to think about the case but too wound up to go to bed.

He laughed quietly at the thought of Rothman and his wife accusing Pete of trying something with her. He turned on the TV and quickly muted it. He knew Karin would have had it blasting while she was doing something elsewhere in the apartment. He pictured her moving about the apartment in an old T-shirt and panties. She rarely wore clothing in the house.

Flicking aimlessly through the channels, Tolya couldn't find anything to divert his attention. "Fuck this," he mumbled, "I'm going to bed." He slipped off his clothes and left them on the back of the leather club chair in the living room, brushed his teeth and washed. Creeping into the dark bedroom, he lifted the covers and slid quietly into bed. He slid up against Karin's back, her warm, soft, smooth skin a comfort against his tired body. He slipped his arm over her, palming the softness of her stomach. She stirred, resting her hand over his, entwining their fingers. He buried his face in her hair, breathing in its scent.

"Tolya, amor. What time is it?" she asked.

"Late."

"How late?"

"2:20."

"Ay, I have to be up at 6. Why did you wake me?"

"I couldn't help myself," he said, kissing her neck, drawing her tighter to him.

"Why are you so late? I thought your shift ended at midnight," she said, removing his hand from her stomach and turning to face him.

"A new case," he said. "I went back at the station after dinner. Pete was late, again."

"Why?"

"He said his wife was late getting back from work."

"Right," she said with a chuckle. "More like the girlfriend."

"Hey," Tolya said, slapping her on the behind. "Be careful, that's my partner you're talking about."

"So what happened?" she said through a yawn.

"This call came in, around the corner from the station house on Bennett. An old man beaten in his bathroom."

"Sounds terrible," she said, caressing his face.

"Your breath stinks," Tolya said. "You've been smoking again."

"No," she lied.

"Yes you have," he said.

"No, yes, OK, a little," she admitted. "Now, what happened with the old man?"

"We tried to interview the son and the daughter-in-law," Tolya said.

"But?"

"They're religious," he said.

"Tolya, why do you hate them so much?" she asked, propping herself up on her elbow.

"I don't hate them," he said, pushing her hair back and caressing her cheek.

"Yes you do."

"No, I just don't trust them."

"Maybe you shouldn't be on this case," she said, running her fingers over his chest.

He turned off his side onto his back. "I was thinking that, but maybe not. The old man wasn't religious at all."

"How do you know that, Colombo?"

Tolya laughed and tickled Karin. "The maid brought him chuletas for dinner."

"Chuletas," she said, snuggling closer to him, "my favorite."

"Something is not right about the whole thing," Tolya said.

"Well, go to sleep now my big detective. It's very late and you can solve it tomorrow."

"I can't sleep," he said, shifting back onto his left side and burying his head in her hair.

"I can fix that," she said, grabbing him between the legs.

Shalom and Rachel climbed the five flights to their apartment in silence. They couldn't take the elevator. It was *yom tov*. After the long walk to and from the hospital — more than fifty blocks in total — and the five flights at the hospital, the stairs were hard, each step an effort. Shalom slipped the key into the lock and turned it. The apartment was dark, except for a light in the bathroom, which Rachel had left on before *yom tov* began.

They continued silently into the bedroom, changing into their nightclothes in the darkness. They couldn't wash or brush their teeth because it was *yom tov*. A rinse with mouthwash would have to suffice. They slipped into bed reciting the Shema in hushed tones.

"What time is it?" asked Rachel.

Shalom looked over at the clock. "2:20," he replied.

"I have to be up at 6," she said. "I have to be at Miriam's by 7 to get Baruch."

"I can get him," Shalom said. "You don't have to get up."

"Thank you," she said, sighing heavily. "I am so tired."

"I know," he said, kissing her gently on the cheek. "How beautiful you are my beloved and how gentle," he said in Hebrew, quoting the Song of Songs.

"Thank you," she replied, turning over and disappearing under the heavy blanket.

Shalom lay back, his head sinking into the softness of the down pillows. He thought of his father lying in the hospital bed in the intensive care unit, his face bloodied and swollen from the beating, a gash just above his thinning hairline. Who would have done this to him? It had to be that boy.

He never trusted those people. His father loved them, the Dominicans. They had saved Shalom's parents. How many times had he heard that speech?

"We had nowhere to go. I was in a concentration camp in Italy in 1940, just after the Germans and Italians attacked France. Your mother was in hiding and the only place that would take us was the República Dominicana," his father would say, pronouncing the Spanish name for the island republic with his thick Hungarian accent, the emphasis on the first syllable of both words instead of on the fourth as it should have been. "We didn't even know where it was. Cuba we knew, but not the República Dominicana. But we didn't care, as long as it wasn't in Europe. They saved our lives. We owe them everything."

Yes, everything. That's why his father was lying in intensive care now. Shalom's mind raced back to the night his father told him that he had agreed to participate in the Hands Across Cultures program.

"A young man will come to help me twice a week," his father said.

Shalom stopped writing out the checks for his father's monthly bills at the large mahogany desk in the corner of the living room and turned toward him. "A young man? What are you talking about?"

"A juvenile offender. It's part of his probation," his father said.

"A juvenile offender, are you crazy? He could be dangerous."

"No. The boy is Dominican, I have to help him, to give a little something to the people who saved us."

"I think this is a very bad idea," Shalom said, putting his pen back into his jacket pocket and turning around in the swivel chair. "I'll get you more help if you need it."

"No. It's not about the money, it's about my life."

Shalom knew there was little more to say on the topic, He was on the other side of that argument many years earlier when he came home from college for break wearing a yarmulke.

"What's that?" his father joked, washing out a glass in the kitchen sink. "You go to a Bar Mitzvah today and forget to take that off?"

"No Pop," Shalom answered. "I wear it all the time now."

His father stopped and looked at him.

"That's what I wanted to talk to you about. Remember I told you on the phone I had something I wanted to discuss with you."

His father put the glass in the yellow plastic drain board next to the sink and walked slowly to the kitchen table. He stood silently for a moment, tracing the outlines of the flowers on the tablecloth with his fingers. "That's what you want to discuss, Steven? A yarmulke?" his father said, then grasped the dining room chair in front of him so hard the veins in his forearms were visible.

"No, not exactly, but yes," Shalom said. "I have become *ba'al t'shuvah**."

His father's mouth was open, speechless.

"I've made a decision about school as well," he continued. "When I'm done at Brandeis, I'm not going to law school. I want to go to study in a yeshiva."

"A yeshiva?" was all his father could muster, pulling out the chair and dropping into it.

"Yes, and Pop, please don't call me Steven any more. I prefer to use my Hebrew name now. Please call me Shalom."

His father rose from the chair with fire in his eyes. "Steven isn't good enough for you? I named you after my brother, my twin brother. He went up a chimney. Your so-called god has taken enough from me already, Istvan," he said, addressing him in Hungarian as he turned and left the room. When he was gone, Shalom's mother rose from the table, walked to her son, placed her hands on his cheeks and kissed his forehead.

"Thank you," she said.

---

* *Ba'al t'shuvah*: A formerly non-observant jew who has become observant (Hebrew)

With that memory playing behind the lids of his closing eyes, Shalom Rothman fell into a shallow, fitful sleep.

5

Tolya sipped his coffee at his desk as he reviewed the incident report he had typed up the previous night. He loved the thick Dominican coffee from the Caridad on 184th Street and Broadway. He became addicted to it as a teenager; after his mother died, he started buying a cup on his way to school each morning. It was easier to stop there to pick up a coffee than to deal with his father's mess in the kitchen, or his shouting when the sound of the coffee grinder woke him. A genius needs his sleep, especially a genius who drinks himself to sleep.

Tolya watched Pete flirt with the duty officer at the front desk on his way into the precinct. He knew Pete couldn't help himself. He liked flirting even more than he liked women. It didn't matter how old they were, or really even what they looked like. Pete would stop and smile and talk to them, often taking their hands. The women, in turn, loved it and smiled whenever he came around.

"Hermano," Pete said, entering the office. He slapped Tolya's foot off the gray metal desk and sat down opposite him, popping his own feet up on the desktop. "The son didn't file a complaint last night on the way out. I just checked."

Tolya didn't look up from the file. "I know. I checked too, and mostly you were just trying to make a little time with the new duty officer."

Pete laughed. "Gotta keep them happy. So what we got?"

Tolya looked up. "We got the interview with the caregiver and whatever I suspect the son didn't tell me last night."

"Any of it dovetail?" Pete asked.

"There's the kid who visits with the old man," Tolya replied. "I imagine he's the best lead."

"Agreed."

Tolya handed the folder to Pete. "The son didn't know his last name. You believe that shit? I called the caregiver. I figured she could fill in a little more." Tolya looked at his watch. "We have an appointment ten minutes ago. She's up on Wadsworth, near 178th."

"Let's go," Pete said. He jumped up and grabbed Tolya's coffee, chugging the rest of it.

"What the fuck you doing?" Tolya said, too late to grab it back.

Pete flashed his big toothy smile at Tolya. "Thank you, that was delicious."

Shalom stood in front of the mirror. Sunlight filtered through the sheer beige curtains. He picked up his *tsitsis** and slipped the garment over his head, then pulled up his pants and fastened them, pulling the fringes out and over. He saw Rachel's image in the mirror at the doorway. Her chestnut hair fell to her shoulders, free of the wig she wore in front of anyone other than him. He loved her hair and the way it framed her face.

"Shalom," she said from behind him.

He turned to look at her and smiled.

"Your breakfast is ready. Baruch is waiting for you." She walked around

---

* *Tsitsis:* Jewish prayer tassels (Hebrew)

the bed and took his left hand. "Thank you for picking him up this morning."

He pushed her hair back and touched her cheek with the palm of his right hand. "There's nothing to thank me for." He smiled at her and kissed her gently. "I have to go, it's already late."

Shalom walked down the hall into the kitchen. Baruch was sitting at the table and staring intently at a book of photographs, scanning the pages methodically before turning them. "Good morning son," Shalom said.

Baruch looked up at him. Shalom picked up a piece of toast from the plate Rachel had left for him, made the prescribed blessing and took a bite. He washed it down quickly with the tea she had left as well.

"Rachel," he called out. "Please get his coat, we're late." He put down the cup and took Baruch gently by the arm. "Let's go, *zindel*[*]," he said.

Pete reached his arm past Tolya and knocked on the apartment door.

"What's that about?" Tolya said, pushing his hand back. "I already rang the bell."

"Maybe she didn't hear it," said Pete.

"Give her a chance, she's an old woman," Tolya said as the door opened. He smiled at María, hoping she hadn't heard him, and held up his badge. "Sorry, sorry we're late. May we come in?"

"Please," María said, backing into the narrow foyer and looking at her watch. "I am expecting you half hour ago."

"I apologize, señora," Tolya said. "My partner here was late."

"OK, I understand. Pero, like I tell you, I have to take my lady to the doctor this morning," she said, leading them into the living room.

"We only need about twenty minutes, Mrs. Leguenza," Tolya said, fol-

---

* *Zindel*: Son (Yiddish)

lowing her.

She stopped and turned again. "Please call me María, everybody call me María."

"OK, María," Tolya said.

"You want something to drink maybe?" she asked, disappearing into the kitchen.

"No," they both answered.

The room was small and cluttered but immaculately clean. The furniture, though worn, was well cared for. They sat down next to each other on a small brown sectional sofa.

María returned with two bottles of Snapple Peach Iced Tea. "Señor Redmond, he love this flavor," she said, joining them on the sofa. "I buy for him at the Costco."

"Thanks," they said, exchanging smiles, then put the bottles down on top of a magazine on the coffee table.

María stroked the worn fabric on the edge of the arm of the sofa. "Por favor, you find the person who do this to Señor Redmond. I like to go to see him today. He is a very kind man." She reached into the pocket of her dress and took out a set of rosary beads and a tissue. She dabbed the tissue at her eyes.

"We're going to try very hard to find that person," said Tolya. "You can help us to do that." He took his clipboard from his bag and grabbed a pen from the inside pocket of his coat. He looked up at María and smiled. "Can you tell us who comes in and out of the house? What's a typical day like?"

"I tell this to the other police last night," she said, clasping her hands tightly around the rosary.

He looked at María's face: tired and frightened. He had seen that look on many old women exhausted by life. "I know," he said, "but we need to go over it again."

"Well," María replied, sighing heavily and leaning back into the corner at the end of the sofa, "I come everyday…"

"About what time?" Pete asked.

"About 8 a.m., after I drop mi nieta at school. I help him to get up from the bed and to wash in the bathroom…"

"Can he walk at all, or he only uses the chair?" Tolya interrupted.

María perked up, a smile crossing her lips. "Oh he walk a little, Señor Redmond, with the walker," she replied. "He only is using the chair when he go out to the street to sit or to the store. Is too far for him, but he no go much to the store anymore."

"I see," said Tolya, noting her answer on the pad. "Who does the shopping?"

"I do, and sometimes Carlos," María said. She smiled at Tolya, the rosary beads sliding silently through her fingers.

"Carlos?" Pete asked. "That's the kid doing community service?

"Sí," María said. "He a good boy except he get in a little trouble."

"Yes, we heard something like that. What kind of trouble?" asked Tolya.

"I sorry, I don't know." She cast her eyes down toward her hands, the rosaries stopping suddenly mid-palm.

"And what's his last name?" Tolya continued.

"Pabon."

"Can you spell that please?"

"Come here, I write it for you." María put the rosaries down in her lap and reached toward him. Tolya handed his clipboard and pen to María. She wrote P-A-B-O-N in slow, deliberate strokes. "There," she said.

"Thank you," he replied, taking back the clipboard.

"De nada."

"How often does Carlos come?" Pete asked.

"He is coming two, sometimes three time a week to sit with Señor Redmond." She hesitated for a moment, dabbing the tissue at her eyes. "They like each other very much."

"What does he do with the señor?" Tolya asked. He looked around the room again, waiting for her answer. The walls were filled with photos in metal frames of various sizes, sometimes with more than one picture in a frame, and small paintings of tropical, pastoral scenes in ornate gilded frames. His gaze shifted back to María as she began to answer.

"He take him in the wheelchair to the park down the block. They sit with Señor Redmond's friend, or sometimes he wheel him over to the schoolyard to watch the boys play basketball."

Tolya caught himself smiling. "He likes basketball?" he said.

"Yes, very much, and the baseball too," she replied, her smile betraying her affection for the old man. The changes in her facial expressions fascinated Tolya. Whenever she mentioned the old man her face would light up. When she thought of his happiness, she became happy. When she thought of his pain, it became evident in her eyes.

"Nobody else helps with the shopping?" Tolya continued.

"Sometimes the son's wife, her name is Rachel," María said, her expression becoming serious again. "She bring things from the store, but Señor Redmond, he no like it because she only buy kosher. He like the regular better."

"So he isn't religious?" Pete asked.

"No," replied María, shaking her head and threading her rosary beads through her fingers. "He no believe in nothing, but I pray for him anyway. He tell me he stop believing in God long ago. I feel sorry for him that he no have faith. I tell him that God love him anyway."

Pete shot a look at Tolya, rolling his eyes. A sardonic smile crept up around the corner of Tolya's mouth. Pete got up from the sofa and walked around the room a bit. Tolya watched Pete out of the corner of his eye. He knew that if María had anything in this room that she took from the old man's apartment, Pete would catch it. He was the best evidence dog in the business.

"So you come about 8 a.m. and you help Mr. Redmond to the bathroom to wash?" Tolya continued, focusing on María to keep her distracted from Pete's movements.

"Sí."

"And he can walk to the bathroom?" Tolya asked.

"With the walker, sí."

Tolya noted her answer. "What time do you leave?"

"Noon, to go to my lady to help her."

"Where does she live?" Pete asked.

"Around the corner from Señor Redmond, on 187th Street."

"What's her name?" Tolya said.

"Mrs. Tombach. Like I tell you, I supposed to go there early today to take her to the doctor, so I have to leave soon," María said, looking at her watch again.

"I understand, María. This won't take much longer," Tolya said. "And then what time do you return usually?"

"About six, to make dinner and help him into bed and then I leave about eight," María said, shifting her weight. She was becoming impatient and Tolya knew it. He wanted to keep her cooperative.

"I see, so who stays with him when you are not there?" Pete interjected, sitting back down on the couch.

She perked up again at this question. "Well, he not a baby, Señor Redmond. He can stay alone."

"I understand that," Tolya said. "But who else comes to stay with him?"

"Carlos. I tell you," María said, looking at her watch again.

"Does anyone else come to help or visit?" Tolya asked.

"Well sometimes Mr. Steven come and sometimes his wife, and sometimes they bring their son, Baruch. He love Señor Redmond."

"They're close?" Tolya asked.

"Yes, he is close with the boy, not Mr. Steven," she said, leaning toward him as if she were delivering damaging gossip to a mutual friend. "You know Baruch, he has a problem."

"No. What's that?" Pete asked, leaning forward himself and smiling at María.

"He is… Cómo se dice?" she said.

"Yo no sé. Diga me en español," Pete said.

"Es un niño que nació enfermo, tiene problema mentalmente."

"He's not normal in the head," Pete translated.

"I see," Tolya said, noting her remark on the pad.

"But he love Señor Redmond, he is very calm around him and he like Carlos too. I never see him act so nice with another boy like he act with Carlos."

"Really," Tolya said, making more notes. "Does he have problems with other kids?"

"Other children? Oh, I no really know, but sometimes I hear them talking that he can't be with other children."

"Does he get violent?" Tolya continued.

"Yes, sometimes I hear that."

Tolya looked over at Pete.

"Excuse me, officer," María said.

"Detective, María."

"Sorry, detective. I have to go in a few minutes to take Mrs. Tombach to the doctor."

"OK," Tolya said, "just one more question then."

"Yes?"

"Who else has keys to the apartment?"

"OK, let me think," she said. She counted out the keys on her fingers, mumbling in Spanish, then looked up at Tolya. "I have one, Mr. Steven, Mr. Steven wife, Carlos, the super, he have a key, and the friend who is with him from Santo Domingo who live on Ft. Washington Avenue."

"Can you write all of their names down for me please?" Tolya asked.

"Por supuesto, and then I can go?"

"Por supuesto," Tolya replied.

María handed back the list to Tolya. He surveyed it as she prepared herself to go. "María, who is Señor Enrique?"

"He is the friend of Señor Max."

"Is he, um, old?" Tolya asked.

"Yes," laughed María. "He even a little older than Señor Max."

Shalom walked up Bennett Avenue with Baruch at his side. The service hadn't been as difficult as he'd expected. Mostly people just shook his hand and wished his father a speedy recovery. And Baruch had gotten through the service without the smallest incident. He had stayed in his seat quietly when Shalom was called to the Torah to make a *Mi Sheberach** for his father's recovery.

---

* *Mi Sheberach*: Jewish prayer for the ill (Hebrew)

"They've made real progress with you," Shalom said, not expecting an answer from Baruch. He didn't get one. Shalom placed his hand on Baruch's shoulder as they continued walking.

"Today is a very important day for us, *zindel*," Shalom continued. "We begin again. Our people have been doing this for thousands of years. We finish reading the Torah and we begin again; our greatest joy, to reveal HaShem's words and thoughts, to remember our special covenant with him."

Shalom paused a moment. Baruch stared intently forward, his shoulders slumped slightly. He took Baruch's hand gently in his and crossed the street, this time in silence. He was happy to be with his son, returning from prayer.

6

"We could have walked here in half the time," Tolya grumbled as they exited the subway station at St. Nicholas Avenue and 190th Street.

"You didn't want to walk," Pete said.

"Right, I didn't," replied Tolya.

They crossed St. Nicholas Avenue and headed down West 190th Street to Amsterdam Avenue. The neighborhood had changed since his youth. The drug wars of the '80s and '90s were long over. The area was still primarily Dominican but now it had a mix of people from all over Latin America. There remained evidence of earlier communities: a Greek church on St. Nicholas Avenue, a sign with Hebrew lettering on Amsterdam, an Irish Pub on Audubon. Rarely was English heard on the street.

"You see that over there?" Pete said as they crossed Audubon Avenue.

"What?" Tolya replied, Pete's voice breaking his concentration.

"Another Mexican grocery." Pete pointed toward a new awning with "just opened" banners and drawings of the Mexican flag hanging from it.

"So?" Tolya said.

"They're taking over the neighborhood."

Tolya stopped in his tracks laughing, his hands on his knees.

"What's so funny?" Pete asked.

"You gotta be kidding."

"No, I'm not. Just like you Russians tried to do in the '80s."

"And where are we now?" Tolya said, straightening up. Smiling, he raised an eyebrow and pointed over the roofs and water towers of Washington Heights toward New Jersey. "Same place these Mexicanos are gonna be in a few years, outta here."

The principal saw them immediately. No, Carlos Pabon hadn't shown up for school today, but that wasn't unusual. No, he couldn't let them interview anyone without a warrant. He'd be happy to cooperate as soon as they had the proper paperwork. There were minors involved. He gave them Pabon's address.

Tolya pushed open the front door to the building at 209 Wadsworth Ave. Where the keyhole should have been was a gaping wound. The interior door was open as well. The glass panel in the door was cracked, held together only by the wire mesh inside.

"What apartment is it?" Pete asked.

"55," Tolya said, looking again at the sheet of paper the principal gave them.

"Of course, fifth floor," Pete said. "And no doubt the elevator has been out of order for over a century."

They proceeded up the darkened stairwell littered with broken glass and cigarette butts. Tolya was disgusted by the condition of the building. He doubted it had seen a fresh coat of paint in twenty-five years. "Damn landlords don't do anything in these buildings anymore," he said.

"Why should they?"

"Nobody should live like this," Tolya said.

"You don't, so don't worry about it," Pete said as he continued climbing, taking the steps two at a time.

"I once did," Tolya muttered under his breath.

"55, there on the left," Pete said, pointing toward a door in the corner of the hall.

Tolya walked up to the door and tapped on it. No answer. He rapped harder the second time, calling out, "Is Carlos Pabon here?" Still no response. He turned toward Pete raising his eyebrows.

"Let me try." Pete smacked his fist into the door several times and shouted in Spanish, "Police, open up now."

"Subtle," Tolya said.

A moment later they heard the lock turn and the door opened a crack, the chain link from the security lock holding it back. Tolya saw the face of a young woman half-hidden behind the door.

"What you want? Stop screaming and banging, you gonna scare the kid," the girl said.

Tolya and Pete held up their badges. "We're looking for Carlos Pabon."

"He's not here, he's at school," she said.

"No he's not, we just came from there," Tolya replied. Her eyes caught his. Dark and deep, they reminded him of Karin's.

"Well I don't know where he is then," the young woman said, her gaze shifting between Tolya and something behind the door. A scream came from the back of the apartment. "I'm coming Nikolito." She tried to push the door closed.

"Can we come in?" Pete said, pushing the door open again as far as he could against the chain lock.

"For what?" she asked.

"To talk with you," Tolya said, trying to peer over the woman's head into the apartment beyond.

"What you wanna talk about?" she said.

"Carlos," Tolya replied.

"You got a warrant?"

"No," he answered.

41

"Then no." She tried to close the door again.

Pete slid his hand against it, holding it open. "You don't know where he is?" Pete pressed her.

"No, I told you and I gotta go."

"You his mother?" Tolya said.

"No, I'm his aunt. His mother is at work. I'm taking care of his brother."

There was another scream from the back of the apartment. "OK Nikolito, I'm coming."

Tolya handed the girl his card. "If you see him, tell him to call us."

"Sure." The young woman laughed and closed the door.

Shalom sat quietly a few feet from his father. Laying back on the hospital bed with his mouth open and his hands crossed over his chest, he looked dead. The thought made Shalom shudder.

He had decided to come alone. At first Rachel wanted to come with him. Then they decided she would stay home with Baruch rather than leave him with her parents. Shalom preferred the solitude. There was much he wanted to say to his father that he hadn't.

The past few months were the most compelling between them since his youth. He had persuaded his father to discuss his basic view of God with him in the hope that he could convince him, no, in the hope he might reignite something from his father's past to reconnect him with HaShem. He knew his father was very old and that the end of his life was approaching even before this happened. He wanted to help him make peace with God before he died.

He would visit his father once a week and spend an hour or two discussing whatever passage of Talmud they had agreed upon the week before. Despite their mutual dislike for each other's beliefs, he found the discussions fascinating and, perhaps more importantly, he felt connected to his father in a way he hadn't in almost three decades. He also realized he could forgive his father's anger against HaShem. HaShem had burdened him, perhaps more than he had the strength to bear.

Shalom got up from the chair and walked to his father's bedside. He took his hand and said aloud, "I forgive you, pop, and I'm sure HaShem forgives you too."

"It isn't for you to dispense forgiveness on HaShem's behalf," Shalom heard from behind him. He turned to see his father-in-law enter the room accompanied by another man he didn't recognize at first.

"This is Assemblyman Levitz," his father-in-law said.

"Yes, good *yom tov*," Shalom replied.

"The super was useless and we can't interview Shalom Rothman or his wife again till tomorrow."

"Did you get anything from the neighbors or this friend of his?" asked Captain Edwin McCloskey, crammed into the small space between his desk and the rear wall of his cramped office. He was a big man, more than six feet tall and well past 250 lbs.

"The neighbors all claim they didn't hear anything," said Pete.

"Which makes sense," said Tolya. "I live in a building like that and the walls are thick. You can't hear much from one apartment to the other and then it would have to be something that caught your attention, not an everyday noise like the pipes clanging."

"And this friend of the victim, Señor Enrique?" said the captain, looking at the short list of interviewees Tolya had assembled.

"The maid says he's even older than the victim. We'll get around to interviewing him, but I doubt he knows anything," Tolya replied.

"And the kid is nowhere to be found," said the captain.

"We need to pick up the kid," said Pete.

Tolya peered absently through the dusty metal blinds onto Broadway. "What would you suggest?" he asked the captain.

"I'd find that kid," the captain answered.

"We tried his mother's apartment, but without a warrant..."

"...there's no way in," the captain said, interrupting Tolya. "And you think he's in there?"

"Yeah," said Tolya. "Can we get a warrant?"

"What grounds?" the captain said.

"Suspicion of battery and probable theft," said Tolya.

"I'll see what I can do," said the captain.

"We looked at the school. He hasn't been there in two days but that's not unusual for him," Pete said.

"He can't stay in that apartment forever," Tolya said.

"If he's there," the captain said. "Do you know where he hangs out?"

"The parks, the playgrounds. The maid says he takes the old man to watch him and the other boys play basketball in the schoolyard over there," Tolya said, pointing aimlessly in the air to indicate a direction correct only in his own mind.

"The old man watches them play basketball?" the captain said.

"Imagine this shit," Tolya replied, leaning against the desk.

"You been watching that yard?" the captain asked.

"Whaddya think?" Pete said, propping his feet on the captain's desk and pushing his chair back on two legs.

The captain looked over at Pete. "I'm sure you have. Now get your hooves off my desk."

7

Tolya and Pete left the station and walked up Broadway toward a small Salvadoran restaurant just past 187th Street. As they passed the schoolyard, Tolya saw a skinny kid practicing his jump shot. "Pete," Tolya said, "slow down but don't stop walking. Look in the schoolyard across the street. Is that him?"

"I'm not sure." He pulled the copy of the mug shot he had gotten from the kid's juvenile file out of his pocket.

"Let me see," Tolya said, grabbing for the picture.

"Wait a fuckin' minute," Pete said, pulling his hand back then holding up the photo. "Could be. What you wanna do?"

"Let's get a little closer."

They cut across Broadway. A cab honked at Tolya drawing the kid's attention. By the time they crossed Broadway the skinny kid was in a full sprint up 185th Street.

Tolya panted running up the hill. Why did it have to be 185th Street? Despite all the hours he spent at the gym, at 38, a hill at this incline would take the breath right out of him. He couldn't catch a 17-year-old on a hill like this, but Pete could.

He watched Pete race up 185th like a gazelle on the African plain. He was 200 lbs. of solid muscle, not an ounce of fat on him. Tolya wished he had the genes to allow for the same ability. The kid moved up the hill quickly. Pete closed in. They momentarily left Tolya's field of vision. As Tolya neared the top of the hill at Wadsworth Avenue they came back into view. Pete had collared him. He had him on the ground, his knee against his back.

"I didn't do nothing wrong. Get the fuck off me," the kid screamed.

A crowd collected around them in nanoseconds.

"Pete, Pete, let him up but hold him," Tolya said, panting. Pete had barely broken a sweat.

"Let me the fuck go!" the kid shouted, trying to squirm out of Pete's hold.

"You Carlos Pabon?" Tolya asked him.

"Yeah, what of it?" the kid replied.

"We just want to talk to you," Tolya said, still winded and bent over. "We've been looking for you for two days."

"You arresting me?" Carols said. "I didn't do nothing."

"Yeah, you arresting him?" someone shouted from the crowd.

"Shut the fuck up and get out of here," Pete shouted back, "or I'll arrest you."

The crowd backed off a little. Tolya took out his cuffs. "You wanna come have a talk with us quietly, or I gotta put these on you?" he asked Carlos.

Carlos looked at the cuffs. "No officer, please, no cuffs. OK, I'll come with you."

"It's detective..." Tolya said.

"Shit Tolya," Pete whispered to him, "you gotta give that up."

"You thirsty?" Pete asked, putting half a dozen bottles of soda down on the gray metal table in the interrogation room. "Take what you like."

"Yeah, thanks," Carlos said, wiping his forehead with the back of his hand then rubbing the sweat on his pant leg. "It's hot in here." He reached over and grabbed a bottle of Inca Cola, popping the top on the table rim. He took a gulp. "Man, that's good. Why you keep it so hot in here?"

"To soften up guys like you," Tolya said with a smile, sitting down opposite Carlos. Pete leaned up against the wall behind him, sipping on a Jarritos Piña. "Listen, sorry we left you here so long, papito. We got tied up on another matter. So tell us about Señor Redmond and you."

"There ain't nothing to tell," Carlos replied. "I help out the old man a couple times a week."

"Why you doing that?" asked Tolya.

Carlos looked at Tolya and chuckled. "Coño, you know why. I'm sure you seen my record."

"Yeah we have. You got in a little trouble, tried to rob a couple of old ladies. But they beat the shit out of you with their canes instead," Tolya said. Both he and Pete broke into laughter.

"Shit," Carlos said. "Who knew that old lady could swing like A-Rod?"

"So did you try the same thing with Mr. Redmond?" Pete said.

"No, never," Carlos replied, snapping his wiry frame to attention in the chair. "First of all, I learned my lesson, and second, he's my friend. That old man is mad cool."

Tolya was intrigued; there was no way this kid should be this impressed with an old man like Redmond. "Why's he so cool, Carlos?" Tolya said.

"Because he listens, man. He knows how to listen."

"Whaddya mean?" said Pete.

"He's the first man in my whole life I've ever known who wanted to know what I was thinking, not just interested in telling me what I did wrong and how I should be fixin' it."

"Did you talk to him much?" Tolya asked.

"Shit yeah, about everything. And he speaks Spanish too, not like you maricones," Carlos said, waving his hand toward Tolya and Pete.

"Vete al Diablo," Pete said, flipping Carlos the finger.

Carlos snapped back at Pete. "Stop that shit,"

"OK, settle down, both of you," Tolya said. "Carlos, when was the last time you saw Mr. Redmond?"

"A few days ago. I been busy, wasn't able to see him since the end of last week," Carlos said.

Tolya pulled a piece of paper out of his rear pocket and unfolded it. "Says right here though on the log from Hands Across Cultures that you were there the afternoon the old man was found all beat up."

Carlos sat back in the chair, his shoulders slumping into his chest.

"Why are you lying?" Tolya asked. He searched Carlos' eyes for honesty.

"Because I know his son gonna try to pin this on me, so I didn't want you to know I was there that day."

"Carlos," said Tolya, leaning forward over the table, "we aren't trying to pin anything on you, we're just trying to find the truth. If you didn't do anything wrong and you liked Señor Redmond, help us out here."

"What you want to know?" Carlos said, placing palms on the table and leaning forward.

"What happened that day?" Tolya asked.

"I told you, nothing."

"What did you do with him that day?" Tolya asked again.

"I went over to his place, he was watchin' some TV and he asked me to take him outside. He likes to go outside."

"So where did you take him?"

"First we went over to the Key Food. I took him in the wheelchair. He bought some stuff."

"What did he buy?" Tolya said. Pete sat down on the edge of the table.

Carlos closed his eyes and mumbled something Tolya didn't hear clearly, then looked up. "I think oranges," he said. "He likes oranges."

"Then?"

"He saw the boys playing ball across the street at the schoolyard."

"The one we just saw you at?" Pete asked him.

"Yeah," Carlos said, pausing to finish the cola and toss it in the trashcan. "He wanted to watch for a while"

"So you took him over there?" Tolya asked.

"Yeah, and I played a little, but I had to pick up my little brother at 5:30 so I brought him home. He was tired anyway."

"Then you left?" Pete asked.

"First I helped him in the bathroom, then I helped him into bed, then we was talking a little."

"What were you talking about?"

"My father," Carlos said, casting his eyes downward, withdrawing his hands into his lap.

"Your father?" Tolya asked. He wasn't expecting that, and by the look of surprise on Pete's face, neither was he.

"Yeah I was asking his advice."

"About what?" asked Pete.

"My asshole father who abandoned us wants to see me and my little brother, and I was asking Señor Max what he thought, whether I should see him or not."

"I'm kinda curious," Tolya said. "What did he say?"

"He told me, 'Life is too short to make enemies of those you love.' He said I need to learn to forgive my father and that's the best advice he could give anybody."

Tolya couldn't get those words out of his head: "Life is too short to make enemies of those you love. Learn to forgive." The case was getting under his skin.

He walked into the bakery and took a number, leaned against the wall and waited his turn.

"61," the old woman behind the counter called out.

He remembered her. She'd been working this counter when they had arrived from Moscow. She must be at least 80 by now. He looked at his ticket: 68. It would be a long wait but he wanted to surprise Karin with the cookies.

"62. How are you detective?" the woman behind asked.

Detective. He loved the sound of it, so much better than officer "Well, thank you," he answered. "And yourself?"

"Fine, thank God," she answered as she took a rye bread off the shelf.

He remembered the conversation with his father like it was yesterday. He had walked in the apartment and dropped his bag at the door. He looked in the kitchen to find it empty. You couldn't see the living room from the front foyer then, as there was still a wall separating the two dining areas. What a stupid design.

"Tolya?" he heard his father call out.

"*Da*, who else would it be?" he called back. He reached into his bag and pulled out the envelope he had picked up that day from the police academy.

"I'm in the living room," his father called back. "Quickly, I have something to show you."

"What do you want to show me?" Tolya expected to find his father at his desk waiting to excitedly explain some elegant mathematical proof that Tolya would never comprehend. Instead, he found his father on the ornate brocade sofa by the window, not his desk. He handed Tolya a white envelope. It was addressed to Tolya but it was already open. He looked at the upper-left corner. It said: Princeton University. He looked at his father.

"I'm sorry Tolya, I couldn't help it. I was too excited."

Tolya's heart sank. He slipped the large brown envelope he was carrying under his arm and lifted a single sheet out of the envelope his father had given him. He already knew what it said. He read it silently to himself.

Dear Mr. Kurchenko,

On behalf of the trustees of Princeton University, I am pleased to inform you that you have been accepted to the University for the fall term.

He refolded the letter and looked at his father.

"Congratulations," his father said, his tall thin frame rising from the couch. He grabbed Tolya's arm to help steady himself. "I told you Ivan would help you."

"Yes," Tolya said, avoiding his father's gaze, "you did…and he did."

"So you will study physics," his father said, taking both Tolya's hands in his.

The envelope under Tolya's arm fell to the Persian rug covering the wood floor. He let go of his father's hands and bent to pick it up. "Papa, please sit down," he said. He knew he had to do this now. "I need to show you something, too." He sat down next to his father on the couch and pulled a colored brochure from the brown manila envelope.

"You don't seem very happy for your good fortune, son. What is this?" his father asked, looking at the materials Tolya was arranging on the mahogany coffee table.

"I don't know how to tell you this, so I'm just going to show you," Tolya said. He could feel his pulse in his throat. He knew he was going to break the old man's heart. "Papa, I'm not going to Princeton."

He saw the anger rise in his father's face as he took the police academy brochure in his hand. "I thought we had been through this. Ivan went to the Dean of Admissions…"

Tolya rose from the couch and took a deep breath, walking to the other side of the coffee table in three quick steps. "I asked you not to do that, Pop."

His father looked at the brochures. He thumbed the pages. "You want to be a policeman? This is what you want? Like a Cossack?"

"Pop, it's not like that."

"We didn't have enough of the KGB in Russia?"

"It's different," Tolya said dropping into the chair opposite the couch.

"You disgrace me," his father shouted. "You disgrace the memory of your mother!"

"I disgrace you?" Tolya said, clenching his fists and leaning forward. "And you have the nerve to bring my mother's memory into this?" He had to control himself. He knew he had to stand up to him now.

"Yes," his father shouted. "I bring your mother's memory into this. She wanted more for you than to turn into one of our tormentors."

"This is America, not the Sovietsky Soyuz," Tolya shouted back, jumping up out of the chair. "I should think about what *you* want? What you think she would want? Did you ever think about us when you stood up for what you claimed you believed in?"

"You want to be a policeman? Go throw away your life. Live a common life," his father said, taking the letter from Princeton and tearing it into shreds. "Not in my house."

Tolya began to pace around the room. After a moment he stopped and looked at his father. He expected it would be bad, but not this bad. His mouth opened and the words came without any ability to control them. "And then big Jew that you were, leader of the Refuseniks, when you finally got out you didn't take us to Israel. No, you decided you didn't like that government either."

"Menachem Begin was a fascist..."

Tolya stopped moving. "Maybe you should have just kept quiet."

His father struggled to push himself up on his cane. He looked at Tolya, his face like stone. "I couldn't."

"You should have. Perhaps Oleg and mother would still be alive."

His father fell back onto the couch. "How could you? I loved your mother and your brother..."

"You loved them?" he screamed at his father. "You loved yourself more! You loved the movement more! Oleg died because of what you did and mother never recovered from it. That's why I found her hanging from my chin-up bar in the hallway." Tolya couldn't believe he had said it. After all these years of thinking it, he'd finally said it. Now he wished he hadn't. He stared at his father's face. It had gone from the usual gray to white.

"You will not talk to me like this," his father shouted, grabbing his chest with one hand and the wooden arm of the couch with the other. "After what you've said, you can get out."

"68," the old woman shouted from behind the counter.

8

"Tolya, amor, you need help?" Karin called out as he scuffled in the doorway.

"No, I'm OK," he called back, slamming the doorknob into the wall as he pushed his way in. "Shit, I'm gonna make a hole there someday," He turned around in the small space to close the door and fumbled with the packages as he pulled his key out of the lock. He felt Karin's arms close around his waist.

"What do we have here?" she said, frisking the packages. "Wine? Let me see. Chateauneuf du Pape, very nice."

"And these are for you," he said, handing her the flowers.

"Qué linda," She held them to her face and inhaled their scent. "Thank you." She leaned up and kissed him quickly on the lips.

"What's in that box?"

"Something special for you," he said, handing her the bakery carton.

"Ayyy," she said. Tolya saw the sparkle in her eyes. "You went to the Jewish bakery and got me those cookies?"

"Yep." Finally free from his coat, he grabbed her and kissed her hard on the lips. "Happy anniversary," he said when they were done.

"And to you," Karin said, hugging him tightly. After a moment, she let go and returned to the kitchen. "Go clean yourself up and open that bottle," she called out to him. "Dinner will be ready in about ten minutes."

Tolya went into the bedroom. He took off his shirt, went into the bathroom and looked at himself in the mirror. Not bad for 38. Despite the thin layer of fat around his lower stomach, he was muscular and defined, the result of almost daily workouts with Pete at the gym on 181st Street. He picked up the bar of soap, lathered his hands and washed the day's grime away. His thoughts from the day's work didn't go down the drain with the grime.

"Life is too short to make enemies of those you love." A heavy thought. He studied the mirror again, searching his face. He tensed a little. He looked more and more like his father each day.

"Come in," Karin called from the dining room. "The paella is ready,"

Karin had set the table with her good china, the plates with the little red roses that were her grandmother's. They were for her marriage, but her grandmother hadn't succeeded in living that long so just before she died she gave them to Karin. In the center of the table she'd placed a vase filled with the flowers Tolya had brought her. Next to the plates were the $5 wine glasses they had bought together at Target on 225th Street. Abuelita hadn't left her any stemware.

"This is really spectacular," he said, taking her hand and kissing it gently. "I'm hungry and need a drink."

Karin poured the rich burgundy into their glasses. The deep red wine swirled around as it filled the goblets. He raised his glass to hers and said, "Thank you my love, this has been the best year of my life."

"Mine too," she replied.

He placed his arms around her waist again, bending over a little to reach her and kissed her on the lips again, gently this time. "And the most fattening," he said, patting his slightly thickened gut as he stood up.

"Bullshit, don't blame that on me," she said, slapping his stomach, both of them laughing. "Sit down, I'll get the paella."

Karin returned with the copper paella pot, settling it on the trivet in the middle of the table between them. The smell of saffron and seafood filled the room. She scooped up a big serving of rice for Tolya and surrounded the rice with goodies: lobster tail, chicken thigh, chorizo and clams. "Disfruta," she said.

"Disfruta?" Tolya repeated.

"Sí, enjoy. When are you going to learn a little Spanish?" Karin teased.

"When you learn a little Russian," Tolya said tickling her leg with his foot under the table.

"Stop that." Karin squirmed and giggled. "Now, how was your day?" She propped her head on her hands, smiling and fluttering her eyelids. "Do I sound like a wife?"

"Are you giving me hints?"

"Maybe. Abuelita is spinning in her grave right now."

Tolya smiled and took a forkful of paella. "This is delicious," he said.

"Thank you," she replied, fluttering her eyelids again. Her thick, dark hair fell in front of her face, partially hiding the perfectly even white teeth in her broad smile.

"Much better than my day," Tolya continued.

"Why what happened?" she asked, taking another swig of the wine. "Mmm, this is good."

"There is a lot of pressure from this case with the old man."

"I thought you were going to have yourself taken off it."

"I can't do that."

"Why?" she said. Tolya focused his gaze on her as she tasted the rice, testing its chewiness with her front teeth as she'd done since she was a little girl.

"Because today it got interesting."

"In what way?" She bit off the end of a Portuguese roll.

"We found the kid today and brought him in."

Karin stopped chewing. "Really," she said, her mouth still full.

"Yeah," replied Tolya, taking another forkful of rice.

"So do you think he did it?" Karin said.

"I'm not sure."

"See, I told you." She leaned back in her chair and chewed on the rest of the roll.

"You should be a profiler." Tolya popped some lobster tail in his mouth. "Excellent."

"Fuck you," she said.

He loved the smile that flashed across her face with those words.

"So what did the kid say?" she continued, taking another sip of wine.

"He said the old man is like a father to him."

"Really?" Karin licked the wine off her lips.

"Yeah. The kid talks to him, confides in him. The old man even speaks Spanish."

"Not like you."

"Fuck you." Tolya smiled and devoured the paella. "Can I have some more, please?" he asked, holding his plate up in front of him like a child.

"Of course," Karin said, spooning more paella onto Tolya's plate. "What does he talk to the old man about?"

Tolya felt like Karin was interrogating him and he liked the feeling of it, of her taking control. "His life. He asks him for advice."

"What kind of advice does he give him?" She put down her fork and leaned back, stretching her arms behind her head. Her shirt pulled upward, exposing the caramel skin of her stomach.

"From what he told me, pretty good advice," Tolya said, putting down his fork and leaning in toward her, arms on the table. He knew he could take her right then and there, but wanted to play along with this a little more.

"What did he say?" Karin asked.

"He told him life is too short to make enemies of those you love."

"That's a pretty big statement."

Tolya got up from the chair and moved around the table. He bent over Karin's compact frame and kissed her hard on the lips again. She rose from the chair to meet him. He took her hand to lead her to the bedroom. He gently pushed her down onto the bed, pulled off his shirt and climbed on top of her. As he breathed in the scent of her skin, she whispered in his ear, "Amor, I'm pregnant."

Shalom opened the door to the apartment deep in thought. He'd just come from the hospital. His father was still in a coma, still hovering between life and death. He kissed the mezuzah absentmindedly, removed his hat and quickly covered his head with his favorite yarmulke, which Rachel always left on the little table by the door. Peering down the hallway, he could see Baruch in the living room caressing and organizing the buttons in Rachel's sewing kit in a silent ritual.

The apartment was spacious yet cluttered, mostly with books. Bookcases lined the walls of virtually every room. They were filled with various copies of the Talmud and commentary in Hebrew, Yiddish and English, stacked helter-skelter into the shelves; some volumes vertical, some horizontal when they didn't fit. Shalom loved his books despite how much dust they collected.

"Shalom is that you? Dinner is on the table," Rachel called from the kitchen.

Shalom walked into the living room and touched Baruch just under the arm to signal him to stand up, as the teacher at the new school had shown him. "Come now, dinner is ready son." Shalom said softly. Baruch rose. They walked back through the living room toward the kitchen.

Rachel had set the table as always: regular dishes for herself and Shalom, plastic for Baruch. A large pot of soup with chicken, vegetables, noodles and matzah balls sat on the stove. She had filled Baruch's bowl earlier so that it would cool a bit before he sat down. If it was too hot he simply wouldn't eat it and once he rejected something, that was it. She had cut up the breast of the chicken and placed it on a plate beside Baruch's bowl of soup. He wouldn't eat either if they were in the bowl together. Shalom straightened the yarmulke on Baruch's head and made a blessing over the bread.

"Did you have a chance to speak with the doctor at the hospital?" Rachel asked Shalom after several minutes.

"No," he answered. "The doctor was gone by the time I got there and the nurse said there was no change."

"Do they think he'll wake up?"

"Only God knows that," replied Shalom, putting down his fork and looking at Rachel.

"Baruch HaShem," said Rachel.

They were silent for a moment, both of them looking over toward Baruch, watching him quietly eat his soup.

"He's really improved recently," Rachel said, beaming up at Shalom.

"Yes, he has."

"Shalom," she continued, "I was wrong to resist so much sending him to that school."

Shalom put down his spoon, reached out his hand to Rachel's and smiled. "You were just acting like his mother, protecting him."

"Thank you. I am sorry though. We should have acted sooner."

"Don't be." He squeezed her hand and looked at her face, simple and full of truth. She was as beautiful as the first time he saw her, a woman of valor and piety.

"Have you heard anything from the police?" Rachel asked.

"No, I haven't. Your father said to let Assemblyman Levitz handle them," Shalom replied, picking up his spoon. "Why?"

"I don't know. What's taking them so long?"

"So long with what?" he asked, taking a bite of the matzah ball. "No one makes a better *kneydl** than you, Rachel," he said.

"Thank you," she said.

He noticed her hesitation and asked again, "So long with what?"

"To arrest that boy."

"They have to finish their investigation," he said. He thought it unlike her to be accusative.

"It's obvious it was that boy," she said. "He was with your father that afternoon. Who else could it be?"

"We don't know that," said Shalom, placing his spoon back on the napkin and covering her clenched fist with his open hand. "We can't accuse him unjustly."

"Why?" Rachel said. "They certainly tried to accuse us."

* *Kneydl* (k-NAY-del): dumpling (Yiddish)

Tolya rolled off Karin. "Are you sure?"

"Yes," she said rolling on top of him. She had taken off her top. Her naked breasts pressed against his skin. She smiled at him. He turned his face away from hers.

"Let's make love."

"How did it happen?" he asked. He realized how stupid he sounded.

"You know how to make a baby, silly boy," she said, straddling him. "You remember that night it was so warm, we'd just taken out the air conditioner and we couldn't sleep?"

He did remember. Tolya felt her hand slip into his unbuttoned pants.

"What happened to little Anatol?" Karin teased.

"Nothing," Tolya said, rolling out from underneath her. "You just caught me off guard, surprised me. Anyway, maybe it's not good for the baby?"

"It's fine for the baby," Karin said, putting her arms around him from behind, her silky skin sliding against his back. He could feel himself getting hard again. All she had to do was touch him. He turned toward her and smiled.

"You're happy about it then?" she asked.

"Yes," he lied.

9

Tolya ran back to the station house. He'd gotten Pete's text only a few minutes earlier. It said, "Get over here now, captain wants you." As he entered the building, he saw Pete outside the captain's office waving at him to follow him in. "What's up?" he asked, a little out of breath from the frantic run back to the station.

Pete didn't answer. The captain motioned to them to sit down.

"See, I told you not to go home. He was asking why you weren't here," Pete said.

"Yes, yes of course, assemblyman," the captain said into the phone.

"Tell me something?" Tolya said.

"It's a murder rap now," Pete said.

"The old man died?" Tolya looked at the captain.

"Pete," the captain said as he put down the phone. "Damn it, I told you I'd fill him in."

"Sorry Cap…"

"Sorry my ass," the captain interrupted. He turned to Tolya. "Where the fuck were you? You left the station while on duty, unauthorized, without telling anyone?"

"I, I had something I had to take care of at home. I was only a few minutes away," replied Tolya sheepishly. He couldn't tell the captain he went home to use the crapper and had been doing so for years because he had an irrational fear of public toilets.

"I should discipline you for that," the captain said.

"OK, Cap, I'm sorry. What happened?"

The captain leaned back, the chair creaking under his weight. "The old man died this morning."

"They gonna do an autopsy?" Pete asked.

"No autopsy. Orthodox belief doesn't permit it. Surprised I knew that?" He shot a confident smile at Tolya.

"No. I assume Levitz just told you," Tolya said, knocking the smile and confidence off the captain's face.

"Don't interrupt … Levitz was out of control. And we aren't about to pick another argument here. We all know how he died. They want us to pick up the Dominican kid and charge him."

"What?" Tolya said. "We don't have any evidence, we can't make a case. We hoped we would find something on one of the private security cams along the street. Nothing. We checked the cams from the synagogue and the co-ops along Bennett. We only confirmed that María and Carlos had been there when they said they were."

"Well you better make a case, one way or another. And you got, as I figure it, a week to do it," the captain continued. "The funeral is tomorrow. And yes, we will be going, all of us, while they sit — whatever the hell they call it..."

"Shiva," Tolya interjected.

"Yes, whatever, for a week. So the son will be out of commission for the next eight days, but I gotta have something by the time they're done. Levitz won't be sitting shiva. Go back to that apartment. Find something."

Shalom sat quietly perched on the couch in his living room, his hat in his hands. He watched Rachel and her father, Rabbi Schoenweiss, whispering to each other. He couldn't hear them and he didn't care. Assemblyman Levitz was in the kitchen on the phone. He kept repeating, "Uh-huh, yes, uh-huh."

His mind raced. His father was 95 years old. He couldn't have survived this. He asked HaShem to forgive him for not returning his father to faith before he died.

He felt the rabbi's hand on his shoulder. "Shalom," he said, "we need to speak about the funeral now. Assemblyman Levitz will have to leave shortly."

"All right," he said. He wasn't sure why Levitz would be involved.

Levitz walked down the two steps into the living room. An unremarkable-looking man, his entire persona changed as he spoke. "I understand how difficult this is for you," Levitz began. "Losing a parent is very difficult at any age, and particularly under these circumstances."

Shalom heard his words, but wasn't sure what Levitz was trying to tell him.

"Unfortunately, Shalom…" Levitz paused. "May I call you Shalom?"

"Yes, of course."

"Unfortunately, because of the circumstances — the all-too-frequent violence against our people and the way the police handled this — it's important that your father's funeral reflect the strength of our community."

Shalom lifted his head.

"I know you are a very private person, but can you consider this?" Levitz said, sitting down next to him on the couch and straightening his tie.

"I'm sorry Mr. Levitz, I am not sure I understand what you're driving at."

"The funeral, Shalom," the rabbi said.

"The funeral?" Shalom repeated, his gaze shifting back and forth between Levitz and his father-in-law. His sudden chuckling caught everyone off guard. "My father hasn't seen the inside of a shul since my mother died, and then only because she requested a Jewish burial. Before that, he hadn't been in a shul since my Bar Mitzvah. What kind of funeral? He doesn't even have a burial plot. He wanted to be cremated."

"God forbid," the rabbi said.

"I don't know. He was born a Jew, but nothing else," Shalom said. "I might not agree with this but it was his wish. How many times did I hear him say he wanted to go up in smoke, like his family did?"

The rabbi sat down next to Shalom and put his arm around his shoulder. "I know all this," he said, "but we can't do what he asked. He was born a Jew. He should be buried as one."

"*Abba*," Shalom said, addressing his father-in-law with the Hebrew word for father. "You yourself have said many times: He was the worst *apikoros** you have ever met."

"I was wrong to have said that," said the rabbi, standing up and smoothing his vest and pants. "May HaShem and your father forgive me."

Shalom's mind raced. Rachel's father detested his father and had never tried to conceal his contempt. Now he was asking for his forgiveness. "What are you suggesting?"

"The congregation will take care of everything," the rabbi said.

Shalom was dumbfounded.

"Let me tell you what we have in mind," Levitz said.

Tolya and Pete carefully removed the police tape blocking the door to Redmond's apartment before letting themselves in.

"You take the bedrooms," said Tolya, handing Pete a pair of Latex gloves and slipping on a pair himself. "I'll take the living room."

"OK," said Pete. Tolya watched him turn the corner and disappear toward the master bedroom. The living room was filled with old mahogany furniture, heavy and carved. The blinds were still drawn and the room had that smell that goes along with old people no matter where you find them. Despite the age and shabbiness of the contents of the room, Tolya noted how clean it was,

---

* *Apikoros*: Non-believer (Hebrew)

everything in its place and dusted. On the windowsill were stacks of magazines, neatly piled in size order. He leafed through them: *National Geographic*, *The Economist*, *The New Yorker*, some publication from the World Jewish Congress and another in an odd language he couldn't decipher. Redmond was no dummy.

"Tolya," Pete called from the bedroom. "Come in here. Look at this."

Tolya found Pete standing over the dresser. Next to an old-fashioned mirrored tray with empty perfume bottles were two photos: One very old, a picture of a couple in a wedding gown and tuxedo. It looked like it dated back to at least the 1930s. "That must be the old man and his wife," Pete said.

The other photo was much more recent: A boy, about 13, in the somber dress of local Orthodox Jews.

"And this must be the grandson," Tolya said, picking up the frame and examining the photo.

"Yeah," Pete said, laughing, "but the clothes."

"That's why you called me in here?" Tolya said.

"No, look at this one." Pete picked up another old black-and-white photo. It was of a young man standing in front of a beautiful beach with palm trees, in a white shirt and slacks and a straw hat in his hand, smiling broadly and holding the hand of a small, dark-skinned boy. At the bottom on the right-hand side, the words "Con Josecito a Bahía Sosúa" were written.

"I think it's the old man," Pete said.

Tolya looked at the photo. The man in the picture looked a lot like the guy in the wedding photo, only a little older and happier. "Interesting life this old man had," Tolya said, putting the photo back on the dresser. "I'm going to check the second bedroom."

"OK," Pete answered as he bent down to check the cubby in the night table.

The second bedroom was small and cramped. Tolya opened the dresser drawers one by one. They were filled with old clothes, magazines, newspapers and trinkets.

"Nothing here," he said out loud as he pulled a box out of the bottom of the closet. He saw Pete come into the room out of the corner of his eye. "You find anything?" Tolya asked.

"Just this," Pete said, holding up the small metal chip he had placed into a small plastic evidence bag.

"Where was it?"

"Just under the bed frame."

"What do you think it is?" Tolya asked, taking the plastic bag from Pete and holding it up to examine the small metal chip inside.

"No fucking idea, but hey, you never know," Pete said, taking the bag back from Tolya.

"Keep looking," Tolya said, "and did you search the dresser in the master bedroom?"

"No, I was about to."

"Could you go back in there and finish up, please? The captain's gonna have our asses if we don't come up with something."

"OK, tranqui," Pete said, gesturing with his palms open toward the floor before leaving the room.

Tolya took the box and sat down on the bed. He removed the worn, black leather orthopedic shoes sitting on the top of the box. "The shit people hang on to…" he mumbled to himself.

He opened the top of the box and found an embroidered black-velvet tablecloth. It was very large, requiring him to stretch his arms to their full six-foot extent to open it completely. He recognized it as a piano cover. His mother had had one like this in Russia. They weren't allowed to bring it with them when they left. The Soviet policeman who monitored their emigration removed it from their boxes when he learned that her grandmother had embroidered it herself. He was a mean bastard that cop.

Under the cloth were a number of leather-bound books. He lifted one up and examined it. No title, no author's name. He opened the book. Each page was filled with script. Every several pages there was a date, written in the old European style: the date first, in Arabic numerals, followed by the month signified in Roman numerals, followed by the last two digits of the year in Arabic numerals. He could tell the thin volumes were diaries, but struggled to determine what language they were written in.

He opened up to a page and tried deciphering the words. He sounded them out, mumbling almost inaudibly, and eventually recognized it as Spanish. He looked through the box at several other volumes. Some were written in English, in that same old-fashioned, flowing script that reminded him of the notes his father would leave him inside the covers of his schoolbooks; others in Spanish, and yet others in a language he couldn't identify at all. Pete's voice broke his concentration.

"Tolya, take a look at this," he said, holding out a much larger clear plastic bag. Inside was a large book with a silver cover and a large blue stone in the center.

"It's a prayer book," said Tolya.

"And it matches this piece of metal I found under the bed," said Pete.

"So?"

"I found the book in the bottom drawer under the sweaters. Way in the back."

"Really?" said Tolya, taking the bag from Pete. "Let me take a look where you found it."

Pete turned and walked back toward the master bedroom. Tolya hesitated as he got up to follow him. He reached into the box, took some of the journals and placed them in the large inside pocket of his overcoat.

"What's that?" asked Karin, walking into the bedroom wrapped in a towel.

Tolya looked at her. He focused on her lower abdomen and the baby he knew was growing there. It changed everything. "Something I found at the old man's apartment," he said.

She stopped in her tracks. "You took something from the crime scene?" she said. "You're kidding me, right?"

"I shouldn't have taken it," he replied, continuing to thumb through the small red volume. "It was an impulse."

"No, detective, you don't act on impulses." Tolya watched her body stiffen as she crossed her arms against her chest. "And do you think you should have told me?"

"It's our secret," he said and flashed a smile at her.

"We can't have any secrets, amor. I work for Internal Affairs, and this could affect my job. I don't want to know anything about this."

Tolya looked up and watched her from behind as she gently placed her hand on her stomach. She moved her hand in a slow circular motion as she focused in the mirror.

"Are you excited, amor?" she asked him.

"Of course," he said, avoiding eye contact in the mirror. Tolya's mind filled with an image of Karin in a few months, her body changed by the pregnancy. He wasn't sure how he felt, what to tell her. In the day since she'd told him about the pregnancy, he had said few words about it and had measured every syllable.

Tolya picked up the diary again, careful not to damage the pages with his large clumsy fingers, hoping it would attract her attention and change the subject. He knew curiosity would get the better of her. She'd want to know what he was reading.

He scanned the old-fashioned writing on the page. This volume was in English, if you could call it that. Tolya remembered how hard it was for him to learn to write in English. The date on the top of the page said: 19 VI '47. June 19, 1947. He began to read.

19 VI '47

We went Davey's seventh birthday party today. Charlotte had bake a beautiful cake, chocolate that Davey likes. The cousins was there. It was very happy till Jack asks me to come into the bedroom. He wants to show me something. We are in the bedroom. He hand me the letter from the Red Cross. I ask him, what is this? I see tears in his eyes. He says in very low voice, I almost not hear him, "Istvan." It is about Istvan, my twin. I open the letter and it tell me he is dead. I cannot continue to read it. I put it back in the envelope and give it back to him. I cannot look at Jack. Another part of me is dead now, one more little piece.

"Tolya," Karin said, sitting down next to him on the bed, "why are you crying?"

He felt his heart beat quicken as he looked up at her. "I'm not crying," he said. He hadn't felt the tear fall from his eye.

Karin wiped the tear off his face with her pinky finger. "Then what was this," she said, holding her wet finger up to his lips.

"I didn't realize."

"Obviously. Let me see that," she said, grabbing for the book.

"Be careful with that," he said, relieved that the subject of her pregnancy had receded.

"Let me see," she said.

"No, wait, I have another one for you. I need your help. This one is in Spanish."

He turned and bent over the bed to the floor, picking up another small, red, leather-bound volume and handing it to her. She opened it and squinted her eyes at the difficult script. "What is this?"

"The old man's journals. I need you to read that one for me, ASAP. I need you to translate it for me."

"I shouldn't be doing this," she said, shaking her head while opening the book slowly to the first page, scanning it. "Interesting. He says right here, 'Yo empiezo libro en español. Español esta idioma nueva de mi vida.'"

"And?" Tolya says. "What does that mean?"

She leaned over him, her hair falling around her face, her breasts hidden by the towel but only inches from him. "First tell me what made you cry, my big strong detective."

Tolya hesitated for a moment. He pushed himself up on his elbow and kissed her. "The tear was for what I read. It was about the death of his twin brother."

"A little too close to home, querido mio?" she said, returning the kiss.

"Sí. Now, what does that say?" Tolya said, drying his eyes.

"It says he is writing in Spanish — and poor Spanish, I might add — because it is now his language."

"Shit Karin, give the guy a break. Can you make sense of it?"

"Por supuesto, amor." She hesitated a moment before continuing.

"Well?" said Tolya.

"This is actually quite interesting. This entry is dated October 30. He says his group left Genoa on September 20 after a farewell dinner given for them by the local Jewish community. He thought this very odd, as all Jews in Europe were under threat by the Fascists. Not exactly a time or place for a party."

She continued, correcting Max's bad Spanish in her mind as she translated free form:

"The Chief Rabbi of Genoa presented them with a Torah Scroll for the community in Sosúa, which he has volunteered to transport himself,"

Karin said. She stopped for a moment then continued, shifting to a direct translation:

"My mood, unlike most of the other refugees, was lifted immediately upon leaving Italy. I stood on the deck, breathing the warm Mediterranean air and anxious to begin a new life.

"The first stop was in Barcelona. We picked up a group of Spanish refugees, communists released by the Franco regime upon their agreement to leave the country. They too are headed to Santo Domingo. I met one of these refugees at the bar the night we set sail from Barcelona. His name was Gustavo. He spoke German fluently, almost as good as mine. Gustavo was a professor of renaissance literature at the university. He supported the Republican regime in the civil war and was imprisoned in a concentration camp for more than a year after the war ended. His family bribed the court to release him on the agreement that he leave Spain permanently.

"He told me his greatest regret is that he might never teach again. I asked him to teach me Spanish to prepare me for our arrival in Puerto Plata. I have been studying with him for a month now, as we have been stuck in Lisbon awaiting a ship to take us to our new lives. This is my first journal in my new language."

Sosúa
Puerto Plata
Dominican Republic
15 XII '40

The palm trees astounded me. I leaned over the rail of the ship to get a better look at them. I had only ever seen them in pictures. The warmth of the sunlight and the coolness of the breeze rushed over my shirt, penetrating the cotton fabric through to my skin. It felt electric. Imagine: It's December and it feels like July. No more winter, ever. We will need new clothes. Almost everything we have is wool.

I called out to Helen. "Come here, you should see this. It's beautiful." She was hiding from the sun under the overhang from the next deck.

"It's too hot," she called back.

"Please, come look," I said, waving at her. "I'll shade you with this." I held up the Hungarian newspaper I had been carrying around since my brother Jack gave it to me a week earlier when we stopped over in New York. I hadn't seen him in nearly 15 years. He was shocked that Istvan and Magda weren't with us. In the few minutes the American authorities gave us, and with no place to have a private conversation I wasn't able to tell him everything that had happened, only that Istvan and Magda had gone back to our family's village in Slovakia, that he should cable the family to make sure they had arrived.

Helen waved me off and feigned a smile. I pouted at her. Finally, she put her wool hat on her head and walked slowly, carefully, toward the rail. I watched her move toward me. Even in these calm waters she couldn't get used to the listing of the ship.

"I'm glad we'll be off of here soon," she said, grabbing hold of the rail with one hand, holding her hat against the breeze with the other.

I put my hand over hers on the rail. "Yes, we'll be off soon. To start our new life," I said turning toward her. The brim of her hat cast a shadow across her face. I knew I had to try to make her happy, to make myself happy with her.

"Yes, our new life," she said. She wiped away the sweat that had formed under the rim of her hat. "Such as it will be."

It was a long first day. We were processed twice: first by the Dominican authorities and then by the Dominican Republic Settlement Association, DORSA. It was DORSA that brought us here. The result of Trujillo's offer to take up to 100,000 Jewish refugees at the Evian Conference in July of 1938. Trujillo donated a defunct banana plantation at Sosúa on the north coast near Puerto Plata as the first settlement site.

DORSA representatives came to the concentration camp in Italy and told us if we agreed to come to the Dominican Republic we would be released immediately and we could bring our families out in one year's time. We had nowhere else to go. Now DORSA is mother, father, teacher and confessor all rolled into one.

They greeted us with a cool drink and a fresh banana. Thin, dark-skinned men removed our belongings from the ship's hold and placed the luggage and boxes into lorries. "Bienvenidos a la República Dominicana," read a large sign that hung against the back wall of the open-air building where we assembled before being taken to the settlement. Helen clung to me. I could sense her nervousness, as she is rarely physical with me, especially in public.

The director of the settlement, Dr. Joseph Rosen, spoke. "Welcome," he said in German, Spanish, Hungarian, Czech and Polish. "We are so delighted to have you here." He continued the rest of the speech in German. I saw strain on Helen's face as she tried to follow the words. "Here you will start your lives anew. At the end of one year, your families will come to join you. Build Sosúa for them. Today we are about 300 people. In a few years we hope to be 10,000."

The settlers applauded. Some shouted, "Bravo, Bravo," as if they were at the opera house in Vienna or Budapest.

"Forget the nightmare you have been lucky enough to escape," Rosen continued. "Look around you at this new place and smile. It is your home now."

I felt Helen buckle a little on my arm. "Are you all right?" I asked her.

"It's just the heat," she said, but I knew what it was. She was frightened and I understand that. She is alone here with me; no sisters, no mother and no servants. I put my hand on the small of her back. She looked up at me with a weak, sickly smile.

"You'll see, *drágám*[*]," I said in Hungarian. "We'll be fine, we've done the right thing. In a year we'll bring them all out."

She sighed and smiled, a bit calmer.

"What is it?" I asked her.

"The sound of Hungarian," she said. "It's like music to me. It calms me."

"See you all at the settlement," the director said loudly into the microphone, the harsh sound of his German interrupted by more applause. We applauded as well. Helen's wool hat muffled the sound of her hands gently clapping.

We stood at the door of a large wooden building. Young men and women moved about the room preparing for the evening's meal. They called out to one another, some even joking, mostly in German with a smattering of Spanish.

"Welcome. May I help you to a seat?" an attractive young woman in a coffee-colored cotton dress asked Helen, her hand outstretched. "My name in Greta."

She had caught Helen off guard. Helen turned toward me, her mouth slightly ajar. I told her with my eyes to relax. I took the young woman's hand

---

[*] *Drágám*: Darling (Hungarian)

and said, "Yes, please. My name is Max Rothman and this is my wife, Helen."

"Follow me, *bitte*," she said, leading us to the middle of a long table where there were two empty places.

The other people sitting at the table were mostly men. Seeing a woman, and being who they were, they all rose. "I'm Fritzy," the man seated immediately to my left said, "and this is my brother, Robert." He pointed to an almost exact, but slightly older replica of himself. "We are from Salzburg."

"And I am Edward," said the man to Helen's right, taking her hand lightly. He, like Fritzy, addressed us in German. "I'm from Sturova. That's what it was called when it was Czechoslovakia, now it's called Sturgau."

"We are from Kosice," I said, taking Edward's hand.

"Which was also Czechoslovakia once," he said, prompting a laugh from everyone at the table.

"But your accent is Hungarian," the man standing directly across from me said.

"Yes. It's our first language," I replied.

"I'm Erno, but here they call me Ernest," the man continued in German, then switched to Hungarian. "*Csókolom**," he said, taking Helen's hand in his and kissing it formally.

"Please, sit. Enough of the politeness," said a young woman as she came up from behind Erno. "I'm Ava." A broad smile on her face revealed a perfect set of white teeth. She took the seat next to Erno. "You could have introduced me," she said to him, flipping back her red hair from her face.

"You didn't give me a chance," he said and kissed her gently on the lips.

Helen rose slightly from her chair, offering her hand. "I am Helen Rothman." Ava took Helen's hand in both of hers and said in Hungarian, "Welcome, I am so happy to have another woman, another Hungarian woman, here."

"Thank you," Helen said, smiling.

"What news of the world do you bring us?" asked Robert. "We only get American papers, which we translate into German, and weeks late at that."

"Not much," I said. "We didn't hear much on board the ship." I took out the remainder of the pack of cigarettes I had in my shirt pocket and

---

* *Csókolom*: Hello (literally, "I kiss it," Hungarian)

offered them around.

"Oh, thank you," said Fritzy, taking one. "Where did you embark from?"

"Italy," I said, offering him a light.

Ava sighed. "Ah Italy. I remember Italy, from before all this."

"When did you leave?" asked Fritzy. He sucked in the tobacco smoke and let it out slowly. "Excellent, we don't get American cigarettes here often."

"We left Kosice in early April. I had a friend, a gentile, he worked for me. He woke us in the middle of the night to tell us the Arrow Cross was coming for us in the morning. We escaped in the darkness. Helen, me, my brother Istvan and his wife," I answered. "Then we traveled to Budapest and stayed there until I was able to arrange passage to Italy. We went to Genoa by way of Vienna, which was very frightening. I had my doubts that we would be permitted to leave Vienna. We arrived in late April of this year, just before the Nazis and their Italian allies attacked France. How long have you been here?"

"About six months," said Fritzy. "Your voyage sounds harrowing."

"To say the least."

Two women placed large white platters of schnitzel and cold vegetables, both cooked and raw, with a pink-colored sauce on the tables. I watched Helen survey the platters.

"Try this," Ava said, pointing to a white mass that looked something like potato. "It's called yuca. We grow it ourselves. Have it with the onions."

"Thank you," Helen said, smiling at Ava.

"Where did you set out from?" I asked Fritzy.

"Switzerland. We were in a detention camp. We had escaped over the border from Austria…"

"Germany," corrected Edward. "There is no more Austria, same as there is no more Czechoslovakia."

"Yes," Robert said. "In any event, DORSA came to the camp and here we are."

"I had a very similar experience in Italy," I said, taking a piece of the schnitzel. I tasted it and knew instantly it was pork. Helen took a small piece of the white vegetable and onions and placed it in her mouth. She then cut a small piece of the schnitzel and tasted it as well.

"Do you like it?" Ava asked her.

"Yes, it's delicious. What do you call it again?"

"Yuca," replied Ava.

"And the veal is excellent," Helen added, placing another piece of schnitzel into her mouth.

"Veal?" Erno said, raising one eyebrow. "It's not veal. We can't afford to slaughter the calves. We need the herd for milk, that's our main business."

"Chicken?" said Helen.

"It's pork cutlet, we raise the pigs ourselves," Erno said, cutting off a large piece from his cutlet.

Helen stopped chewing. I knew she had never eaten pork. She is not strictly observant but she would never eat pork. I also knew she would never spit it out in front of a table full of strangers. My heart sank as she forced herself to swallow, knowing this would only serve to confirm for her that she didn't belong here.

"Pork, really?" she said, putting down her knife and fork, then folding her hands in her lap. "I've never tried it before."

An awkward silence enveloped our group, the din of the dining room surrounding us. Helen looked at me. I said nothing, kept eating and watched her face redden. I felt sorry for her, but our future depends on our ability to adjust to life here.

"In a few more months we can bring out our parents and our sisters," Robert said, breaking the tension.

"If they last that long," said Erno.

A dark expression crossed Robert's face.

"Erno, that's enough," Ava said, jabbing his arm. Ava turned toward me and smiled. "Well, Italy is still beautiful, despite Mussolini, I imagine," she said.

"What we saw of it," I replied. "We were there only a short time before the attack on France. Mussolini declared all non-Italian Jews enemy aliens. We were ordered to leave the country immediately or face internment in a concentration camp. My brother and his wife were traveling with us. They returned to Slovakia. I was interred in a camp."

Ava's eyes turned and settled on Helen, the look of terror evident behind them.

"No, no," Helen said, "I wasn't in the camp. I went into hiding. A very kind woman protected me."

Ava sighed.

"And here we are," I said, lifting my glass. "It's only water but here is to our new life."

"You know, we Hungarians never toast on water," Erno said raising his glass as well. "It's bad luck."

I pulled back the mosquito netting and slipped into the narrow bed. The sheets are rougher than at home. The light of the candle flickered on the small, rough-hewn table under the window. The window was open to the darkness outside: no glass pane, no screen, the wood shutters held back by rope tied to the wall inside the room.

Because we are married, we've been given private accommodations. Single settlers have to sleep together in the large dormitories; one for the men, the other for the women. Our "suite" consists of this room, a cordoned off corner that functions as the bathroom (a huge luxury here), and a small porch.

"Helen, are you all right in there?" I called out toward the bathroom. It has merely a toilet and a sink with only one faucet for cold water.

"Yes, I'm fine," she answered from behind the thin cloth separating the alcove from the rest of the room. I watched her pull the nightgown over her head, her shadow cast against the cloth by the light from the candle. I surveyed the room in the dim light. How different than anything I could have imagined. Now I will become a farmer. No father-in-law checking my books every week.

"Max," Helen called out.

"Yes?"

"Can you help me?" she said, pulling back the curtain. "It's so dark."

"Just hold the candle out in front of you and walk toward the bed," I said. "I'll pull back the netting."

I watched her walk toward me, almost ghostlike in the darkness, the nightgown trailing behind her. The candlelight softened her face. She was never what I'd thought of as pretty. She was sweet, my father had said, demure, a woman of valor, and she came with a big dowry. I needed the dowry. As the fourth son — or fifth, as I was a twin — I wouldn't get an education like Zoli and I wouldn't inherit the business like Julian, nor would I get a steamship ticket to America like Jack. I needed a wife whose father could supply me with one. Helen's father did that. She came to me with a house, a business, a bank account and a partner: her father. All that is gone now. In a year I will bring them all out. They will be in my debt this time.

"Where should I put this candle?" Helen asked, standing next to the bed.

"There," I answered, "next to the other one on the table. Or better yet, blow it out."

Helen hesitated for a moment, then with a quick breath blew out the candle. She took the netting from me and sat on the bed, shifting her legs under the sheet. "It's so warm," she said.

"Why do you have on that heavy nightgown?" I asked, feeling the wool material rub up against my skin. I was naked except for my underwear, something I would never have done at home.

"I could never sleep…uncovered," she said, waving her arm in my direction, "like that." Even in the dim light of the single candle, I could see her face flush with embarrassment.

"Why?"

"It would be…improper."

"We're not in Europe anymore," I said. "You're my wife. We make our own rules here."

"I never wanted to make new rules," she said, laying back on the small pillow the settlement supplied us. "Anyway, it seems there are no rules here."

"What do you mean?" I asked.

"Ava and Erno. Did you see the way she kissed him, how he touches her in public?"

"Yes, it was sweet."

"She has no rings. They're not married."

"Perhaps they took her rings in Vienna," I said, withdrawing my arm from her waist. She had to adjust, if we are to survive here.

"Perhaps," she said.

The noises of the jungle filtered into the room and filled the silence between us. I focused on her breathing, shallow and nervous. "Helen, are you all right?" I asked.

"It's very warm, that's all. I'm not used to the climate."

"You'd be much more comfortable if you took off that nightgown," I said, my hand moving to the button at her neck.

"I, I couldn't," she answered.

"You won't sleep this way and you need to be rested for tomorrow."

"I don't know."

"Oh come now," I said, moving my hand under her breast, cupping it.

"Stop," she said.

"Why?"

"Because I don't want to."

"Why?" I said, gently undoing the buttons. "You'll be much more comfortable."

"And sweaty," she said. I could feel the perspiration forming between her breasts as my hand brushed against them pulling back the nightgown.

"Here, sit up. I'll help you with this," I said slipping off the gown.

She immediately covered her breasts with her arm.

"There, isn't that better?" I said. I noticed then, laying on the bed, how her body has changed over the past few months. She's lost weight since we left Italy. We had been in separate beds almost constantly since leaving Kosice eight months ago. She is not only thinner, but less lumpy. Her body is almost pleasing.

"Better?" she said, pushing her hair off her forehead. "I'm not sure about better, but…certainly cooler."

I placed my hand on her breast again and leaned toward her, kissing her gently on the lips. She turned her head slightly away from me.

"What's wrong?" I asked.

"Nothing is wrong," she said. "It's just all so new. Not tonight Max, please."

"All right, not tonight. There will be many nights," I said, moving closer to her, placing my arm over her waist, feeling the skin of her back against the skin of my chest. I will make her happy. I will make us both happy.

10

The view from the corner of West 186th Street and Broadway enabled Tolya to watch the growing crowds outside the precinct and the synagogue at the same time. Juan Carlos Guzmán, head of the Alianza Dominicana, stood in front of the steps of the station house dressed, as always, in an impeccable dark-blue suit, his hair and beard perfectly trimmed. Crews from all the local TV stations milled about the outer edges of the crowd. Behind Guzmán stood a large group of people. From his vantage point, Tolya couldn't estimate the number. Two teenage boys dressed similarly to Guzmán stood directly behind him, each holding a pole to a banner that read, "Innocent Until Proven Guilty" in both English and Spanish.

"Look," said Pete, standing just behind Tolya and pointing toward the door of the station house. Tolya watched as the captain walked out of the front door of the station house with two other men he didn't recognize, both dressed in suits. They stopped at the edge of the first step. Guzmán picked up a small megaphone and turned toward the crowd.

"Theatrical enough?" Tolya said.

"Almost like it's been rehearsed," said Pete.

"Mis amigos," Guzmán began, alternating between Spanish and English, the TV crews moving in closer to catch every word. "We've come here today to accomplish three things."

Shouts of "sí" and "claro" rose from the crowd.

"First, to let the police department know that we support their efforts to find the perpetrator who attacked Señor Redmond, a man close to our community as well as his own, a man who lived among us both here and in Santo Domingo. A man whose life was saved by the generosity of our homeland and in return worked with us to save our youth."

Applause rose from the crowd.

"Second, to make clear to our friends in the NYPD that Carlos Pabon is innocent of any wrongdoing." He turned from the crowd toward the captain and the two men standing with him in front of the entrance to the station. "Do not railroad this young boy for the sake of a quick resolution to this terrible crime. Find the real killer and bring justice to our communities."

More shouts of claro and sí rang out from the crowd.

"With that said," Guzmán continued, "we have come to present Captain McCloskey with this petition, signed by hundreds of local residents, to continue the investigation into the attack against Señor Redmond until the real killer is found. We can never believe that a heartless crime such as this would come from within our community."

Guzmán turned and put down the megaphone, climbing the three steps up to where the captain was standing. He reached the top step and extended his hand, then turned toward the cameras. Guzmán faced the cameras with a broad smile and said something to the captain as he handed him an envelope.

"Can you believe this shit?" Tolya said.

"Only sorry I can't hear what he's saying right now," Pete replied.

They watched as Guzmán walked back down the steps and picked up the megaphone again. "Lastly, but of no less importance," he shouted into the megaphone at the growing crowd, "we have come to assure our Jewish neighbors they have nothing to fear from us."

"So he's really gonna do this?" Tolya said.

"It appears that way and his timing is impeccable," Pete said, pointing toward the synagogue on Bennett Avenue. "Here they come."

Tolya looked toward the synagogue. A sea of men in black hats and coats, many wrapped in prayer shawls, streamed into the street. The women poured out from the side doors.

"We'd better get over there," Tolya said.

Shalom stood silently in front of the synagogue with Baruch at his side. He scanned the growing crowd for Rachel. Almost everyone stopped to offer him condolences for his father's death. He was so distracted he couldn't spot her.

"Look down the block," he heard someone say from behind him. He turned his head to see a large group of people with a banner walking toward the *Shabbos*[*] crowd milling around in front of the synagogue. The banner waved unsteadily in the wind. In front of the marching crowd was a man with a megaphone shouting something he couldn't quite make out. As the crowd grew closer the chant became clearer. "Pabon is innocent, find the real murderer," alternating between English and Spanish.

Shalom felt his stomach turn. He was a very private person leading a quiet life. He knew now that had changed. He turned back toward Baruch, who was oblivious as always. He then felt a hand on his back. It was Rachel.

"What's going on?" she asked.

"I'm not sure," he answered, "but it has something to do with my father. Watch Baruch, please." Shalom climbed back up two steps of the synagogue portico to get a better look at what was happening. From behind him, he heard Levitz's voice. "Who does that man think he is?" Then louder, "Excuse me, let me through please."

Shalom watched Levitz push his way through the crowd. He walked back down the two steps to where he had left Rachel and Baruch. "Wait for me here," he said.

He followed Levitz through the crowd several paces behind him. Sha-

---

* *Shabbos*: Sabbath

lom recognized the two detectives handling his father's case moving quickly through the opposing crowd to the front of the demonstration. They stepped in front of the man with the megaphone just as Levitz broke through the crowd of his own people.

"How can we help you, Señor Guzmán?" Levitz shouted at Guzmán.

"I think the customary greeting is 'Good Shabbat,' Assemblyman," replied Guzmán.

"Good *Shabbos*," Levitz said, correcting Guzmán's pronunciation.

Shalom watched them as they sized each other up. Guzmán offered his hand. Levitz didn't take it. "And I ask you again," Levitz said louder than before, "how can we help you?"

The web of men tightened around Levitz. The crowd around Shalom began to grumble. He forced himself forward through them to get closer to where Levitz was standing.

Guzmán straightened himself before responding. "We came to show solidarity with your community for the terrible crime that was committed against Señor Redmond," he said. The crowd behind Guzmán began to buzz as well. He turned and gestured for them to be quiet. They responded almost immediately. The sudden silence was eerie.

"I'm sure Mr. Rothman would have appreciated your concern," Levitz shouted, and grinned to the crowd. "Though I'm sure he wouldn't have approved of your disrupting our *Shabbos* observance."

"We apologize for that," Guzmán said. He lifted a small envelope and attempted to hand it to Levitz. "We'd like you to have a copy of this…"

Levitz drew back. "I'm sorry I can't accept that from you. I can't carry that on *Shabbos*."

Shalom had heard enough. He stepped through the crowd, pushing his way past Levitz. "Excuse me," he said. "I'm Shalom Rothman." He extended his hand toward Guzmán's and shook it. "Señor Redmond was my father. I'll be glad to take that from you and thank you."

Levitz's hand appeared between Shalom and Guzmán. "Shalom, it's *Shabbos*."

Shalom turned toward Levitz. "Of course, Assemblyman, I know that. We have an *eruv*," he said, pointing toward the nearly invisible line of string that ran between streetlight poles above them. Then he turned toward Guzmán. "So that you understand, we have many proscriptions for the Sabbath. That simple line of string," he said, pointing above them, "enables us to do many things on the Sabbath we otherwise couldn't. It's evidence of the wisdom of our rabbis."

"Thank you," Guzmán said, handing him the envelope.

"You're welcome," said Shalom. He looked toward the crowd in front of him and caught the gaze of the detective who had interrogated him a few nights earlier. Their eyes met. He sensed a respect he had not seen there before.

11

"Sounds like a circus," said Karin.

"It was," Tolya replied, stretching out on the black leather couch. "You'll see on the news at 6."

"Hmm," she said, curling up into the corner of the sofa. "My boyfriend on TV. How exciting. I think I'll call my sister."

"Don't do that." Tolya waved his hands. "I wasn't interviewed. I'm hoping they didn't get me on camera."

"Amor, you were right in the middle of it and the cameras were right on top of you. Why are you so shy?"

"You know I hate all this attention," Tolya said, sinking further into the couch.

There was a long silent moment between them. Karin smiled at him. She touched her stomach subconsciously. When she did this, her expression would change. Her eyes would wander off somewhere far away, then she would touch her stomach and smile. He loved her deeply when he saw her like this, then the reality of the baby would send a shiver through him. "Did you tell your sister about the baby?" he asked.

"What?" she said, snapping out of her reverie.

"Did you tell your sister about the baby?" he repeated.

"No, not yet," she said. "I was going to wait till after I saw the doctor on Monday. I wanted to see her and tell her, not on the phone."

He was surprised. They were very close and told each other everything. Their relationship reminded him of how close he had been with his brother. Sometimes he felt that old loneliness come back. "So it's still our secret?" he said, leaning toward her and kissing her gently on the mouth.

"Yes." She took his hand and placed it on her stomach. "For now."

"Can I change the subject?" Tolya asked, taking his hand from her stomach and laying his head down in her lap.

"Por supuesto, mi amor," she said. "I am so happy." She kissed him harder than he had kissed her.

"Did you read any more of those diaries?"

She slapped him on the head playfully. "All business, Detective Kurchenko," she said, then saluted him.

"Well?" he said, sitting up.

"As a matter of fact, I did."

Sosúa
Dominican Republic
10 I '41
8 p.m.

We walked through the thick underbrush, the sun beating down on us. Erno was in front of me, Fritzy behind with Robert next to him. The Dominican workers walked in a group about three meters in front of us.

"They don't sweat," Fritzy said, tugging at his formerly white shirt and swatting at the tiny flies circling around us. He had sheared off the arms of his shirt at the elbow and removed the collar. The soaked cotton clung to him.

"That's because they know how to pace themselves, and they're half naked," said Erno, walking slowly and leaning on a large cut of sugar cane he used as a walking stick.

He was correct. They wore no shirts. Their pants were sheared off just above the ankle, loose about the legs and waist, held up by rope instead of our leather belts. They wore open shoes with flexible soles and straw hats with broad brims to shade them from the sun.

We, on the other hand, tried ignorantly to convert our Mitteleuropean wool clothing and leather shoes to work clothes appropriate for the tropics. Our wool pants, while cut off at the middle of the calf, guaranteed to keep us sweltering. Our modesty, plus our fear of severe sunburn, prevented us from removing our shirts. We covered our heads with our homburgs, which made us look doubly ridiculous.

"You'd have thought DORSA might have told us what kind of clothing we would need," I said.

"Had they," said Erno, "you wouldn't have believed them."

"Probably true," I said.

"And where would you have bought it anyway?" added Robert.

"Also true," I said. We walked through the last of the brush into the partially cleared area we had created the day before.

"Please form an orderly group on the perimeter of the clearing," the so-called agricultural expert from America shouted at us in badly accented German. We did as we were told. The Dominicans stood where they were, as they hadn't understood a word of the German. I laughed to myself. This idiot was giving us instructions. We had no skills. Without the Dominican workers nothing would get done, yet he treated them as if they were pack animals, not the least bit of recognition.

One of the Dominican men looked in my direction. He was about a head shorter than me. His complexion was dark, darker than most of the other men. He was shirtless and nearly hairless, his face and head clean-shaven. He smiled broadly at me.

We repeated the same wordless ballet we had practiced the day before. I motioned with my hands and my eyes that he and his men should follow our lead and form a circle around the edge of the clearing. He transmitted the message to them in hushed, rushed Spanish and they quickly and quietly assumed positions satisfactory to the agricultural expert, as evidenced by his lack of criticism or disgust.

"Today we will continue clearing this area to create a field. We will plant corn here to feed the herd," he shouted through his bullhorn. "First we will remove the large stones that would make planting and hoeing impossible."

We settlers looked at one another and at the ground full of stones. With some quiet mumbling, a few of us walked toward the truck we had left in the field overnight and began removing the equipment. My Dominican friend looked over toward me again, shrugged his shoulders and raised his eyebrows. I pantomimed taking a shovel, digging it into the ground and removing a large stone. He smiled and nodded. He told his men what was needed and before we could sort out the process of choosing equipment and assigning jobs they were diligently clearing the field.

As the sun reached its zenith and the heat became more intense, we quit work and settled in for lunch. DORSA sent us with sandwiches and fruit and bottles of purified water that had become tepid in the sun. We had enough for everyone, including the Dominicans. Lunch was part of their pay and they graciously accepted it.

As had happened the day before though, about a half-hour before we stopped work for lunch, a half-dozen native women appeared out of the brush with baskets on their heads carrying food for their men. They quietly, and with great dignity, placed the baskets under the shade of a mango tree and built a large fire. They removed simple wooden bowls from one of the baskets. From another, they took a large clay pot filled with slices of what looked like sausage and something white, like cheese. They covered it with a white towel with red stripes. When the baskets were empty they took the sandwiches and fruit we had given their men and neatly placed them inside. A third pot came out filled with a yellowish mass that resembled mashed potatoes. Finally, another basket, handled very carefully, was placed near the fire. It held fresh eggs. A woman placed an oiled pan on the fire, in which she would later fry the eggs to perfection.

I grabbed a sandwich and sat next to Erno in the thin strip of shade on the side of the truck. I took a swig of the lukewarm water and nearly gagged. "Sliced beef with horseradish again," I said, peeking under the dark bread at the interior of my sandwich.

"Yes, that's what we have so that's what you get," Erno responded. "From each according to his ability, to each according to his needs."

"Still a communist," I said, laughing and taking a bite of the sandwich. "This is terrible."

"I know," Erno said, handing me a banana. "Eat this, you need what it has."

"Thank you." I peeled back the skin and took a bite of the overly ripe fruit. It was cloyingly sweet but instantly energizing.

"We could learn from them," Erno said, tipping his head toward the Dominicans.

"What do you mean?" I asked.

"They live very simple lives, the way we are supposed to live. They're more than happy, they're content."

"Then why don't you mix with them?" I asked.

"Because I don't speak their language and I'm a Mitteleuropean snob. Honestly Max, I don't intend to stay here. When this nightmare is over, communism will triumph and I intend to return to Europe to build a new world."

"I'm never going back to Europe," I said. "They hate us. That will never change. I never want to see Europe again. I'll bring them all here. That's why we came."

"And your brother in New York?"

I laughed. "My brother in New York? He couldn't get anyone out, save for our very aged mother who is too sick to travel. America doesn't want us either. They made that very clear when they kept us penned up like animals on that island in New York Harbor for three days."

"So you propose to stay here?"

"Yes and build the Worker's Paradise," I said, picking myself up and dusting off my pants.

"Where are you going?" Erno asked.

"To practice my Spanish."

I walked across the open field to where the Dominican workers were eating their lunch. When they saw me approaching, they put down their bowls and got up one by one. "No, por favor. No levantomos," I said, using the wrong verb ending and mispronouncing the word. They looked at one another, then toward my "friend." He said something to them and they sat down but he got up. He extended his hand to me.

"José," he said.

"Max," I said, taking his hand. His grasp was loose and his hands were rough like leather.

"Tú tienes hambre?" he said, waving his hand toward the pots of food.

At first I didn't understand what he had asked me, then I realized from his gesture what he was saying. Yes I did want to eat, I was starving but I felt uncomfortable taking their food. "No," I said, "no tienes hambre."

He smiled. "No *tengo* hambre," he said.

I realized my mistake. "Sí," I said. "No *tengo* hambre."

He turned toward the other men and said something I couldn't catch. They smiled and applauded me. I felt the redness rising from my neck into my face. José slapped me on the shoulder and pointed toward the shade under the tree where he had been sitting, then spoke to the woman who had set up the fire. She rose and went off toward it. I sat down next to him under the mango tree and, before I could get the first word of broken Spanish out of my mouth, a bowl appeared in my lap. It contained a big lump of whatever the yellowish mash was, topped with slices of the sausage, the white cheese and two fried eggs smothered in pickled red onions. I stared down at it.

"Comemos," he said.

"Qué…es?" I asked.

"Mangú," he said, pointing toward the yellowish mass.

"Mango?" I asked suspiciously. It didn't look like mango so I thought he might be making a joke.

"No, mangú," he said, emphasizing the "u." "Plátano verde."

I translated in my head: green plantain. I looked up and saw Erno, Fritzy and the other men standing now, all of them looking at me. José picked up his spoon from his bowl, wiped it off with the bottom of his pants and passed it to me. They all stared at me, Erno silently daring me with his eyes and his smile. I took the spoon and scooped up some of the mangú with some egg and popped it into my mouth. It was delicious. Warm and comforting.

"Excellent," I said. José smiled and gestured toward the woman who had given me the bowl. "Gracias," I said to her.

"Tres golpes," José said, pointing to my bowl.

I had no idea what he meant.

"Tres golpes," he repeated. "Esa comida se llama tres golpes."

I realized what he was trying to tell me. The dish is called tres golpes. Three something, but I had no idea what golpes meant. I filed the term away for later explanation.

I wolfed down the contents of the bowl. The salami-like sausage and the white cheese had been fried, creating a salty, crisp exterior, satisfying and filling. But most of all the eggs, warm and runny in the middle, satiated my hunger. "Gracias," I said again as I finished the meal and rose to leave.

José reached up and took me by the arm, pulling me down. "No, no," he said. "Ya tomamos café."

I thought for a moment. Tomar, to take, also to drink something. He was offering me coffee. "Sí, gracias," I said, sitting back down under the tree. Out of the corner of my eye I saw Erno and Fritzy gesturing for me to come back. I ignored them. "Tú tienes un familia?" I asked José.

He grinned. "Una familia," he said. "Sí, tengo una familia. Mi mujer," he said, pointing toward the woman who had set the fire and given me lunch, "y tengo tres hijos y una hija."

Three boys and a girl, I quickly translated in my head.

"Tienes una familia?" he asked before I could respond to him.

"Solo…una mujer," I answered. "No niños." He looked at me curiously but before he could respond the agricultural expert walked briskly into the center of the clearing, the brim of his hat casting a shadow directly over his feet, and shouted in German through the bullhorn, "Lunch break is over."

José looked at me. "Trabajo," he said.

"Sí," I said, "ahora."

Sosúa
Dominican Republic
8 VII '41
9 p.m.

My friendship with José has grown as the weeks have passed. I asked to be placed with the Dominican work team but was ignored, at which point I simply stood with them in the field, ignoring the agricultural expert.

My Spanish improved quickly, far beyond what I learned from Gustavo on our transatlantic voyage. Rather than depend on the classes we were supposed to attend in the evening, when I was entirely too tired to concentrate, I listened to the Dominicans speak and tried to use the phrases I heard them use. For the first few weeks I let my ear become accustomed to the cadence of the language, to recognize when one word ended and another began. Then, as I had done with Slovak as a child, I identified words with objects or actions and began repeating what I heard. Within a few more weeks I was speaking haltingly, but well enough to understand the conversation and to be understood.

I walked quietly along the path through the trees to the native village at El Batey on the other side of the horseshoe-shaped bay. You can reach the village along the beach, but the path cuts about twenty minutes off the trip. Helen was working in the kitchen, despite it being Sunday. We all worked one Sunday a month in the commissary.

The silence of the jungle suits me. There is so little of it at the settlement. The settlers never stop speculating. Will the Germans attempt to invade England? What would happen to our families? Would the Americans enter the war? I can't listen to it any more.

I breathe in the warm moist air. It smells of guanaba and the sea. I feel at home here. The underbrush, still wet from last night's rain, scraped against my feet. I had traded two pairs of leather shoes in Puerto Plata for sandals like the Dominican men wore, along with some local clothing. The other settlers thought I was insane. "Going native," they called it, most of them insisting they would need their wool clothing when they returned to Europe after the war. Erno just looked at me and laughed.

Regardless, I feel more at home this way. I have no intention of ever going back to Europe. I only wish Helen could adjust more easily. She has no intention of returning to Europe either, but she clings to the hope that eventually we will go to America along with her wool clothing.

I smelled the village before I saw it. The scent of meat roasting on a wood fire filtered into my nostrils. Next I heard the sound of children playing. That is the other thing I hope for: that Helen will finally conceive, that we will have a child of our own.

I have come to love José's village, a few houses built around a common clearing in the forest, some fields out in back and across the road. No stores, no church, no nothing, just a few families living together. Whatever they need that they can't grow themselves has to be brought in from Puerto Plata, a two-hour walk. They don't have the luxury of a horse or a truck, as we do in the settlement. They have a donkey though, which belongs to none of them and all of them, good only for carting things on its back. José, told me that the donkey can turn a two-hour walk into four. Being a Dominican donkey, it is very stubborn.

"Blanquito. Blanquito," the children screamed as I emerged from behind the trees and into the clearing in front of the village. Four boys ran toward me — Josecito, José's youngest son, in front of them — all of them jumping on me, knocking me to the ground.

"What do you have for us?" Josecito demanded, the rest sticking their hands in my pockets.

"Nada," I said. I had hidden candies in the small bag I carried with the tools I needed to build the still with José.

"Nothing?" they all shouted back as they got off of me, the disappointment showing on each of their faces.

I kneeled in front of them, slapping each on the head gently with both hands. "Nothing in my pockets," I said, grabbing the bag and pulling out the candies. Their eyes lit up as I tossed the candies in the air and they ran after them.

"Spoiling them again?"

I heard José's voice from behind me. "Sí," I said. "Y por qué no?" We have become easy friends, a brother-like connection between us. One day in the fields I asked him how old he was, he had said he wasn't sure. We went to the priest in El Batey and he figured out through the baptismal records that we were the same age.

He grasped my hand and pulled me up. He embraced me tightly. "How are you, hermano?"

"Bien," I said.

"Where is Helen?" he asked, looking around.

"Working in the commissary today."

"She couldn't switch with someone?" he asked.

I had switched my day with Fritzy. "No," I lied. "She tried, but no one likes to give up a day at the beach." I had asked her to come with me. She said she's uncomfortable staying alone with the women because her Spanish is so poor.

"Nereida will be disappointed," José said.

"She will be stuck with just me."

We walked across the clearing toward the modest wood shack José and Nereida share with their children. We passed a small, eviscerated pig roasting on a wood spit over the open fire, the fat dripping into the charcoal. I have grown to love pork in all its forms over the past six months.

"That pig gave its life in your honor," José joked.

"Gracias," I said, bowing toward it.

We walked a little farther to his shack then up the two stairs to the porch.

"Sit down." He motioned toward the wood bench against the wall, then disappeared inside. I breathed in the heavy air, stretched my legs out and smiled to myself. I felt calm, not like at the settlement.

José returned with a large glass in each hand. "Take this," he said, sitting down next to me with his arm up against mine. He removed a flask from the deep pocket on the left side of his pants.

"What is this?" I asked, sipping the brownish liquid.

"Nothing much yet." He uncorked the flask and poured a bit of the dark amber liquid into my glass. "It was tea with pineapple. Now it's tea with pineapple and rum. Much better." He clinked his glass to mine. "Salud."

"Salud," I said, taking a sip of the drink. Though the rum burned on the way down, it was refreshing. "Rico."

"And after we finish building that still, we'll have more than enough rum to drink this every day," José said, a smile creeping up around the corners of his mouth.

"I have the tools right here in this bag, pana." I jiggled the sack, clanging the tools inside. "When do you want to get started?"

"In a while," he said, staring off into the distance. "After lunch. Nereida and the others will be back from the church soon. Then we'll eat and after lunch we'll build the still. If it gets too late you can stay here with us tonight."

We looked at each other and laughed. There was a sparkle in his dark eyes. "I know," he said. "You're thinking about Fritzy. If you don't show up for work tomorrow he'll get crazy."

"Yes, and what about my wife?"

"Don't worry. If you need to stay I'll send Josecito to tell her."

The prospect of spending the night excited me. I wanted to immerse myself in their world. I could do without the weekly concert of Handel or Mozart arranged by the cultural committee to provide our "orchestra" with a sense of purpose. I also knew Helen would be upset. She would be embarrassed in front of the others. They would suspect the worst of me if I disappeared overnight. "OK," I said. "You've got a guest."

"Bueno," he said. He looked at me and put his hand on my forearm. His expression became more serious. "Now, hermano, tell me the real reason Helen didn't come."

He could read me like a book. I hesitated, then told him the truth. "She's uncomfortable with her inability to speak Spanish."

"But that's not all. I can see it in your eyes." He took a long sip of his drink and settled back against the wood wall of the shack.

I leaned forward and thought for a moment before answering. I missed my brother Istvan. It was good to have someone to talk with. "She's uncomfortable with me, with who I'm becoming."

José smiled and laughed a little. He took another sip of his drink and asked, "Do you like who you're becoming?"

I thought for a moment, picturing myself a few months earlier. "What do you think? Yes, of course."

"Then what's the problem?"

"She's frightened. She thinks I'm growing away from her. Coming here helped us at the beginning. It made things better between us. Now she sees me changing."

"And she's not changing?"

"Not in the same way."

He put down his cup and leaned toward me. "Entonces, you have to help her change too. That's why you should bring her here. Let her see what you see." He waved his hand at the village in front of us. "Help her fall in love with you, with this you."

I raised my glass and touched it to his. "It's not like I haven't tried. She's stubborn."

"Try harder. She'll come around. You'll see. Treat her with love. You know that's all they really want, women. They want to feel loved. If they think you don't love them or that they'll lose you, they turn away, become afraid."

I knew he was right. Everything was so simple for him. My marriage was difficult to begin with, but in the past few months I have fallen in love with Helen in a way I hadn't in all those years back home. Here it is just us. No parents, no expectations. We have left the many things that came between us behind.

José pointed through the trees toward the distance. "They're coming," he said.

I rose from my seat, like the good Hungarian boy I was raised to be, to greet Nereida.

"Hermano, sit down," José said. "No need to get up."

I sat back down and watched as they came one by one out of the forest, women and men with a smattering of children. "Why don't you go, José?"

He smiled at me. "For the same reason you don't."

"How do you know I don't?"

"Because many times I have been at your settlement when your people go to prayers, yet I've never seen you go in or come out of that building."

"I'm surprised you noticed."

"I notice everything," he said, leaning toward me and placing his hand on my forearm again. "I believe in El Todopoderoso, hermano, pero I don't need to go to the church to speak with him." He gestured toward the sky. "He's everywhere. I talk to him when I need to. Alone."

I felt the same way.

Nereida came up the two steps to the porch. Her slight frame swayed from side to side as she climbed the steps. Her skin is the color of cinnamon, her hair black as coal. She smiled at me. I got up and embraced her. "Cómo tú ta?" I asked her.

"Bien, bien," she said, "and spoken like un Dominicano verdadero. Where is Helen?"

"She couldn't get anyone to cover for her and it's her day at the commissary."

"Perhaps next time, then," she said. I saw the disappointment in her face. She hugged me again. "Excuse me, I have to go inside to change. Then we can eat." She turned toward José. "Oye, check that pig. We have a guest."

"Of course," he said. He got up and smiled at me. "She loves to boss me around," he whispered as she entered the house. "I was going to go myself, but I let her order me around. I let her think she's the boss."

The pig was excellent, as was everything else Nereida and the other women had prepared. Rice, beans, yuca, maduros, tostones, avocado and fruits I still haven't identified. After the meal, the men brought out their instruments: guitars, congas, smaller drums, simple instruments made from cowbells, and washboards and gourds.

Only the men played and sang. The women sat around them holding their children in their laps. It was the first time I'd heard these children quiet. They sang a cappella at first, a slow mournful tune about amor perdido, love lost.

I didn't understand all of the words, but enough to get the meaning. A steel guitar twanged along with the rhythm of the percussion. This music was so different from ours. No symphonies here, just a simple beat and an opening of the heart. When the singer finished, the others clapped for him.

"Do you like it?" Nereida asked me.

"Yes, very much. What is it called?"

"Musica de amargues," José said. "It's very sad and sentimental, full of bitterness and regret."

It reminded me of the Fado we had heard in Lisbon while we were waiting for DORSA to arrange passage for us to Santo Domingo. I would sneak out alone at night to the dark, smoky clubs near the harbor to hear the local women sing their sad ballads. I loved the way that music moved me inside.

"You'll only hear it in the campo," Nereida said.

"Or in the brothels," José added.

Nereida rolled her eyes at José. "Coño," she said. "Anyway, El Jefe doesn't care for it."

José spat at the mention of Trujillo's moniker. "He prefers the rumba of the upper classes. This music is our soul."

The men began playing another tune. This time Nereida and José both began clapping out the rhythm along with the other people listening.

"Like this," José said, showing me the beat by taking my right hand and slapping it into my left palm so that I would feel the rhythm. "It's called clave."

"Clave," I repeated. The musician began to sing again. This time the melody was a little faster but just as sad. Everyone stood up and some couples began to dance. The dance was very sensual; the couples entwined in each other's arms, their bodies touching and hips moving together to the rhythm.

It was so different from the way we danced. We rarely touched one another in public and kept a safe, respectable distance between us.

One by one they began singing along with him. This time the song was about a young man from the country who falls in love with the daughter of the local landowner, but knows he can never even speak with her. Though I didn't know the words, I quickly picked up the tune, which I hummed as I continued to bang out the clave in the palm of my hand. I felt the music in my heart. I felt at peace for the first time in so many years. I felt at home.

12

Tolya, Pete and the captain stood outside the synagogue on Bennett Avenue waiting for the doors to open. Assemblyman Levitz stepped out of his car. The sea of bearded men parted to let him through, but the TV news crews flooded the space to shove microphones and cameras into his face.

"This guy is gonna make our lives miserable," Pete muttered under his breath.

"Shut up," the captain said as Levitz walked right past him without so much as a nod. The mass of black hats began moving up the stairs and into the synagogue as the front doors opened.

Tolya's skin crawled as they entered the sanctuary. He had been here before. It didn't bring back good memories. He tried not to think about it, instead practicing the slow-breathing exercise Karin suggested, slowly counting out his breaths as they moved with the crowd toward the pews.

"Stay toward the back, guys," the captain said. "And turn your phones to vibrate."

They followed the captain farther into the sanctuary. He stopped abruptly at the second row of pews from the back. "This should be good," he said. "Go in."

"I wanna sit on the end," Pete replied.

The captain looked at him, a small smile creeping up one side of his mouth.

"You gotta be kidding?" Tolya said, nudging Pete with his shoulder to move into the pew.

"Hey," Pete said, "I'm the tallest. I can't get my legs in there."

"Yeah, well, I'm the fattest, and I'm the captain. Get in."

Tolya squeezed into the pew between lanky Pete and the paunchy captain. He folded into himself, hunching his shoulders the way he did when he was a teenager on the subway ride to Stuyvesant High School, desperate for a seat so that he could finish his reading or catch some sleep on the way downtown. He looked around the room and continued to count his slow, deliberate breaths.

The men continued to file into the sanctuary, filling every available seat and standing against the walls under the stained-glass windows when the seats filled up. Tolya looked at the women's gallery upstairs. He looked around for María but didn't see her. He found her absence strange. She was so dedicated to the old man.

The balcony was as crowded as the main floor. Almost all of the women had their arms crossed and were dressed in the same somber tones as that night a few days earlier when this nightmare of a case started.

Their wigs fascinated Tolya. He thought it unnatural for almost every woman of almost any age to have almost exactly the same hairstyle. He breathed deeply again, fighting the feeling of claustrophobia.

"What's with the breathing, detective?" asked the captain.

"Nothing, captain. Just helps me to stay calm."

"Boy, you have some issues," the captain said, patting Tolya on the knee.

"Sorry sir," Tolya said, taking yet another deep breath.

Tolya noticed Pete pressing his knees against the pew in front of them as if his superhero strength could move the pew forward.

"Man, they build these seats for short people," Pete said.

"Actually it's only the back seats. The farther forward you go, the more room you get. Like on a plane, you know, biz class, first class."

"Don't fuck with me."

"No seriously, and over there by the window is the emergency exit aisle."

"Fuck you," Pete whispered in Tolya's ear. He spread his legs to relieve the pressure on his knees, cramping Tolya in even further. "How long this gonna take?"

"Not sure. Depends on how many eulogies."

"Jeez," Pete said.

"That will be enough, Detective Gonzalves," the captain said, sticking his legs into the aisle.

The rabbi ascended to the podium at the front of the sanctuary. The crowd became immediately silent as he stood before them. A chill passed through Tolya as he remembered the rabbi. It had been a long time, nearly twenty-five years.

"I thank you all for coming, for taking time out of your day to show your support for my son-in-law and his family in this time."

"She's his daughter. I should have guessed," Tolya mumbled.

"What's that detective?" the captain said.

"Nothing, captain," Tolya said.

"It's very important," the rabbi continued, "that our neighbors know — that our city administrators know — how much pain this terrible event has inflicted on our community. It is not the first time we have been threatened and it will not be the last. Our community was born under threat. We will not run. We will not live in fear."

There was a low murmur in the crowd. The rabbi stopped and took a breath, leaning his heavy frame against the podium.

"Please, quiet, please, the family is about to enter," said an elderly man off to the side of the room.

Tolya followed the rabbi's head as it turned toward the left corner of the room. A large door opened in the wall. It was made of the same wooden material that paneled the walls as high as the windows. Shalom and Rachel entered with their son between them. Tolya watched them, their body language stiff and uncomfortable. That stance, the son between the parents, holding their hands, the traditional approach to the wedding canopy in a Jewish ceremony.

They walked to the front pew and sat down. The rabbi came to them along with several other men who had been sitting on the *bema* and offered their condolences. As the men returned to their seats, a coffin covered in a beautifully embroidered white cloth was wheeled into the room. The attendant removed the cover. The coffin was more like a crate, really, as tradition requires: plain pine, no adornments, no nails.

The rabbi returned to the podium. He leaned in toward the microphone. "Friends, congregants. May I introduce our first eulogist," he said, "Assemblyman Yehuda Levitz."

Levitz rose from his chair and approached the podium. He shook the rabbi's hand as they passed in the aisle. Levitz adjusted the microphone, surveyed the crowd and removed his hat, placing it on the podium. Left on his head was a large black-velvet yarmulke.

"My dear friends," he began. "May I first offer the traditional condolence to the family?" He turned toward Rothman and said, "May HaShem comfort you, along with all the mourners of Zion and Jerusalem."

"Thank you," Rothman said, barely audible.

Tolya noted how Baruch fidgeted in his seat. Rachel distracted him quietly.

Levitz looked at the crowd and continued. "Max Redmond was all of us. He was born Moshe Rothman, in a far away empire that no longer exists. He was run out of his country by a vicious madman who would have killed every last one of us." Levitz stopped for emphasis, moving his clenched fist to the center of the podium. "He endured years in a harsh jungle to preserve a life for his family." He stopped again and waved his hand above his head. "In the end he came here to be secure, the same right we seek today."

Tolya sensed that Levitz was going to milk this for everything he could. He looked back to the doorways where he could see reporters with notebooks hanging on every word Levitz uttered. Security, Tolya chuckled to himself. What did this guy know about security? Live as a Jew in the Soviet Union, then come talk to me about security.

Tolya tuned Levitz out and focused instead on the rabbi. He had aged a lot in twenty-five years. The beard was mostly white now, but the pasty complexion was the same. He was much fatter and he had age spots on his cheeks. But the eyes, the eyes had not changed. They were a cold, light-blue color, like the shells of robins' eggs in the Ukrainian countryside, where he and Oleg would visit their grandparents as children. Only they didn't offer hope. They offered only tired sadness. He could hear his father's voice when they visited the rabbi's study all those years ago.

"We would like him to know something of his culture," his father said in thickly accented English.

"How old is he?" the rabbi asked.

"He is 12 last week," his mother answered.

"He should be Bar Mitzvah," his father added. "You want that, yes Tolya?" his father said, turning toward him and placing his large hand on Tolya's knee.

"Yes," Tolya said, absently. He really wasn't sure what a Bar Mitzvah was. He knew, though, that it would require him to study yet another language, another alphabet. He was having enough trouble with English.

"How long have you been here?" the rabbi asked.

"Almost a year," his mother replied.

The rabbi fell silent for a moment, his eyes lost in thought. "Well, OK. I need to ask you a few questions."

"Questions," his father repeated, shifting in his chair.

"Yes, just a formality really, so we know where our starting point is."

"Certainly," his father replied.

"Do you observe anything at home?"

"What do you mean?" his father asked.

"Do you light candles? Do you make *Shabbos*, holidays?" The rabbi spoke quickly and in low tones. Tolya had trouble following his English.

His mother and father exchanged looks. "No, Rabbi. I am afraid we don't, but…" His mother interjected, "You see, we want to learn too."

The rabbi paused. He placed his two index fingers together and touched them to his lips, nodding almost imperceptibly. "Did your son have any religious training in Moscow?"

"Religious training?" his father said, shifting nervously in the hard wood chair. Tolya caught the look his father gave his mother. It wasn't a good sign. "Rabbi, do you understand how difficult life was for us after I asked for permission to emigrate?"

"I am sure it was," the rabbi said. "We have heard many first-hand accounts. Many people taught their children in secret though."

"We couldn't teach him what we ourselves didn't know," his father replied.

"I see." The rabbi stopped questioning them for a moment. He got up from the desk and moved toward the window, turning his back to them for a long moment. When he turned back he said, "Mr. Kurchenko…"

"That's Dr. Kurchenko."

"Sorry, Dr. Kurchenko, I am afraid I am going to have to ask you some very difficult and personal questions."

Tolya watched his father react. He stood up. His suit, which was too big, accentuated his tall, thin frame. The months in the prison camp outside Arkhangelsk had taken their toll. He said the cold had settled into his bones, that it had become a part of him, and he couldn't gain weight no matter what he ate or did.

"And what would those very personal questions be, Rabbi?" his father said, drawing out the last syllable in "rabbi."

"This is not meant to offend you," the rabbi said, sitting back down in his chair, "but I have to ask."

"Please, Boris," his mother said, touching his father's sleeve to suggest he retake his seat, which he did.

"Did Tolya have a circumcision?"

"Yes," his father said.

"A circumcision?" Tolya asked his mother. She explained it to him, whispering Russian in his ear.

Tolya shuddered inside. Circumcision. That was like a curse, a mark. Every time he had to go swimming at school the boys would make fun of him.

"Do you have a *bris* certificate from the *mohel*?[*]" the rabbi asked.

"No, Rabbi, I am sorry. We don't have a certificate," his father said, laugh-

---

[*] *Mohel*: Person authorized to perform a circumcision

ing nervously. "*Mohel?* There was no *mohel*. A doctor we knew did it very quietly. You had to be very careful of these things."

The rabbi hesitated again. "I understand," he said, "but these things have to be done properly."

Tolya watched his father become even more agitated. "Who does this man think he is?" his father said to his mother in Russian. "Who does he think he is talking to? How dare he question me about my son's Jewishness?" His mother answered him in Russian, telling him to calm down.

"I'm sorry doctor, I didn't mean to upset you," the rabbi said.

"Then be careful what you ask me," his father replied, rising from the chair.

"I am afraid I have one more difficult question then."

"And that would be?"

"Is your wife Jewish?"

Tolya saw his father's face stiffen. "My mother was a Jew and my father a Ukrainian. His family hid her during the war. They saved her life."

"I'm sorry, but that's not what I asked. Is Mrs. Kurchenko Jewish?" the rabbi repeated, turning toward Tolya's mother.

"My father was a Jew but my mother was not," she replied, avoiding the rabbi's gaze.

The rabbi placed his hands on the desk, clasping them together. "I'm afraid we have a problem. We cannot educate your son or Bar Mitzvah him because he is not a Jew. He would need to be converted first."

His father leaned forward over the rabbi's desk. "My son is not a Jew?" he said.

Tolya followed his father's laser-like gaze directly into the rabbi's eyes, surprised by their intense and unusual shade of blue.

"No. I am sorry, but your son is not a Jew because your wife is not a Jew. She was not born of a Jewish mother, therefore neither is he."

"Excuse me?" said Tolya's father. "You are going to tell me who is a Jew?"

The rabbi averted his gaze. "Our laws are very clear and very simple…"

Tolya's father slammed his fist down on the desk. The rabbi slid back in his chair, hitting the bookshelf behind him. Some small volumes fell onto the floor.

"You are going to tell me who is a Jew?" his father shouted again. "What do you know of being a Jew? You live here in this country, free to do whatever you want, and you judge me? I spent eleven months in a work camp north of the Arctic Circle because I dared to stand up for my beliefs. We were humiliated, all of us. My other son died when we couldn't get medical care for him because we are Jews, and you are going to tell me who is a Jew?"

The mention of Oleg struck Tolya in the heart. He could feel his pulse quicken. He only wanted to get out of here.

"I am sorry doctor…" the rabbi said, fidgeting with the papers on his desk. He avoided looking at Tolya's father.

"Sorry?" He leaned over the desk until he was inches from the rabbi's face. "This is what I stood up to the Soviet Union for, to come here and be insulted by you? You think you are more of a Jew than me, than my son, because of your beard and your clothes? Try living in Russia. You have no idea how lucky you are that you were born here."

Tolya's mother got up and settled her husband back into his seat. Tolya didn't move. He didn't understand all of what had happened. He watched his father shaking in his seat, his shrunken frame lost in his suit jacket.

The rabbi rose laboriously from his chair. He turned the gaze of his cold blue eyes on Tolya, then at his father. "I wasn't, sir," he said. "I was born in Germany. I was smuggled out in a suitcase, sedated, with my mouth taped shut."

13

The afternoon sun streamed through the open blinds into the captain's office. He, Tolya and Pete leaned over the coffee table at the far end of the room listening intently to the technician's explanation.

"This fragment is the corner of this book," the tech said, pointing first to the small silver piece Pete had found on Redmond's floor and then at the book he had found in the drawer.

"Any indication of how it was broken off?" Tolya asked looking up.

The tech whistled through his teeth. "Not specifically. Some sort of blunt force. And it would be difficult to break this." He picked up the book in its plastic bag. "What's more interesting is the residue I found just under the setting of this large blue stone here," he continued, pointing to the spot with a stylus.

Tolya leaned closer to get a better look at the cover of the book. "Residue of what?" he asked.

"Hair and skin," the tech replied.

"And what's this stain on the edges of the book?" the captain asked.

"Blood."

"You've checked these residues against samples from the old man?" Pete said.

The technician smiled at them. "Yes. We're waiting for confirmation of a match."

"When will you have it?" Tolya asked.

"By tomorrow."

Tolya found Karin curled up on the couch with one of the small red diaries when he walked into the apartment.

Karin jumped. "Tolya," she said, "I didn't hear you come in."

Tolya tossed his coat over the black leather club chair as he crossed the room. He knew her. Once she got a look at the diary she would have to read it, IA or no IA. He bent over her and kissed her gently on the lips. "Tell me what's in there," he said as he settled next to her.

She poked his ribs. "You know I shouldn't be doing this, but I have to admit it's very interesting, engrossing, even. But first," she said, closing the book and putting it on the coffee table, "tell me how things went today."

"Went with what?"

"The funeral."

"How could it go? It was a funeral," he said, lying back, putting his head in her lap. "But I do have something to tell you."

"What?" she said, stroking his hair.

He thought for a moment before bringing it up. He looked up at her enchanting smile and thought better of it. Now wasn't the time. "I used that breathing technique you taught me to calm me down and it worked."

She leaned back into the corner of the couch. "That's what you have to tell me? Why on earth would you need to do that at a funeral?" she said, slapping him lightly on the head. "You didn't even know the man."

"All those beards, it made me tense."

"My god, Tolya," she said, pushing him off her lap. "You need to lighten up with these people."

"I can't."

"Then you should take yourself off the case."

"Then I realized who the rabbi was," he said, sitting up.

She rolled her eyes. "Who?"

"The same guy my father had that fight with about whether I'm Jewish, that one I told you about."

"Small world," she said. "And seeing him made you tense?"

"I guess."

"Papi, you need some therapy," she said and gave him a quick kiss on the cheek as she got up from the couch.

"Maybe I do." He watched her cross the room. "How are you feeling?"

"Fine, why?" she asked.

"From the pregnancy."

"It's a baby, not a tumor," she said, laughing.

"I thought women get sick when they're pregnant," he replied.

"Some do, I might." She took a paper bag from the top of the desk. It was from Barnes & Noble. She walked back across the room and handed it to him. "Tolya, you have to learn a little about this."

He took the bag and removed the book: *What to Expect When You're Expecting*. "Thanks," he said. "It's not what I was expecting."

"You're welcome," Karin said and sat back down on the couch next to him. "There's nothing to worry about, Papi."

He could feel the tension rise into his shoulders. "Papi?"

"Sí, I'm going to call you that all the time now."

"I don't think so," he said, chuckling and thumbing through the book. He thought he had said doon't instead of don't.

"We can read it together," Karin said.

"OK," he hesitated. "But first, tell me what's in the diary."

Karin got up on her knees and faced him on the couch. She lowered herself onto his lap and kissed him hard on the lips. "Paciencia, Papi."

Sosúa
Dominican Republic
8 XII '41
9:30 p.m.

When I awoke yesterday morning I turned in the bed and reached for Helen, surprised to find she wasn't there. The breeze through the window floated over me as I stretched. In the year since our arrival I have grown to like the climate, even in the summer months. I would be happy never to feel the cold again. I called out to Helen, knowing full well in the tiny space that she wasn't there. She must have gone down to the dining hall to help with breakfast.

I got out of the bed and looked at my nearly naked self in a mirror I hung on the opposite wall. It took more than a little of my Hungarian charm to get DORSA to give me a mirror. "Non-essential merchandise," they had called it. I cajoled them until they agreed, telling them it was my wife who needed it. How could a woman go out every day without properly preparing herself? In fact, the mirror was for me.

I admired my lean frame. I lost the fat that had padded me through hard, snowy Slovak winters all my life. The physical labor in the fields has laid muscle over my frame. I liked what I saw.

I slipped on some pants and a white cotton shirt, stopped at the sink in the bathroom alcove to brush my teeth and headed out to the dining hall. It was Sunday, no work, just a day at the beach with our friends.

I wandered through the palm trees on the dirt path that is now more like a road. There are almost 600 settlers now. As I passed the new school, I admired my handiwork: the portico in front of the building.

There was a line in front of the new clinic. I realized that the doctor from Puerto Plata must be at the settlement. The villagers from El Batey waited with their children. What a fight that had been to get the DORSA administrators to agree to let the local dairy workers use the clinic. The kids saw me and waved, calling out to me. Their parents slapped their hands gently to quiet them and nodded silently in my direction. I am always amazed at how different, how formal, their behavior toward me becomes when they visit the settlement.

I took a deep breath. The scent of the sea filled my nostrils as I turned the curve in the road toward the dining hall. I will miss all this. Soon we will move out of the barracks to a homestead. I will have my own farm. Helen is apprehensive about it. As soon as we are settled, I will apply to have our siblings come from Europe.

I saw Helen through the door of the dining room. The large, wooden, open-air structure was nearly empty. She was sitting with Ava and Erno. She waved at me as I walked in and Erno grabbed another chair for the small table.

"Good morning," I said, bending over to kiss Helen, then Ava. I slipped my hand into Helen's as I sat down. Sosúa is good for her. It is good for us. She has lost weight in the year since our arrival. Ava has transformed her as well, teaching her the secrets of putting herself together, secrets that her mother and sisters had never thought important. Even here, Ava is still a lady amidst the cow manure, mud and jungle.

"You snuck out this morning," I said to Helen.

"Yes," she replied, smiling. She glanced over to Ava. Ava smiled back at her.

"What's all the smiling about?" I asked.

"Never question a smiling woman," Erno said.

I picked up a banana fritter from the plate in the center of the table with my fingers. "Did you make these?" I asked Helen.

"No, I did," said Ava.

"Well, I hope you know how, *drágám*, because you'll need to make these for me when we move out to the homestead. They are excellent."

"Thank you," said Ava.

I felt Helen's hand on my thigh. "I can make them for you now," she said, the smile continuing to light up her face.

I smiled back at her. She has become beautiful.

"Coffee, Max?" Erno asked.

"Of course," I answered. Erno poured a cup from the porcelain pitcher.

"Milk as well?"

"Yes please," I said. "It's ours, best on the planet." I raised the cup to my lips, the full aroma of the coffee wafting into my nose. I looked at Erno and

Ava. Though tan and healthy, they still have that expression behind their eyes: the fear of a refugee. I wonder if my eyes look the same way. "What news this morning?" I asked.

"I was talking with Fritzy earlier. We've done a very good job," Erno said. "We've increased the yield on the herd by more than 50 percent in one year."

"Excellent," I said, taking another bite of the fritter, "but not as excellent as this fritter."

"Stop," Ava said, blushing.

"And our banana yield is up 100 percent as well," Erno added.

"Enough business talk," Helen said, letting go of my hand. "We're going to the beach, should we pack a lunch?"

"Absolutely," said Erno.

"And bring a few of these," I added before popping another banana fritter into my mouth.

"At the rate you're going, we're going to need to double the banana yield again," Helen said, patting my stomach and laughing. I looked at her, her smile even broader than before. I have fallen in love with her here and hope she has with me as well.

"*Elég volt,*[*]" I said. "That's enough from all of you on the subject of my, I will have you know, very flat stomach. I was admiring myself before I left the barracks."

"Admiring yourself?" Ava said, all of them laughing now. "We need to get you away from that mirror."

"What other news from Fritzy," I asked, the laughter subsiding. "Has he heard from his sister and brother? Are they on their way?"

"Yes," Erno said. "It appears they left for Marseilles last week and should be in Lisbon by now. There's a whole new group leaving from Lisbon before the New Year."

"I hope I can get our brothers and sisters into the next group," I said. "Next week I can apply for the immigration visas, we will be here one year on Wednesday."

"I'm happy for you," Ava said, reaching across the table and touching

---

* *Elég volt:* Enough! (Hungarian)

116

Helen's hand. Her expression darkened through her smile.

"You still haven't heard from your sisters, have you?" Helen asked, letting go of my hand and taking Ava's.

"No, not since September," Ava said, taking her hand from Helen's. She turned her face away and subtly wiped a tear from her eye while feigning fixing her hair. Her expression changed again to a broad smile, as quickly as the first time, as she took Erno's hand in both of hers. "I am sure they're fine. You know how difficult communication is here. Let's go to the beach. Go, the both of you, and change. We'll meet you at the path in twenty minutes."

I put my arm around Helen as we walked through the village back to the barracks. The air had become thicker and more humid since earlier. The scent of guanabo in the air was citrusy and sweet.

"Why did you run off to the kitchen this morning?" I asked. "It's not your day."

She stopped walking and pulled me toward her. "Mishka, I didn't go to the kitchen this morning. I went to the clinic."

"You aren't feeling well?"

"I am feeling fine, but I have something to tell you."

I pulled in closer, sensing what she was about to say. I put my arms around her waist and pressed against her. "What could that be? What did the doctor say?" I said, kissing her neck.

"I am going to have a baby," she whispered in my ear. I leaned back and laughed, then kissed her hard on the lips. The scent of her skin mixed with the guanabo.

"Mazel Tov," Erno shouted, jumping up from the blanket, sand flying as he landed.

Ava grabbed Helen and hugged her, the two of them on their knees in the sand. "I didn't know how much longer I could keep this to myself," Ava said.

"When did you find out?" Erno asked.

"This morning," Helen answered. "I went to the clinic to see the doctor. He confirmed it but I suspected."

"Max, I'm so happy for you, for both of you," Erno said. "This calls for schnapps. I'll run back to the dining room."

"No, no, not necessary," I said, reaching into the small wicker basket I had brought with me. "I brought this. Not quite schnapps, but not bad either." I pulled out an unlabeled bottle with a caramel-colored liquid. "José gave it to me a couple of months ago. I keep it in the room." Helen took the bottle from me.

"Rum?" Erno asked.

"Yes," I said. "I helped him build the still."

"You know how to build a still?" Ava said.

"That was our business back home," Helen said, unscrewing the top from the bottle.

"I thought you had a hotel?" Ava said.

"We did, but we had to serve the guests something," I said, pulling four small glasses from the basket.

"And from where did you pilfer those?" Erno asked.

"The bar behind the social hall. I'll need to return these, so be careful."

Helen poured a shot for each of us.

I looked out over the curve of the broad, white-sand beach meeting the calm bay of Sosúa. A feeling of power flowed through me. I, we, have been transformed by this place. And now a new life, perhaps even a son. The memories of our escape and of the camp still haunt me, especially the goodbye with Istvan. I will send for him soon. We will build this farm, our farm, and a new life together.

"To my wife," I said, raising my glass, "and to our new baby, and to our friends, Salud."

"L'chaim," they shouted and downed the shots.

"And now how about a swim?" I said, taking a step toward the surf. I saw Helen hesitate as Ava and Erno ran toward the water.

"What's wrong?" I asked.

"I, I don't know," said Helen.

"Why?"

"Do you think it's safe? In my condition?" She said, her hand resting on her lower abdomen.

"*Drágám*, why not?" I took her hand in mine and pulled her gently toward the water. I looked into her eyes and kissed her again. I knew I had done the right thing by coming here. We are alive. We have created a new life.

"Are you coming?" Erno shouted from the water. "It's beautiful."

"Will you go ahead with the move to the homestead?" Ava asked. The four of us lay on the blanket, our bathing suits still damp from the swim.

"Of course," I said. "If we don't move to the farm I can't bring my brother out. That was the deal with DORSA." I am always cutting a deal with DORSA, whether for a mirror or a farm. They control everything here. I felt Helen's body tighten under my arm a bit as I said this.

"I wanted to talk to you about that," she said, turning onto her side to look at me.

"Talk about what?"

"The farm, moving to the farm."

"What's to talk about?" I picked up a small pebble and tossed it toward the calm waters lapping at the sand.

"Max," said Erno. "Not to interfere, it's not my business, but a new homestead with a pregnant wife? Perhaps you should wait till after the baby comes."

I sat up and brushed the sand off my knees. "It's only a few miles away."

Helen sat up as well. I could see the look of fear in her eyes, that same look she had the day I was arrested in Genoa. "But I should be nearer to the doctor," she said, "and the other women. It would only be six or seven months."

"I can't put it off, that was the deal with DORSA. We go now and they move Istvan and Magda up on the list. You'll be fine, I'll take care of you," I said. I reached over and took her hands again. "Besides, we'll have the wagon and horses." I watched her face. A weak smile grew around the corner of her lips. I knew that expression. "Trust me," I said, reaching toward her.

"I do," she replied and drew back her hands.

"Another shot of that rum?" Erno said, breaking the silence.

"Sí, comó no?" I said. As I reached around to retrieve the basket and the rum I saw Fritzy running across the beach toward us. I stood up and waived at him. "Fritzy," I called out. "We have some news."

When he arrived he leaned over, hands on his knees, trying to catch his breath. "I have news too," he said, still panting.

"We go first," Helen said. "You want to tell him, Mishka?"

"No, no you go ahead," I said, slipping my arms around her from behind.

"I'm pregnant," Helen said.

Fritzy stood up. He took a step toward Helen and kissed her on the cheek. "That's wonderful. I'm afraid I don't have such wonderful news."

"What's wrong?" said Erno.

"The Japanese have attacked America," he said, still out of breath.

"What?" I said. "Where?"

"In Hawaii, in the Pacific."

"Then they will enter the war, that's good," said Erno.

"Not so good," said Fritzy.

"Why, what's not good? They'll fight the Germans as well," I said.

"True," said Fritzy. "But the Caudillo, Trujillo, he is puffing his chest. He is threatening to declare war on Germany as well."

"What?" said Erno. "That's ridiculous."

"Yes, it is. He's demonstrating his solidarity with Roosevelt."

"Will we be called up?" I asked.

"No," Fritzy answered, "but there will be no more emigration permitted from Germany either."

14

"We have a murder weapon," the captain said, the forensic report in front of him on the desk.

Tolya turned the metal-bound book in the plastic baggy around in his hand. "Killed by a prayer book," he said, fighting back a smile.

The captain picked up the bound folder and read:

The hair and skin residue found lodged in the setting between the large blue topaz stone and the silver-plated cover of the Hebrew prayer book, as well as the blood stains on the edge of the pages, positively match the samples taken from the victim of the attack, Max Redmond. The broken corner of the book cover and the resultant disassociated matching fragment are confirming evidence of blunt force of substantial strength.

"Creepy," Tolya said.

"Now let's figure out who hit him with it," Pete said.

"That's what I wanted to talk to you about," the captain said. "Turn to page five. We have some prints."

Tolya beat Pete to the folder and opened the report to page five. "No way," he said. "The kid's prints are on the book? There's gotta be an explanation for that."

"I know you think he's innocent, Tol, but it's most likely the kid," the captain said.

"I don't agree," Tolya shot back.

Pete leaned over toward him. "Tol, he was the last one to see the old man. He's got a history. The kid is trouble."

"Nah, I don't think so. No fucking way. Not the way he was talking about the old man."

"Tolya, think about it," the captain said. "No one else has a motive. The kid probably needed some cash, knew where it was stashed, or maybe took something else, maybe the dead wife's jewelry."

Tolya pressed his hands against his eyes and sighed. "Go on," he said.

"We need to interview the Rothmans again to find out what might be missing from the apartment," said Pete.

"Not till next week," Tolya said.

"Right," said the captain. "I think you gotta interview the Pabon kid again too."

Rachel peered into the living room. The men were crowded around Shalom, studying the commentaries on this week's torah portion. She knew it was a good diversion for him.

"Amen," they said. The learning was over for now.

They would leave soon. Shalom would rest a bit and she would clean up the living room with Miriam's help, only to have the men return later for evening prayer. She was tired and unhappy about how the shiva was affecting Baruch's routines. He was uncomfortable with so many strangers in the house.

She heard one of the men say, "Did he steal anything, that Spanish boy who worked for your father?"

"We don't know if anything is missing," Shalom replied. "We haven't been through the apartment yet."

"It's obvious he killed your father," another said.

"No, no, that's not right," Shalom insisted, his voice low and steady. "There's no evidence that he did it. He claims he's innocent. The *mishna** clearly states that you should not accuse a man without sufficient evidence."

"They should arrest him, who else could it be?" another of the men said.

"We don't know. We have to let the police do their investigation," Shalom replied, then sighed. "I went along with what Levitz wanted for the funeral, but now he is just using this for his own political ends and I don't like it."

"And Shalom, is it so bad if that helps us a little?" Mendy Weisskopf said. "If he can get us some additional security from the police and we don't have to pay for it privately anymore?"

"It's just not right," Shalom insisted, "and I don't want to be involved."

Rachel pulled back the stiff white sheet from the bathroom mirror and stared at herself. She wasn't sure she recognized her own face. Her complexion was paler than usual. The red around the edges of her eyes accentuated their blue color. She had been crying, but not for her father-in-law. She was glad he was gone. Would HaShem forgive her for that?

Everyone wanted a part of this. Her father-in-law had become a symbol. How ironic, considering what contempt he had for their community. She would be happy when it was over and their lives could return to the way they had been. She didn't know if that was possible though, when she considered everything that had happened in the past few days. She herself would never be the same. She took some Kleenex from the box on the top of the toilet and

---

* *Mishna*: A collection of Jewish laws, originally passed down orally, that now make up the first part of the Talmud.

dabbed her eyes. She placed the sheet back over the mirror, walked back to the kitchen and sat down at the table.

"You don't look well," Miriam said. "You're very pale, *mamele**. Would you like some tea?"

"Thank you, yes. Tea would be good," Rachel said. She shifted in the chair, pushing back the bangs of her wig from in front of her eyes. "Miriam," she said.

"Yes?" Miriam answered, placing the tea bag into a cup with a small wedge of lemon. "Sugar?"

"Yes please, it's on the second shelf," Rachel said.

Miriam dried her hands in the *fleischik*** dishtowel, sat down at the table and took Rachel's hand. "What's wrong, darling?"

"It's just, just that I think sometimes about HaShem and forgiveness..."

"We all do."

"Sometimes I think I can't do it anymore," Rachel said, her eyes brimming with tears, "take care of Baruch, keep a home for Shalom. I failed at the one thing I should have been able to do."

"You haven't failed. You're a good woman, a good wife and mother," Miriam said, stroking Rachel's arm.

"Yes I have, like Sarah in the Torah. I couldn't give Shalom the one thing he wanted more than anything: a son." Rachel began to cry more deeply.

"You gave him a son," Miriam said, moving closer.

"HaShem forgive me, but what kind of a son did I give him? He is my child, I love him, but I don't understand what happened to him."

"Shhh, shhh," Miriam said. "Rachel, calm down."

Her gasps grew more pronounced through her weeping. "He was such a joy, such a precocious child. Then, all of a sudden..."

Miriam wrapped her arms around Rachel. "It's all right," she said.

Shalom entered the room. The other men standing behind him craned their necks to see what was going on in the kitchen. "Miriam," Shalom said, "what happened?"

---

   * *Mamele*: Dear girl (Yiddish)
   ** *Fleischik*: Designated for meat products only, under Kosher rules

Washington Heights
NYC
5 April, 1993
1 p.m.

Rachel stood in front of the teak cabinet, looking out the window into the courtyard. The afternoon sun peaked over the roof of the building opposite her, warming the light-green walls of the dining room. She opened the lid to the wooden case that held the silverware her mother had given her on her wedding day.

It was a special gift. It had been in her mother's family for more than 100 years.

Her grandfather smuggled it out of Germany with them in 1934. Her grandmother couldn't part with it, though it was used only one night a year, on Pesach for the Seder. She held up the dinner forks, examining each one. They would need a polishing before they could be used tonight at the Seder, their first time hosting Seder in their home.

She was nervous. This day meant so much to her. Shalom had even managed to teach Baruch the first of the four questions. It had taken less than an hour and most of a bag of chocolate kisses, but he had memorized the words, ten words — a great mitzvah for their only child, already showing much promise as a scholar and not quite 3 years old. She had invited her in-laws. Her mother-in-law, Helen, would be here, but she doubted her father-in-law would come. She recalled the first time she met Shalom's mother and father. They had to meet in a kosher restaurant in mid-town because she couldn't eat in their house. Max was unhappy enough that she was Orthodox, but the fact that she came from a family of rabbis made it all the worse. He let her know all too quickly that he had no use for rabbis or for religion in general.

Helen had tried to make her feel comfortable. She was happy, she said, if Shalom and Rachel loved each other. To love each other was the most important thing. The one thing Rachel knew for certain, besides her faith in HaShem, was that Shalom loved her.

She reached into the bottom drawer of the cabinet for the silver polish and the cloth, and got to work on each fork. Polish, buff, rinse, repeat.

At some point, she noticed things were too quiet for a small apartment with a 3-year-old. "Baruch," she called out toward the back bedroom. He didn't answer so she called out again. "Baruch."

Still no answer. She put down the fork and walked down the hallway, dodging Shalom's ever-growing pile of books. She found him sitting on the floor playing with his plastic animals. She loved his room. She had picked out each piece of furniture herself and painstakingly matched the paint and the bedsheets with the blue tones in the carpet. She touched him on the shoulder from behind.

"Hi *Ima**," Baruch said, turning his face to her.

"Didn't you hear me calling you?"

"Yes," he answered, turning back to the pile of animal figures on the floor.

Rachel sat down next to him and put her arm around his shoulder, drawing him to her. "What are you doing?"

He pushed her back and wiggled out of her embrace. His yarmulke slipped off his head. He picked it up and kissed it, holding it up toward HaShem they way they had taught him.

"I'm organizing Noah's Ark." He continued to group the animal figures two by two, placing them in neat rows and humming.

"You are doing a very good job," she said, stroking his hair. She sensed him pull his shoulders down to lower his head after the first stroke. "What's that tune you're humming, *tatele*?" she said

"It's from *Rechov SumSum***," he answered without looking up at her.

"I know that, but what's it called?" she asked again.

"I don't know the name, but it's about not all things being the same as the others," he said, pulling two plastic horses from the pile and placing them in line with the other Ark-bound figurines.

"I know the song," she said. "Can we sing it together?"

"Sure, if you want," he said, stopping his sorting for a moment and looking up at her with a big grin. "OK, sing with me, *ehad, shtayim, shalosh****."* They sang together:

> One of these things is not like the others,
> Which one is different, do you know?

---

* *Ima* (ē′• mah): Mom (Hebrew)
** *Rechov SumSum*: Israeli version of Sesame Street
*** *Ehad, shtayim, shalosh*: One, two, three (Hebrew)

Tell me which thing is not like the others,
And I'll tell you if it is so.

Rachel bent over to kiss him on his cheek. She caught his ear instead as he turned his head returning to his sorting.

"What a beautiful table you've set," Rachel's mother said as she lifted the freshly polished fork from its setting next to the delicately patterned china. The small rose-like design on the stem of the fork complemented the tiny roses in the china pattern. "Your grandmother would be so happy to see you use this."

"I miss her very much," Rachel said.

"Perhaps you'll have a daughter, Baruch HaShem. You can name her for her."

Rachel felt her face flush. "Perhaps," she said. She couldn't go through the fertility treatments again, the ordeal of becoming pregnant — an ordeal she could never have shared with her parents. Her father would never have approved. HaShem alone was responsible for the blessing of children. Doctors shouldn't interfere.

"Good *yom tov*," Rachel heard from behind her.

"I didn't hear the bell," she said, turning around to welcome her brother Menaham and his wife Leah. "Good *yom tov* to you, and a *zissen Pesach*[*]," she said, reaching out and embracing them both.

"Where are the boys?"

"Shalom sent them down to Baruch's room."

"A *zissen Pesach*," Rachel heard again. Her mother-in-law, Helen, peeked through the swinging door from the kitchen to the dining room.

Rachel sensed a bit of apprehension in Helen. "And the same to you,"

---

[*] *Zissen Pesach*: Sweet Passover (Yiddish)

she said, letting go of Leah and reaching for Helen. As she embraced her, she realized that she had lost weight. Her small frame was more frail than usual. "Is Max with you?" Rachel asked, already knowing the answer.

Helen's eyes turned downward, avoiding Rachel's gaze. Rachel noticed the half smile Helen forced whenever Max had disappointed her.

"No, no, *drágá lányom*," Helen said. It was one of the few Hungarian phrases Rachel understood. It touched her deeply to hear Helen refer to her as dearest daughter. "You know how he is."

"I know," replied Rachel, hugging Helen again to lessen her embarrassment. "We have some exciting news though."

"What?"

"Baruch can recite the first question."

"Wonderful. You know, I taught Shalom in Hebrew and in Hungarian," Helen said.

"We used to do them in German as well," Leah added.

"I can't wait to hear him," Helen said. "You must be so proud. Not even 3 years old."

"I am," said Rachel.

Rachel beheld her family gathered around the table. Shalom sat at the head of the table with Baruch on his lap. Rachel's father had insisted that Shalom lead the Seder, despite their relative ages. Shalom had resisted, saying that the tradition clearly states that the oldest male present should lead the ritual retelling of the Exodus. The rabbi overruled.

Her parents had insisted that Helen sit between them. They always tried to make her feel like part of the family. Rachel didn't understand how Max could do this to his wife and son. He was simply selfish.

Shalom began reciting the first verses from the Haggadah. The sounds of the words were like music to her. The American-accented Hebrew sounded different from her father's, but the effect was the same. A warm, timeless feeling of security rushed over her.

"*Ha lachma anya*, the bread of affliction," Shalom said, holding up the plate of matzah, "all who are hungry come eat. Whoever is in need, let him come and celebrate with us. This year we are slaves, next year we will be free."

The words flowed through Rachel's mind. It's in the present, as her father had taught her. It's happening now, to us, not to them in the past. HaShem is freeing us now, choosing us now, to be his people forever.

"Baruch," she heard Shalom say. "Baruch, are you ready?"

Rachel watched everyone at the table. Almost in unison, they leaned toward the head of the table to find Baruch slowly, methodically moving a fork back and forth across his plate.

"Baruch," Shalom said again, this time tapping him gently on the shoulder. "Stop playing with the fork. Let's ask the first question, as I taught you."

Baruch was silent.

"Come, *eynikleh*[*]," said Rachel's mother. "I'm so proud of you. I want to hear you say it."

"No," said Helen, touching Rachel's mother's hand. "Don't force him. He's just a little boy. He's shy."

"Mom, he did it perfectly," Shalom said.

Baruch looked up at Shalom. He started to sing absently. "One of these things is not like the others, which one is different, do you know?"

"What's he singing?" Rachel's father asked.

"It's from *Rechov SumSum*," said both Rachel and Shalom. Rachel got up from the table and picked up Baruch from Shalom's lap. She hugged him tightly and he loosely placed his arms around her neck. "What's wrong, *tatele*?" she said in his ear. "Now we should sing the first question, not the song about what's different."

"But something's different, *Ima*," he said.

"What darling, what are you talking about?"

"The kisses, I can't sing the question without the kisses."

---

* *Eynikleh*: Grandchild (yiddish)

Shalom raised his eyebrows in Rachel's direction.

"The chocolate kisses?" asked Rachel.

"Yes, *Ima*."

Rachel looked toward Shalom, her eyes catching his, pleading with him to make this all right. "There is a bag of *pesadich** kisses in the top drawer," she said.

"But we can't eat anything now, you know that," Shalom said.

"Do you want him to do this?" Rachel asked, feeling a room full of eyes focused on her. She picked up Baruch from Shalom's lap and put him on hers. "Please Baruch, say the question like we taught you. Everyone will be so proud of you."

His body stiffened. "No!" he shouted. "It has to be the same. It has to be with the kisses. I want to go back to *Abba*** and I want the kisses," he shrieked, his face tightening and reddening. He began to cry uncontrollably. His fists waved in the air, his breathing turned to long, sucking gasps. One of his fists caught Rachel over the eye, dislocating her wig.

She handed him back to Shalom. Her eyes filled with tears. She felt like she was going to throw up. She ran out of the room and into the bathroom to do just that.

Rachel and Shalom sat nervously in the doctor's office. Baruch played on the floor with the animal figures Rachel had brought to keep him entertained. He paired up the animals one by one.

Dr. Steiglitz entered the room from behind them. "Sorry to have kept you waiting."

"No, that's all right doctor," said Shalom, closing the thin volume of Tal-

---

* *Pesadich*: Kosher for Passover (hebrew)

** *Abba*: Dad (hebrew)

mud he had been reading. He took Rachel's hand. "Well, what can you tell us?"

He looked over at Baruch, who sat cross-legged on the floor consumed with the animal figures. "I can tell you first of all that you have a very bright son."

"Thank you, doctor," Rachel said, sitting up and smiling. The tension in her shoulders eased a bit at the news.

"I can also tell you that, by my examination and by the examination from your pediatrician, he is physically healthy and developing normally."

"So there is nothing wrong with him?" Shalom said, squeezing Rachel's hand.

"Well, let's not fall into the trap of using the terminology, 'wrong,'" said the doctor. "Perhaps we should start with a question."

Rachel shifted back in her chair. "A question?"

"Rachel, let the doctor talk," Shalom said.

"I am."

"Have you ever heard of autism?" Dr. Steiglitz asked.

"Autism?" she repeated.

Shalom answered, "I have."

"He's not retarded," Rachel said, straightening in her chair. "You just said he's very bright."

"No, he's not retarded at all. He is quite bright, actually, but that's not uncommon with autism."

"Doctor, please forgive me, but more to the point..." Shalom said.

"Yes, sorry. Baruch has all the early signs associated with autism. The repetitive behavior and rituals, doesn't care for physical contact, declining speech patterns."

"And you've determined this by?" Rachel said.

"By the testing we've done with him, observing him during our three meetings, and by what you've reported to us."

Rachel's mind was racing. This couldn't be the case. He was talking at 12 months. "What kind of declining speech patterns?" she asked the doctor.

"You reported to us that he doesn't respond to his name when called," the doctor said, picking up his notes and surveying them. "And you reported that he speaks with a smaller vocabulary than he did, say, six months ago."

"Yes, but he's a little boy. He becomes engrossed in what he's doing," she said, the sound of her heart beating in her ears.

"Like now?" The doctor pointed toward Baruch sitting on the floor at the other end of the room.

"Yes, he doesn't want to be interrupted," Rachel said, turning toward Baruch, her hands outstretched in supplication.

"Rachel, darling, calm down. If there's something wrong…"

"There's nothing wrong with him. You heard the doctor, he's healthy, he's brilliant," she snapped back at Shalom.

Shalom tried to take her hands in his as he spoke to her. "Rachel, please, let's hear what the doctor has to say."

Rachel didn't know where to look, where to put her body. She wanted to grab Baruch and leave the room, run out, run home. She leaned back into the seat, took her hands from Shalom's and crossed her arms over her chest.

"Doctor," said Shalom, "what exactly did you mean by 'like now'?"

Steiglitz put the folder back down on the desk and leaned forward. His pale-gray eyes focused on Shalom. "Well, you see," he said. "By this age, his play should be more creative. He should be interacting with the animal figures, making sounds, causing them to interact."

"He does that," Rachel said, her eyes peering out the window behind the desk, avoiding both the doctor and Shalom.

"He did that," Shalom interjected, turning to Rachel. "He doesn't anymore, we both know that."

15

Tolya took a worn green-leather journal from inside his backpack. He had brought the journals written in English to read during the day as time permitted. The old man's diaries fascinated him. He wished he had both the ability and patience to write as Max had. And yet he felt like he was reading about a part of himself.

"Kurchenko, get your feet off that desk," the captain said as he walked by Tolya's office.

"Sorry captain," he called after him, waiting till the captain was out of sight to open the diary.

June 10, 1953
Washington Heights, NYC

My emotions have overtaken me. I have been like stone these past few years. Not wanting to feel anything, not wanting to get close to anyone. The miracle of Steven's birth, no I still want to call him Istvan, has changed everything. It has even changed my relationship with Helen. I can forgive her now. No, that's not even it. I don't need to forgive her anymore, nor do I need to forgive myself either.

Tolya stopped reading and looked up for a moment. He was impressed by how much Redmond's English had improved. He rechecked the date on the entry and realized Max had been in the country six years by the time he wrote this. He looked at his watch. The kid would be here in about ten minutes. He continued reading.

> There was too much death for us in Santo Domingo. Neither of us wanted to dredge that up again. But somehow this has brought us closer. Maybe we can move on now. I have no right to resent her, we both did plenty to hurt the other. We have a new life now and the child deserves a clean start.
>
> To look at him now in the bassinette. So tiny, so helpless. I want everything for him. But I have to admit to myself, there is pain in my heart when I think of the other one. I know I have to forget, it was never meant to be.

"Tolya," Pete called out from the hallway.

"Yes," Tolya said, putting the diary in his lap.

"C'mon, the kid is here with his lawyer. Room C."

"OK," Tolya replied, "be right there." He put a small piece of paper in between the pages of the diary to hold his place.

"This is Linda Cavato, Carlos' attorney," Pete said as Tolya entered the already cramped interrogation room. He put down his clipboard and coffee and extended a hand toward the attorney.

"Hello detective," the attorney said.

"Hello counselor," Tolya answered.

He looked the attorney over as she rose from her chair to take his hand. Tall and thin with model looks and long, jet-black hair. She was expensively dressed, not what Tolya would have expected for Pabon's defense. As she released his grip, Tolya realized she had very big hands for a woman. Tolya turned toward the kid. "How are you, Carlos?"

Carlos sat with his shoulders hunched, his hands clasped on the table, his eyes cast downward toward his shoes. "Fine, fine," he said. "Can we make this fast? I ain't got nothing new to tell you and I gotta get to school."

"School?" Pete said, laughing. "You putting on a little show for your attorney here, papito?"

Cavato stiffened. "Don't speak to my client in that manner."

"In what manner?" Tolya said, hoping to diffuse the situation.

"Referring to him as 'papito.' It's derogatory."

"Not really," Pete said. "It's a term of endearment."

"Not coming from you and not in the way you used it," she said, standing and putting one of her files back into her briefcase. "They warned me about you at the Alianza."

"About me?" Pete said.

"You're from the Alianza. That explains…" Tolya mumbled, then stopped himself.

"Explains what, detective?" Cavato clasped her large hands on top of her briefcase. "And they warned me about you, too." She unclasped her hands and pointed her large index finger at Tolya. He stared at it.

Tolya rose from his chair. "Counselor, please, let's not get off to a bad start."

"I'm afraid we already have."

Tolya took a deep breath. He knew this wasn't going to be easy. "My apologies counselor, let's just get started." He turned toward Carlos. "Carlos, could you run through the events of the afternoon Señor Max was attacked again?"

"You mean can he tell you what he and Mr. Redmond were doing that afternoon before Mr. Redmond was attacked?"

Tolya looked at Pete. He wanted to roll his eyes but caught himself. "Yes," he said.

"I told you," Carlos began, his eyes still focused on his shoes. "We was in the house and el señor wanted to go to the Key Food, so I took him. Then he wanted to watch the boys play some ball. Then I had to take him home, 'cause I needed to pick up my little brother, and we was talking in the apartment. Then I left."

"OK. So when you left, he was in his room in bed?" Tolya asked.

"Yes, like I told you."

Cavato rolled her eyes. "Do you plan to ask my client anything new?"

"Actually, yes," Tolya said. He placed the plastic bag containing the silver-bound Hebrew prayer book on the table. "Carlos, have you ever seen this?" Tolya asked.

Carlos saw the book and smiled. "Yeah, sure," he said.

"I bet you have," Pete said under his breath.

The attorney stiffened up again in the chair. "What does that mean, detective?" she snapped. "And what exactly is that?" She reached for the prayer book.

"It's a Jewish prayer book," Carlos said.

Tolya caught Pete's eye. A hint of a smile peaked up around his mouth.

Cavato signaled for Carlos to remain silent. "I want a moment to speak to my client alone," she said.

"Fine, counselor," Tolya said. He and Pete got up and left the room. They watched through the window in the door as Cavato questioned Carlos.

"See, I told you Tolya, he did it. See how he looked at that book? And she knows, she's telling him not to answer any more questions."

"No, you're wrong," Tolya said. "He never mentioned that thing to her, that's why she wants to speak to him alone."

Tolya saw the attorney wave at them through the glass. "C'mon, she's ready."

"Mr. Pabon will answer your question now," she said as Tolya and Pete retook their positions around the table.

"OK, so let's try this again," Tolya said. "Carlos, you ever seen this before?"

"Yeah," Carlos answered, his hands still clasped and on the table in front of him.

"Where?" Tolya continued.

"In the closet in the back bedroom in el señor's apartment."

"Why were you in the closet in the back bedroom?" Tolya asked.

"Because about two weeks before this shit happened he was telling us about his life when he was in the DR and he wanted to show us some pictures, so we..."

"Who's we?" Pete interrupted.

"María and me. You know, the cook. So he wanted to show us the pictures and they was in an album that was in this box, and this book was on top of it. So when we took out the box, I took this out and that's when I saw it."

Tolya fixed his eyes on Carlos. He knew instinctively the kid was telling the truth. "Did you put it back?" he asked.

"No, I asked him if he wanted me to put it back and he said no. He was going to give it away."

"To who?" Pete said, leaning forward over the table.

"I think he said he was going to give it to María 'cause she's very religious."

"It's worth a lot of money," Tolya said.

"No shit," replied Carlos.

"I'm surprised you didn't steal it," said Pete.

"I didn't steal nothing, I told you," Carlos snapped back.

"I think that's enough, detectives," shouted Cavato as she got up from the chair, slapping her large hands down on the table.

"I would never steal nothing from el señor, I told you that," Carlos shouted again, on his feet, his fists clenched at his side. "OK, so sometimes at the beginning, when I started to work for him, I would pocket some of the change sometimes when he sent me to the store. I figured that old Jewish guy got plenty of money, so I take a couple of bucks from the change to buy myself some loose smokes or something, but not lately..."

"Carlos, that's enough," Cavato said.

"No miss, let me talk. I got nothing to hide. I told you, he treated me like a man and like a friend. You see this coat here?" He pulled the lapel of the jacket he was wearing out in front of him. "He bought it for me so that I wouldn't be cold. He said it was the least he could do because the Dominicans had saved his life and he wanted to help me save mine. He said he knew what it was like to feel cold. He said if I wasn't cold I wouldn't steal nothing to get warm."

Pete got up from the chair and leaned against the wall, his arms crossed against his chest. He turned and looked over toward Carlos. "You say you handled this book, Carlos?"

"Yes."

"And María was there?"

"Yep."

"Pete," Tolya said. "Could you do me a favor and try to track down María?"

"Sure," Pete said. Tolya watched as Pete left the room without looking back at either Carlos or the attorney.

"Carlos, can I ask you one more thing?" Tolya said.

"Sure, what?" Carlos said.

"You told me Señor Max told you to see your father."

"Sí."

"Did you?"

"Sí, I did, and he was right."

"Right about what?"

"I'm still pissed off at the man, but at least now I know why."

Tolya looked around the hallway for signs of the captain before settling back into his chair. He took Max's diary out of the drawer. He held the book in his hands, closed his eyes and leaned back in the chair, thinking about what Carlos had said. "I'm still pissed off at the man, but at least now I know why." For a troubled teenager, Carlos had insight beyond his years.

Tolya thought of his own father. How long had he been angry with him before he had come to forgive him? Truth was, not till he was dead. He so wished he had forgiven him, made that peace, but the both of them were so stubborn.

The passage from the diary flashed through his mind again. He wants everything for him. Isn't that the way it's supposed to be with fathers and sons? Isn't that the main reason he didn't want Karin to have this baby? He didn't want to do that to any life, to ruin it. He knew he was too selfish and too stubborn to be a better father than his was. Or Carlos'.

Tolya sat in his bed in the dark listening to his parents. They spoke in hushed tones, and his mother tried to control his father's increasing anger. Oleg slept soundly in the bed against the other wall buried in his down blankets. Tolya strained to hear his parents.

"I cannot, Zoshya," his father said. "I cannot continue to do this. They take my work and they use it to develop weapons systems for the Arabs. I can't continue to help them destroy my own people."

"Boris, please. I understand, but you have to calm down, you have to think about this. If you refuse to do the work, it will go very badly for us. Look what's happened to Sakharov and Sharansky."

Tolya had heard these names. In school his teachers had denounced both of these men, especially Sakharov. They were enemies of the people. Why was his father involved with people like them? Tolya knew there were Jews in the family, but his father never made much out of it. His parents were Party members. He and Oleg were members of Komsomol. No one ever called him a Jew, except that stupid kulak Nicholai Tserverin at school when they were naked in the pool and then Oleg bloodied his nose.

"I know what they did to both Sharansky and Sakharov, but I can't go on cooperating with the government all day then sneaking off to meetings every other night. They are going to find out I'm a Refusenik sooner or later. They watch, you know."

Tolya was shocked. "A Refusenik?" he whispered to himself.

"Boris, think of the children. You will lose your job. I'll be dismissed from the university."

"You could divorce me," his father said. Tolya's stomach tied into a knot. "If you denounce me, you and the children can stay here. You'll be safe. They'll put me in prison for a little while."

What was he talking about? Tolya got up from the bed and slipped on the warm fuzzy slippers his father had brought for him from Budapest a few weeks earlier and walked out into the living room. The brightness of the lights made his eyes squint. When he opened them, the big cluttered living room was blurry through the tears welling in his eyes.

"Tolya, darling, what are you doing up?" his mother asked when she saw him at the door of his room. She was sitting in the corner of the red brocade couch, her knees drawn up to her chest, her blond hair tied back in a ponytail.

He wasn't sure what to say. He looked at his father sitting in the chair opposite her, his elbows on his knees, his hands holding up his head through his thick blonde hair. Tears rolled down Tolya's cheek. He tried to speak but the words caught in his throat. He felt his face redden under the wet tears. Finally, the words popped out. "You are a traitor," he said, his eyes focused on his father.

"Tolya," his mother said, rising from the couch.

"I heard everything," he said. "I heard what papa said. He's a Refusenik."

His mother came across the room to him. She bent down on one knee and tried to put her arms around him.

"Don't touch me," he said, pulling back from her embrace. Then he heard his father's voice.

"No Zoshya, it's all right. He, they, were going to find out at some point."

"Then it's true, papa, what you said. You are a traitor?" Tolya said, the tears turning to weeping.

"No, Tolya, it's not true, I'm not a traitor. But I am a Jew and I can't work against other Jews."

Tolya panicked. He didn't know where to run. He backed up against the wall, punching it with the back of his fist. He could hear Oleg in the other room waking to the shouting. "You're not a Jew. I don't want you to be a Jew. I don't want to be a Jew."

His father came toward him and placed his large hands on Tolya's shoulders.

Tolya looked into his father's eyes and screamed. "I don't want you to be divorced. I don't want you to go to prison. They'll put you in Lubyanka with the other Refuseniks. We'll never see you again."

He saw the tears streaming down his father's cheeks. His father looked into Tolya's eyes and fell silent for what felt like a very long time. When they embraced, Tolya smelled the familiar scent of his father, a scent he had always found comforting and reassuring. Now he felt only fear. His father released him, but kept his hands on his shoulders. He quietly said to him, "Sometimes our duties are more important than our desires."

16

S halom thanked the last of the shiva callers as they filed out of the living room. Miriam walked them to the door. He rose from the low bench he had been sitting on all evening. His knees and back ached. He stretched, lifting his arms above his head, reaching for the ceiling. It only made the pain worse.

He wanted to check on Rachel. She had been in bed all evening. She had become so distraught she couldn't stop weeping. Shalom was surprised at how deeply affected Rachel was by his father's death. It had always seemed she barely tolerated him. Perhaps he had misjudged her. After almost an hour, Miriam had to call the doctor. There was no way to calm Rachel down, so the doctor sedated her.

As Shalom passed in front of Baruch's room, he cracked the door and looked in. He was asleep. Thank HaShem for Miriam.

"Shalom," Rachel's father called from down the hallway.

Shalom put a finger over his lips and gently closed Baruch's door.

"Assemblyman Levitz wants to talk with you before he goes," the rabbi said, ignoring Shalom's gesture.

Shalom walked a few steps back down the hall and said, "Let me check on Rachel."

"She's sleeping, I was just in there. Please come back to the living room before the Assemblyman has to leave."

Shalom hesitated, he wanted to check on Rachel himself. Then he thought better of it. Perhaps he should just get this over with first. He would be delighted when this was over. Levitz would disappear from his life as suddenly as he had entered it.

They were settled comfortably waiting for him, his father-in-law on the couch and Levitz in Shalom's reading chair. Shalom sat back down on the shiva stool.

"You don't have to sit there to make a show for me," Levitz said.

"I'm not doing it for you," Shalom said. He was offended by Levitz's hypocrisy. "I'm fulfilling my duties as a *Kaddisher** ."

"Have it your way, Shalom. Sorry, I didn't mean to offend you and please just call me Yehuda."

"I think I'll stick with Assemblyman Levitz," Shalom answered, shifting his weight to relieve the pressure on his lower back.

"Shalom," his father-in-law said, "the Assemblyman was only trying to make you feel more comfortable. It's OK to sit here on the couch if you want." He patted the seat next to him. "Just remove the cushion."

He was surprised to hear his father-in-law say that. He would regularly criticize anyone who suggested any kind of modern interpretation of Jewish custom. "I'm fine here, *Abba*," said Shalom. He turned toward Levitz. "Now what was it you wanted to speak with me about? I was going to check on my wife."

Levitz removed his glasses and cleaned them with his tie. "We've had a very interesting development in your father's case."

"You've had an interesting development?"

"Yes."

"I'm not sure I know what you mean?" Shalom said. He looked over at his father-in-law.

"The Assemblyman has a witness."

Shalom straightened his back again. "Has this witness spoken with the police?"

---

* *Kaddisher*: Mourner (Yiddish)

"The police are dragging their feet and the good rabbi is not entirely correct in using the term 'witness.' What we have is more like evidence."

"What kind of evidence?"

"Let me ask you a question first, Shalom."

Shalom looked at Levitz. He sensed something was not right, that Levitz was up to something.

"Did your father, your parents, have a large silver candelabra?" Levitz asked.

"Yes. Why?"

"We have the Dominican kid on film carrying one out of the building."

The Monkey Room was dark, noisy and crowded. "Beer OK?" Pete asked.

"Sure, why not?" Tolya said, waving over the bartender.

"The usual, Tommy," Pete said.

The bartender popped the caps off two bottles of Corona and pressed a wedge of lime into the top of each.

"You still convinced Pabon did it?" Tolya followed his question with a healthy swig of beer.

"Not entirely, but I'm not convinced that he didn't ," Pete said, pulling the bar stool under him and sitting down. "You want a stool?" Pete asked. "There's another one behind you."

"No, I'll stand." Tolya popped a handful of nuts into his mouth. "Why aren't you convinced?"

"I don't have another suspect," said Pete.

Tolya took another swig of his beer and smiled. "Sure you do," he said.

"C'mon Tolya. Who?"

"The maid, the son, the daughter-in-law…" Tolya ticked off the possibilities on his fingers.

"Or was it Colonel Mustard in the dining room with the candlestick?" Pete said and laughed. "Why are you so convinced it's not the kid?"

Tolya became serious. "He's got no motive."

"Of course he has a motive," Pete replied. "He's also got a history."

"Except he didn't steal anything." Tolya finished the bottle and slammed it on the bar.

"You don't know that," Pete said.

Tolya hesitated for a moment. "I feel it."

"You feel it?" Pete said, still nursing his beer.

"Yeah. The same way you find evidence, I feel motive."

Pete chuckled, Tolya looked at him. "I'm not laughing at you, Tol. You've got a keen sense for sniffing out perps. But we don't know if something's missing from the apartment."

"Like what?"

"Maybe he knew where the old man stashed his cash and just took it. No one would ever know, except maybe the son."

Tolya nibbled on more beer nuts. "There would have been a mess where he was looking for it."

"Maybe he knew where it was, didn't have to look and wouldn't have made a mess."

"He would have been in a rush, would have at least left some prints."

"Maybe the maid cleaned it up."

"The timeline doesn't support it, Pete. She didn't do anything in that apartment from the time she arrived and called 911 till the first uniforms got there."

Pete took a long swig of the beer, finishing it. "Tolya, you and I both know your gut feeling is not enough here."

This is what he loved about Pete: Despite Pete always being late and his generally lazy attitude — which was the complete opposite of Tolya's obsessive promptness and preoccupation with minute details — Pete always challenged him, pushed him, tried to convince him he was wrong.

"I know. I gotta find something. What time is the maid coming in tomorrow?"

"11:30."

"Let's see what we can get out of her."

"Tolya, you don't think she…"

"Get real, Pete," Tolya said, slapping him lightly on the back of the head. "Jeez."

Shalom sat on the edge of the bed. Levitz's security tape showed the Dominican kid carrying the silver candelabra out of his father's building in a brown paper shopping bag. Seeing it left him feeling both relieved and deeply guilty. What more could he have done? He had warned his father not to let that kid into the house. He knew it was trouble. At the same time, he felt in some way disappointed that the kid had done it. He knew it all along, but had wanted to be proven wrong. Or, rather, he wanted to be proven right, but differently. To have real evidence, a witness, someone who could have testified to the last moments of his father's life, not a video tape pointing a finger at motive without definitive proof.

Shalom pulled back the blanket and slipped into bed. Rachel lay on her side facing away from him. Her breathing was regular but shallow. That must be the sedatives. He lay back and looked up at the darkness on the ceiling. Why should he care? Why should he care what happens to this kid? He killed an old man. He killed his father.

17

"Captain, that's just not possible," Tolya said, squinting at the laptop on the captain's desk.

"It's on camera, Tolya," Pete said.

"I thought you agreed with me," Tolya replied, taking his hands from his eyes and looking directly at Pete.

"I was almost there last night, but with this…" He waved his hand toward the desk.

"It clearly indicates a motive," the captain said.

"Run it again," Tolya demanded.

The captain clicked the mousepad. Tolya leaned forward to get a closer look. It was clear: Carlos was walking down Bennett Avenue carrying a brown paper shopping bag. A large silver candelabra was sticking out of the top of the bag. The date on the lower right-hand corner of the video read: October 24, 2005.

Tolya slouched back into the chair. "They had this tape?" he asked.

"It's from the synagogue's security cameras," the captain said.

"You know we asked them if they had any security cameras filming the street," Tolya said.

"And they said?" asked the captain.

"The cameras didn't film close enough to 105 Bennett to pick up any-thing," Pete answered.

"Well, they were correct about that," the captain said. "This video has him walking down Bennett toward 181st Street. He's more than fifty feet from 105 Bennett."

"When did they go looking for this?" Tolya asked.

"After the pawnbroker brought the ticket to Levitz, they checked their tapes," the captain said. "This makes us look pretty inept."

Tolya looked at the receipt lying next to the laptop on the captain's desk. He wondered how the hell Levitz pulled this off. "This proves nothing," he said. He got up, walked around the desk and paused the video. "The old man was attacked on the 25th. The date stamp says the 24th. He took the damn thing the day before."

"I know, Tolya," the captain said, easing back into his chair, "but it speaks to motive."

"What motive?"

"Theft. If he stole the candelabra, what's to say he wasn't planning on stealing the prayer book as well?" Pete said.

"Maybe the old man caught him trying to take it and that's when he killed him," the captain added.

Tolya shook his head. "I can't believe this shit. How the hell did the pawn-broker get involved in this anyway?"

"Levitz said the pawnbroker thought he recognized the piece. Apparently, the old man sold some stuff to him a while back. The pawnbroker came to Redmond's apartment to give him an estimate. He saw the candelabra and offered to buy it. Redmond said no. Said it had sentimental value. He recog-nized it when the kid brought it in. He'd seen the news reports on NY1, etc. He called Levitz's office."

"Not us?" Tolya said.

"Nope. Can you get your head around that shit?" Pete said. "We got a little PR problem here, Cap?"

"Ya think?" the captain said, closing the laptop.

Tolya picked up the pawn ticket. "Cap, this is dated the 29th. He had it since the 24th. The old man died on the 28th. Something's not right."

Tolya felt Pete's hands on his shoulders. "I know you don't want to believe it but it makes sense," he said. "He probably emptied whatever cash was in the house too. I know you feel really strongly about this kid. But face it, you're wrong."

"I just don't buy it," Tolya said, brushing Pete's hands off his shoulders and getting up from the chair. "Why didn't he take the prayer book too? That silver binder is worth a fortune."

"Maybe he got scared. Who knows?" Pete said.

Tolya frowned at Pete then turned toward the captain. "Please, Cap. I gotta have a little more time. This doesn't make sense."

Tolya watched the captain push back against his already strained chair, shaking his head slightly from side to side. "Kurchenko, you're killing me. I just want this nightmare over."

"Tolya, he's right," Pete said.

Tolya flipped Pete the bird. "Captain, how much time can you buy me?"

"Not much. And I don't see why I need to buy you any."

"We've got the maid coming in this morning. Let me question her again to see what she knows."

"She won't tell us anything, even if she does know something," Pete said.

The captain sighed. "We better call the kid in again too," he said. "In any event, we'll need to contact his lawyer."

"And drag that pawnbroker in here for a statement too," added Pete. "The schmuck."

"Yep," Tolya said.

"You got today, maybe tomorrow," the captain said. "Levitz is all over me. The DA is involved now too. Unless you come up with something else, I gotta get an arrest warrant."

Tolya turned to Pete. "You with me on this?"

Pete laughed. "Not really, but I'll humor you anyway. I get to interview the pawnbroker."

"Buenos días, María," Tolya said.

"Buenos días, detective," María replied, looking around the tiny interrogation room. Pete pulled out a chair for her and helped her with her coat. "You know I never be in a police station before, but I watch a lot on TV, especially Law and Order. It look just like this."

Tolya fought to keep a grin off his own face. "How are you, María?" he asked.

"Oh, no so good since Señor Max is died," she said, settling into the chair. "I am very upset."

"I can understand that," Tolya said. "I looked for you at the funeral."

"You go for the funeral?" María said, looking up at him.

"Yes," Tolya answered. He watched María carefully.

She smoothed her skirt with the hand that held a tissue. "No, I no want to go."

"Why?" asked Pete, leaning against the wall in the corner of the room.

"Because I know they are telling many lies."

"About you?" Tolya said.

"No about me." She pursed her lips and shook her head.

"About what, or who?" Tolya asked.

She hesitated a moment. "About el señor," she answered.

Tolya thought she was going to say Carlos. "What kind of lies?" he asked.

"I no want to talk about this señor, por favor," she said, touching a tissue to her eyes.

Pete pulled a chair out and sat down next to Tolya. He put his large hands over both of María's. Tolya had never seen him do anything like that in the years they'd been partners.

"María, please. You've gotta help us here," he whispered in Spanish. "Why didn't you want to go to the funeral?"

María lifted her head. She moved one small hand from under Pete's and placed it on top of Pete's, then smiled at him. "I see on the TV, they talk about el señor and the family and about his life and how the family, is how you say, devastada…"

"Devastated," Pete said.

"Sí, devastada, and I know this a lie. The son, he never come to see el señor, only maybe once or twice a month, and then he act like he better than his father. He no show no respeto. Y the wife, she come more, but every time she is fighting with him over the food. He an old man, leave him alone, let him eat what he want. He suffer enough in this life."

Tolya let her ramble without interruption. He realized she had been bottling this up. He thought she was finished and was about to ask her a question when she suddenly started up again.

"And then she is fighting with him about the boy."

Tolya turned his head toward Pete. "What boy?" they both said, almost simultaneously.

"The grandson."

"The grandson?" Tolya repeated.

"Sí."

"What was the fight about?" Pete asked.

"Porque, she no want the boy to go with el señor and Carlos to the park, or to the schoolyard to play the basketball."

"Hmm." Tolya stood up. "María, could you excuse Detective Gonzalves and me for a moment." He heard his accent thicken on the word moment, shortening the "o" to sound like a "u." "I'm never gonna get rid of that," he mumbled almost inaudibly.

"Por supuesto," she said.

"Get rid of what?" Pete asked.

"Forget about it. Could I speak to you outside please?"

Pete followed him out of the interrogation room into the narrow, dark hallway. "There is no way Pabon killed that old man," Tolya said.

Pete hesitated for a moment, rubbing the top of his head. "I think I agree, but all the evidence…"

"Fuck that evidence, we need new evidence," Tolya said.

"What's the story with the grandson?" Pete asked. "Maybe that would lead to something."

"I don't know," Tolya replied. "Redmond and Carlos were taking him out to the schoolyard to play basketball."

"And the mother didn't like that. We should ask her about that," Tolya said.

"Let's go back in," Pete said.

Tolya put his hand on Pete's shoulder. "Then you're with me on this now? Not just humoring me?"

"I'm with you, it's not that kid." Pete placed his hand on the doorknob. "Probably not."

Tolya rolled his eyes. "Wait," Tolya said. "One more thing."

"What?"

"What was that with the hand-holding and the questioning in Spanish?"

"She reminds me of my grandmother," Pete said, twisting the knob.

"Then it was the boy," said Rachel. She was sitting up in bed. The morning sun sneaked in through sheer curtains, warming the bedroom. "You can't blame yourself."

"It's not that I blame myself. There was no dealing with him on the subject of anything Dominican. I feel embarrassed that I was so difficult with your father and Levitz."

Rachel took Shalom's hand in both of hers. She hoped, now that the police were going to arrest someone, they could return to a normal life. "There's nothing to be embarrassed about with my father, you know that. You're like his own child."

Shalom pulled the blanket up around his chest and sat up. "And Levitz? I practically accused him of exploiting my father's death. Maybe he was just looking out for me."

"Didn't we all try to tell you that?" Rachel said, stroking his hand.

"Yes."

Rachel nestled her head in between his chest and arm.

"Are you feeling better?" Shalom asked.

"Yes."

"What came over you yesterday?"

"I don't know, I'm sorry. I was just so overwhelmed," she said, snuggling closer to him. "Tell me again, how did they find him carrying away your mother's candelabra?"

"On the tape from the *Beis Medrash**, down the block."

"Were they looking?"

"No, it was only after the pawnbroker called Levitz."

"The pawnbroker?"

"Yes, the boy tried to sell it."

"Baruch HaShem, He brings justice."

Shalom smiled at her and stroked her cheek. "But you are better, Rachel?"

"Much better."

"María, could you tell us more about Carlos and the grandson?"

She smiled and shook her head. "There is no much to tell, they like each other. I never see Baruch play so nice with another children."

"What do you mean exactly?" Tolya said. He caught María's gaze as she lifted her head. He knew she would make a great witness.

"They have many problem with him at the Jewish school. But the mother,

---

* *Beis Medrash:* Jewish school and continuing education center (Hebrew)

she refuse to send him to the special school because she no want him around the children who are no Jewish."

"How do you know that, María?" Tolya asked.

"Because I hear Señor Max try to talk to her about it many times."

Before Tolya could ask, Pete said, "What happened when Señor Max tried to talk to her about it?"

"She get very angry."

Pete nodded at Tolya. "Sorry to have interrupted you."

"No problem." He turned his gaze back to María and smiled. "What happened at the Jewish school?"

"He is getting in fights with the other children. The teachers, they no can control him," she said.

"Did they change schools?" Pete asked.

"Yes."

"When," interjected Tolya.

"Finally last year in the winter. I hear Señor Max talking to his son about it many times."

"What did his son say?" Pete asked.

"He say Baruch is better off with his own people. God make him this way and they will take care of him."

Tolya felt the anger rise in his chest. What a schmuck. It was always about their hallowed god and his people. Out of the corner of his eye, Tolya saw Pete's mouth open but no words came out.

"Why did they finally move him?" Tolya said.

María's face opened into a broad smile. "El señor tell me the Jewish school say they could no handle him anymore."

Tolya laughed to himself. He knew she was loving this. It was like gossip.

"He is very happy about it," she continued without prompting. "Señor Max say the boy need professional teachers, no professional Jews."

"He was right about that," Tolya said.

Pete flashed him a sardonic smile.

Tolya leaned in toward María and asked, "So what happened between Carlos and Baruch?"

"He very different with Carlos. Carlos, he know how to keep him calm." María said.

"How come Carlos is able to handle him?" Pete asked.

"Porque he have a brother just like that. I ask him the same thing the first day he meet Baruch."

Tolya looked at Pete and raised his eyebrow. He recalled the screaming from the back of the apartment the day he and Pete went looking for Carlos and his aunt refused to let them in.

"When was that first meeting, María?" Tolya asked.

"A few weeks after Carlos start with el señor."

"María, can you tell us exactly what happened that day?" Pete asked.

"Por supuesto. I remember. The Señora Rachel come by with Baruch after school that day. She is there for a few minutes and she jump up and say she have to go, she forget to do something. She want to take Baruch but I see el señor is so happy to see him. He showing Baruch pictures of himself when he is younger. Baruch love that, so I say no worry, I watch him with Señor Max, you go now and come back for him later."

"So she left him?" Tolya asked.

"Sí, she is very nervous about it but I convince her. She leave and then a little while later Carlos come and Señor Max say to him, 'Come take us to the schoolyard to watch the boys play basketball.' Carlos say, 'Sure, why not, is too nice to sit in the house.'"

"Had Carlos met Baruch before?" Pete asked.

"Sure, a couple of times. But Señora Rachel, she no let them talk much. She no like Carlos."

"Why?" Tolya said. He knew the answer.

"I don't know, maybe she afraid of him because he was in trouble? But now he a good boy."

"So Carlos took el Señor and Baruch to the schoolyard?" Pete said.

"Sí, and then Señora Rachel, she come back before they are back and she is very angry with me."

"Why?" Tolya asked.

"Because I say I would watch Baruch, but I let him go out. She is scream-ing at me that she will tell her husband and he will fire me."

"Did she?" Pete asked.

"I don't know," María said, chuckling a little, "but I no worry because I know how much Señor Max like me."

"Did she go look for them?" Tolya said.

"No, just when she is going they come back. She grab Baruch and she start screaming at Señor Max."

"Because he took Baruch out?" Tolya said.

"Sí, that, but mostly she want to know if they feed him anything that is no kosher."

Tolya leaned back, attempting to stretch his legs under the table without crowding María.

"Her kid disappears and she's worried about what he ate?" Pete asked.

"She always worry about that when he visit," María said. "I no allowed to give him anything, only water."

The recounting of Rachel's behavior confirmed for Tolya what he already thought: These people are insane. "So what did el señor say to her?" Tolya said.

"He tell her she need to let go a little with Baruch. He tell her Carlos is showing him how to throw the ball at the basket and that it good for him."

"And she said?" Tolya asked.

"She tell Carlos he is never to take her son anywhere again. Then she grab Baruch and they leave."

"Did the grandson ever come back?" Pete asked.

"Yes, after that, many times. He come by and she leave him and he go with el señor and with Carlos to the park and the schoolyard, but you could see she no like it much."

"Maybe Rothman reacted differently than she expected?" Tolya said to Pete.

"Maybe, we'll have to ask them about that." Pete replied.

"Detective," María asked, looking at her watch, "is there anything else you want to know. I need to go to my lady now."

"One more thing, María."

"Qué?"

Tolya nodded toward Pete. Pete pulled the silver-bound prayer book in the plastic bag out from under the table. "Have you ever seen this before?" he asked.

"Sí."

"Where?" Tolya said.

"It belong to Señor Max."

"When did you see it?"

"A few weeks ago. He wants to show us, me and Carlos, some old pictures from Santo Domingo. You know Carlos, he come from near where el señor lived, and this book is in the same box."

"Did he tell you what he was going to do with it?" Tolya said.

"Sí," María said.

Tolya noticed her shoulders tense up. "What?" he asked.

"I no want to say," she replied. She picked up her bag and drew the handles up near her chest.

"Why?" Tolya said.

"Because you will think I am lying," she replied

"No we won't. Tell us, please," Pete said, taking her hand again.

"He say he wanted to give it to me."

"What did you say when he told you that?" Tolya asked.

"I tell him no, is no right, is too, how you say, caro."

"Expensive," Pete said

"Gracias, but he insist." She turned her head away and let go of Pete's hand.

"But he didn't give it to you," Tolya said.

"I tell him he should keep it till he die and then I take it."

"So you left it in the dresser?"

"No, I leave it on the night table," María said.

Tolya looked at Pete.

"I tell him maybe he should read it," she added.

"What did he say?" Tolya said.

"Nothing. He just laugh."

"Was that the end of the subject?" Pete said.

María hesitated.

"Is there something else María?" Tolya asked.

"Yes," María said, crossing herself. "Dios mío, forgive me."

"María, whatever it is, please tell us."

"I no like to gossip."

Tolya laughed to himself. No, not much.

"María, please," Pete said.

"OK. A few days before I find Señor Max in the bathroom, he is sending Carlos to fix the candlestick from his wife that I break."

Tolya looked at Pete and nodded. "Go on."

"Again he say, 'Please take the book.' I say no. It worth too much money. He say he would rather I have it to remember him when he is gone."

"He didn't want to give it to his son?" Pete said, reaching over to touch her arm again.

"No. He say his daughter-in-law no deserve it, the way she treat him."

Tolya stood up. "Thank you María. You have been very helpful," he said, extending his hand.

"De nada, detective. You see I call you detective, no officer, because I know you like that," she said.

Tolya looked toward Pete and saw he was stifling a laugh.

18

Tolya was standing with Pete by the coffee machine at the end of the long hall in the station house when he spotted them. "Shit, just what we didn't need," he said.

Pete turned around to look. "Damn, the captain's not going to be happy about this."

Juan Carlos Guzmán, elegantly dressed as always, followed Carlos, Cavato and another woman into the station.

"Who's she?" Tolya said.

"I dunno," Pete answered. They both put down their cups and walked down the hallway toward the reception area.

Cavato approached them, her posse in tow. "Detectives."

"Counselor," they said in unison.

"This is Juan Carlos Guzmán, director of the Alianza Dominicana."

Guzmán extended his hand to Tolya and Pete. "Officers, I'm supervising Ms. Cavato and will be joining you today."

Tolya bit his tongue. "Welcome," he said.

"Mucho gusto," Pete said, shaking Guzmán's hand as well.

Guzmán moved slightly to the right, holding out his hand toward the small woman behind him. "May I introduce you to Leonora Santender, Carlos' mother."

"Nice to meet you," Tolya said, extending his hand again.

She took it formally and held it only briefly, repeating the process with Pete. "Encantada," she said.

Tolya's eyes followed her as she receded back behind Guzmán. He imagined she must have been very beautiful once. What was it his father used to call women like her? A woman of a certain age? No, he realized, she was too young for that.

"Is the captain here?" Cavato asked. "Director Guzmán would like to speak with him."

Tolya turned to Pete again. He didn't want to escalate the tension of this interview. He raised his eyebrow, knowing Pete would get his message. "Do you know where the captain is?"

"I think he's out but I'll check," Pete said.

"Can we go on back to, um, one of our meeting rooms while he looks for him?" Tolya suggested.

Cavato looked at Guzmán. Guzmán nodded affirmatively. "Certainly," she said.

"Looks like we're going to need a larger room," Tolya replied.

Tolya grabbed the two chairs from the smaller interrogation room and brought them into the larger one. It was tight. Pete came in as he was shuffling the chairs behind the table.

"Is he gone?" Tolya whispered to Pete, his back toward the group.

"He is now," Pete whispered back. "I'm sorry, seems the captain has left the building," he said to Guzmán.

"I will have to try to reach him later then," Guzmán said through his ever-present poker face. "Ms. Cavato informed me you have new evidence in Carlos' case."

Tolya looked over toward Carlos sitting in the corner, arms crossed, eyes staring at the opposite wall, mouth tight-lipped. He'd turned his collar up around his neck like a teenage hood in the old black-and-white movies Tolya used to watch on afternoon TV when he first arrived in the United States.

"Officers, what's the evidence?" Guzmán asked. Tolya and Pete exchanged glances, each waiting for the other to begin. Guzmán placed his hand on Cavato's forearm, leaned over and whispered something in her ear. She eased back into her seat. "Officers?" Guzmán said again.

Tolya bit his lip. He caught Pete smiling out of the corner of his eye.

"Actually, it's detectives, director," Pete said.

Tolya smiled to himself. Thanks Pete.

"My apologies…detectives," Guzmán said.

Tolya flipped open the laptop sitting on the table and positioned it so everyone could see the screen. "We'd like to show you something." He inserted the disc into the laptop and clicked play. As Carlos' figure walked from one side of the screen to the other, Tolya watched the expressions of everyone at the table. Carlos deflated, Cavato inflated, the mother smirked, but Guzmán's face remained unreadable like a blank stone tablet.

"What is this?" Cavato said, getting up from her chair.

"It's surveillance footage," said Tolya.

"Big deal, detective. So you've got a tape of my client walking down the street."

Tolya clicked play again. "Please notice what he's carrying," he said.

Cavato and Guzmán watched the video again. Carlos stared at the wall.

"He's carrying a shopping bag, so what? Since when is that a crime?" Cavato said.

"Carlos, what's in the shopping bag?" Tolya said.

"I don't know, you tell me," Carlos replied, still staring at the wall.

"Don't be a wise ass," Pete said.

"That wasn't even the same day," Carlos said, swinging around in his chair to face them.

"Carlos, don't say another word," Cavato said. "What exactly is this?"

Tolya got up from his chair and leaned back against the wall of the cramped room. "This is a surveillance tape from the Yeshiva down the street on Bennett Avenue. It was taken the day before the attack. The victim's son has identified the item sticking out of the shopping bag as a silver candelabra that belonged to his parents."

Cavato's mouth opened but no words came out. Guzmán turned toward Carlos and his mother and said something to them in Spanish.

"Can we see that again please?" he asked Tolya.

Tolya clicked play on the laptop again. They all leaned in to watch the video one more time.

"This proves nothing," Cavato said.

"It kinda proves motive," Pete said.

Tolya shot him a look. What was he doing?

"Motive to do what?" Guzmán said.

"Theft, for starters," Pete said.

"Pete, please," Tolya said.

"I didn't steal nothing," Carlos said, still crouched in his chair. "El señor sent me to get the thing fixed."

"What was wrong with it?" Tolya said.

"María was cleaning it and she dropped it, and one arm was bent."

Tolya pulled the pawn ticket out of the case folder and placed it on the table. "Then what's this about?"

The attorney picked up the ticket and looked at it. "Carlos, don't answer any more questions," she said. She picked up her briefcase and turned to Tolya. "Officers, I think this interview is over. If you want to proceed further, charge my client with something. Otherwise, leave him alone."

Guzmán reached up and touched Cavato's arm again. "Linda, please sit down for a moment. No one wants Carlos to be charged with anything. Let me talk to him, let us talk to him." He turned to Tolya and Pete. "Detectives, might we have a moment alone with Carlos?"

"Of course," Tolya said. He and Pete left the room. They watched from the hallway through the interior window as Guzmán questioned Carlos.

"I wish I could hear this," Pete said. "Look at the kid, he's terrified of Guzmán."

"I suppose it's good he's terrified of someone," Tolya replied.

"Watch the mother, I think she's going to take a swing at the kid," Pete said as she raised her hand, Guzmán holding her back.

"You can see she hasn't had it easy. How old do you think she is?" Tolya said.

"He's 17? Probably no more than 35. She looks like she was a beauty."

Tolya smiled. "Still is."

Pete smiled and slapped Tolya on the back of the head playfully. "You know, hermano, I don't know any Dominican guy who likes our women as much as you do."

Tolya looked at Pete and they both laughed. "I think we played this the right way. They don't realize we don't think it's the kid. Makes them fight harder."

"See, I told you," Pete said.

"Come on, Guzmán is waving at us. They must be ready." Tolya opened the door.

"Carlos has something he wants to tell you," Guzmán said.

"OK Carlos. What's the story?" Tolya asked.

Carlos sat up straight, his arms crossed against his chest. "It's like I told you before, I didn't steal nothing and I didn't hurt nobody and I would never hurt Señor Max."

"OK, I believe you Carlos. Now what happened?" said Tolya, taking a seat.

Carlos hesitated for a moment before he started. "El señor, he asked me to take this to a guy down on 47th Street he found who could fix it."

"OK," said Pete.

"But since I had to go downtown to do that, he told me to do it whenever I had time."

"So you never took the thing downtown to the get it repaired?" asked Tolya.

"No. I was gonna do it the next day," Carlos said. He stopped for a moment and took a deep breath. "But when I heard he was beat up, I got scared and I hid it in our apartment. But I was afraid if you found it there you would say I stole it. And I was right."

"Why didn't you just return it to Señor Max's son?" Tolya asked.

"You kidding, man?" Carlos laughed nervously. "They hate me, especially the wife. They'd say I stole it and beat him up."

That's exactly what they were saying.

"Why did you try to sell it then?" Tolya said.

Carlos looked at his mother. "Cuz my moms over here was scared to death you guys would come to search our apartment and find it."

Tolya shifted his gaze to the mother. Until now she hadn't said one word. He watched her mouth open as the words tumbled out.

"I figured we needed the money more than they did anyway," she said, her face expressionless. "I got a sick child, you know?"

"Captain, the kid can clearly explain what he was doing with the candelabra and the maid's testimony will confirm it," Tolya said.

The captain looked up from the stack of papers he was reading. "And Levitz's people will say that he lied and she's covering for him. He was the only one who was in the apartment that afternoon. He had the candlestick, or whatever it is." He put down the pen he was holding and looked directly at Tolya. "He tried to get rid of it. I don't buy it and I doubt a jury will either."

"But the kid and the maid have the same story," pleaded Tolya. "She dropped it and he was supposed to get it fixed."

"Cap, what more do you need?" Pete asked.

"I need something that implicates someone else. Who might have gotten in there?"

Tolya looked at Pete, then back to the captain. "How much more time do I have?"

"Tomorrow afternoon."

"Why did you want me to meet you here?" Karin called out as Tolya turned the corner from 186th Street onto Bennett Avenue.

"Shhh, not so loud," he said.

"Who's gonna hear? And why are you acting like an undercover cop?"

"Because this is kind of undercover." He slipped his arm around her waist and kissed her quickly on the lips. "I need your help."

"Wait, wait," she said, pulling away from him. "What are we doing here?"

"I need to go back in there and I need some help." Tolya grabbed her hand and tugged her gently forward.

She dropped his hand and stopped in her tracks. "You know I can't go in there, I'm not on this case."

"Please, Karin, they're going to arrest the kid."

She dropped her arms to her sides and looked at him.

"Please," he said again.

"You're so sure this kid is innocent?"

"Yes."

"Why me?"

He wrapped his arms around her, pinning hers down playfully. "Because you were the best evidence cop the precinct ever had," he whispered in her ear.

"True, but..." she said, wiggling out of his hold. "Pete's pretty good too."

Tolya took a step back and looked at her. He took her hands gently in his. "Please," he said.

Tolya followed Karin into the second bedroom.

"I hope we have better luck in here than we did in the other rooms," she said.

"We'd better, or we've got nothing," he replied. He watched her slowly slide open the dresser drawers, scan the room, then open the door to the closet.

"What's in that box?" she asked.

"That's where I found the diaries."

"Are the rest of them in there?"

"Yep."

"Well it might pay to take a look at those." She reached into the closet to pull the box out.

"Whoa, stop," Tolya said, taking her hand off the box.

"Why?"

"You're pregnant," he said.

She rolled her eyes and turned back toward the box. "Ay papi, I'm not a china doll."

"Stop calling me that." The words popped out of his mouth before he could stop them.

Karin stood up. Tolya could see the change in her expression. "I don't know why that bothers you so much."

"I'm sorry," he said, sitting down on the edge of the narrow bed. "I don't know, it's all just so new to me."

"You know it's a term of endearment with us," she replied, sitting down next to him. "I could call you that if I weren't pregnant."

"I know, I hear it on the street all the time. But you never did."

She reached over and touched his face. "Because it's so ghetto."

At that moment, he realized again what it was he loved about her — her easiness, her sincerity. If only he knew how to be this honest with her about how he was feeling.

She looked toward the window out onto the airshaft. "Tolya," she said. "Can I ask you something?"

"Por supuesto."

"Hmmm, español." She smiled at him. "The way to a woman's heart."

"So go ahead, ask."

She touched his hand. "Are you OK with this, with the baby?"

"Of course," he said, withdrawing his hand. "What kind of question is that to ask me?" He was sure he had said "vhat."

"I was just worried."

"Nothing to worry about," he said. "I'm just stressed out from this case. Let's grab those diaries and get out of here." He reached into the box and took out the rest of the diaries. He opened the first one. It was in Spanish but he could read the date: 15 VI '42. He handed it to Karin. "You can start with this one as soon as we get home."

"Yes detective," she said, saluting him.

Sosúa
Dominican Republic
Rothman Homestead
15 VI '42
8 p.m.

The heat was intense, even at 7 in the morning. It beat down on my back and head, penetrating my hat and shirt as I weeded the small garden plot behind the house. The breeze off the water doesn't carry this far from the beach. I stood up to stretch. The cows were so much easier to tend to. Then I heard something move to my left. I saw the long tail of a rat slide between the stalks of corn, picked up a small stone and threw it into the thicket. I missed. I bent over again continuing to pull the weeds from between the plants. They grow faster than the corn does.

"Max," I heard Nereida call from the porch of the house. I stood up again, took the straw hat from my head and wiped my brow with the tattered sleeve of my shirt. "Your coffee is ready, Helen is up," she called to me in Spanish.

Nereida has been with us for two months. I am paying her in milk and a few vegetables, siphoning off a bit from the yield every day. Erno covers for me at the co-op, fudging the numbers on my deliveries to the dairy.

Helen can't work, the pregnancy has been difficult and the doctor had sent her to bed. Nereida is a midwife. If there are any problems, she will know what to do. I certainly don't. My only experience with birth was with calves, and I'm not going to risk the safety of my wife and our first child to inexperience.

"Ya voy," I called back, dropping the small shovel to my feet. I stopped to inspect the squash as I walked back to the house. There were small bite marks in two of them. Damn rats.

Crossing the fifty yards between the vegetable garden and the house, I climbed the small rise I had chosen as its site. I remember how happy I was the day we cleared the brush before digging the holes for the stilts on which the house sits. I looked out over my homestead, mostly low brush with some mango trees and wild banana plants. It is our future. With Istvan's help, I will build it into a real farm.

I took off my hat and placed it on the hook by the door as I entered the house. Helen sat at the table wedged into the hard chair, her hands under her large belly. It was as if she was trying to hold the baby in her arms now. I sat down at the table I had built myself. I do all kinds of things now I would never have thought myself capable of. Nereida brought me coffee.

"*Drágám*, why are you out of bed again?" I asked Helen. "The doctor clearly said to stay in bed."

"I was up anyway, Nereida helped me to the bathroom," Helen said. She reached across the table and took my hand. "Besides, I didn't want you to eat alone."

"Eat?" I said, a smile creeping up my face. "We have nothing to eat."

"I made you some mangú," Nereida said, placing the plate of mashed green plantains topped with pickled onions in front of me.

I looked at the plate. It was too hot for mangú. "Gracias," I said. "Is there more coffee?"

"You have to eat something," said Helen. "You can't work like this on no food. You'll pass out in the field or the barn."

"I'll have a mango," I said, reaching for one from the wooden bowl I had traded for on my last visit to Puerto Plata with José. It was an impulse, something we didn't need. But it had taken my fancy, carved into a perfect oval with palm trees painted on the side. Helen had smiled when she removed the brown paper wrapping I had put around it. She loved things like that. She was devastated when we left in the middle of the night, leaving everything behind.

"She'll be insulted if you don't eat it," Helen said in Hungarian.

"No she won't," I said. "She'll just place it into a bowl, cover it up and take it back to her house for the children. It won't go to waste." I took a small knife from the sheath attached to my belt and cut a large X into the ripe mango. I sucked out the fruit, eating it from the inside the way José had shown me almost eighteen months earlier, those first days in the fields.

The mango had a marvelous flavor — sweet and tangy at the same time, almost like the peaches that grew in the backyard of my father's house, but somehow more satisfying, meatier, never mealy the way a peach could be. Helen watched me as I devoured the fruit. I hadn't realized how hungry I was.

"You can't keep pushing yourself like this," she said.

"I have to keep going. The baby will be here soon and we need to be ready. When Istvan arrives it will be easier."

At the mention of Istvan's name, a silence descended on the two-room hut. Nereida walked briskly past the table, picked up the uneaten plate of mangú, placed it into a bucket full of dishes and walked out the front door.

"Max, we haven't heard from them since March and that letter was dated the end of December."

I stiffened in the chair. "Letters are impossible now. You know that. And they are in transit. They're coming," I said, getting up from the table and walking over to the window. I swung the wood shutters open, letting in more light and what little breeze there was. "I know it, I feel it."

"Close that please, it'll stay cooler in here with it closed," Helen said.

I walked away from the window, the shutter still open. "I'm sure they're on their way." I turned back toward Helen as I reached the door. "I've got to get back to work. The cowshed needs cleaning. Nereida, por favor, ven aqui, ella necesita ayuda." I walked back down the steps toward the barn. I felt my shoulders hunch over. For a moment I felt like I was back home barking orders at the help. I forced myself to stand straight.

Later that day, I heard Erno calling my name. I wasn't expecting him.

"Max," I heard a second time.

I looked out of the opening in the wall of the cowshed. It was Erno and he had come in the truck, not on horseback. I put down the broom I was holding, wiped off my hands and walked toward the flat afternoon light at the door of the cowshed. I called back. "I wasn't expecting you."

"You're not happy to see me?"

"I didn't say that," I answered as I embraced him. "I'm delighted to see you. You don't make trips for no reason, though."

"Ava wanted to see Helen," Erno said.

I knew there was something else on his mind. "Ava is here too?" I asked.

"Yes, she's inside with Helen."

I turned to walk toward the house, then felt Erno's hand on my arm. "Wait, let's walk a little. Show me what you've done here lately. I haven't been here in a while."

He knew what I had done. He had been here within the month. "Sure," I said. "What would you like to see?"

"Everything," he said waving his outstretched arm toward my homestead.

"Is something wrong?" I asked.

"No, why would you think that?" he replied

"Because you were here last month. How much do you think I could get done since then?"

"Nothing's wrong," he said, putting his hand on my shoulder. "My wife wanted to see your wife, that's all. Let's give them a little time alone."

"Certainly," I said. "Come then, let's sit down under the mango tree. I can show you something new. I built a bench there." We walked down the gentle slope through the cleared area. I cleared the brush myself before I brought Helen to the homestead. I left the largest mango tree in place, about fifteen meters in front of the house. With the brush gone, you can see the Bay of Sosúa in the distance shimmering beyond the trees.

"So, Rothman," Erno said as we arrived at the bench. "I see you have become a carpenter. Who would have thought that a clumsy Jew such as you would have learned to make furniture like a peasant?"

I laughed. "A miracle, thanks to José," I said as we sat down on the bench. "It even has a back."

"Very impressive," said Erno.

We sat together in silence for a moment. A breeze broke the heat.

"You can see the bay from here," Erno added, taking his handkerchief from his pocket and wiping his forehead. "I'll never get used to this heat."

"And I love it," I said. "It's funny, sometimes I think I was born for this."

"An old innkeeper like you?" he replied, fanning himself. The handkerchief fluttered like a white flag of surrender.

"Not so old," I said.

"How is Helen handling it?"

"She's doing well enough," I lied. "Mostly she stays in bed all day, or outside on the porch. Nereida tends to her."

"I can't imagine how difficult this is for you, the physical labor, the isolation. Perhaps you should…"

I leaned forward and put my hand on his forearm. "Don't even say it. I can't come back to the settlement."

He looked at me and sighed, wiping his brow again. "Maybe just until Helen has the baby?"

I knew that was why they came, to convince me to return to Sosúa. "The whole place would go back to wild," I said. "I would have to start all over again, and then the money I owe DORSA…"

He leaned against the back of bench. "They won't ask you for the money now."

"Erno, please, I can't go over this again. We'll be OK. Tell me about the news at the settlement."

"What news? We get three-week-old newspapers in English. Thank God for the family from Hamburg who came just before the Americans entered the war. The daughter was so sure she was going to America she studied nothing but English for a year before they left. She can translate almost anything from English to German, with the help of her dictionary."

"Really?" I replied.

"Yes," he replied with a smile. It was good to see his face change from serious to playful. "So we have her translate the newspapers and set up the settlement newsletter. Because she's so clumsy, we can't let her near the equipment or the farm animals in the dairy for fear she'll hurt herself, or the cows or the machinery."

"Has she?"

"On her first day she reported to the cow barn with white gloves and a perfectly matched ladies suit. Robert asked her if anyone had explained to her what she would be doing. She said yes. He then asked her why she had come dressed so formally. She said she wanted to make a good impression."

"What happened then?"

"Robert suggested she go back to her bungalow and change. She didn't want to do that because she was already on duty and didn't want to shirk her work responsibilities. He proceeded to teach her to milk a cow the old-fashioned way. She insisted on wearing her gloves, which of course irritated the cow and were ruined from the milk and the dirt. Then the flies were so aggressive with her that she tipped over the milking stool while shooing them away and landed in the mud. So much for her suit."

We both laughed. "Thank you, Erno," I said through the laughter.

"For what?"

"For that story. I haven't laughed so hard in many months. There's not much to laugh about out here."

His mood turned more serious again. "You should come into town more. It would be good for you, though there's not much to laugh about there either."

I have little interest in returning to the settlement for any reason. I have no connection to it anymore. Except for Erno and Ava, I have no strong bonds to any of the settlers. When I need a friend, I go to the village to visit José. My world is here now, not in the tropical incarnation of central Europe that is Sosúa. "Perhaps after the baby comes," I lied. "When Helen can travel." I rose from the bench and picked a mango off the tree. I used the large knife sheathed in my belt to slice off half of the fruit and score the ripe flesh before handing it to Erno. "Here, refresh yourself. I've had two already today." I sat down again and asked. "What other news?"

Erno bit into the mango's flesh. "Fritzy and Robert heard from their brother and sister," said Erno.

"They're on their way then?" I asked.

"No. They never got to Lisbon, they were sent back to Salzburg." Erno bit into the mango again. The juice trickled down his chin. He pulled his handkerchief from his pocket again and wiped if off. "Now they've been deported to Warsaw."

"Warsaw?" I said.

"Yes."

"This all sounds very strange. Did he get a letter from them?"

"Sort of. DORSA traced them through the Red Cross. They had visas, never showed up in Lisbon. It took weeks."

"Why Warsaw?"

"No one knows."

"So he didn't actually hear from them?"

"I'm not sure how to explain it. He got a letter from the Red Cross saying they had been located in Warsaw. In the same envelope was a short letter from the brother saying they were fine and were awaiting work and housing assignments and that they would write as soon as they were settled."

I looked at Erno. He handed me the rind of the mango and wiped off his hands with his handkerchief. "How old was the letter?" I asked.

"There was no date on it. The Red Cross letter was dated last month."

"Work assignment? But they're emigrating here."

"Not anymore. The Germans won't let them out."

I cut away the flesh from the remaining half of the mango and gave it to Erno. "Here, have some more," I said.

"I've had plenty," he said, continuing to wipe his hands.

I threw the remaining half into the bush.

"Come, let's go up to the house," he said. "I want to see your wife."

We walked back across the open area in silence. At the steps I stopped him and said, "Before we go inside, I wanted to ask you something."

"What?"

"Did Ava hear from her sisters?"

"Yes, I will let her tell you the news. It's quite a story."

My vision was affected by the change from light to darkness as I entered the house. I could see Ava from behind. As she turned toward me, her features were obscured by the shadows. Then my eyes adjusted. She was more beautiful than ever.

"Buenos días," she said as she approached me with open arms.

"Buenos días," I replied. "Sorry, cara, don't hug me, I stink."

She embraced me anyway. "You do. Like a peasant." She let go of me and held her nose, laughing.

"He is a peasant," said Helen from her chair at the far end of the table. "And I a peasant's wife."

"It suits us both," I said, sitting down next to her. "Did Nereida prepare something for them to drink?"

"Yes, she's a marvel." Helen poured some of the murky, light-green liquid from a large glass jar into a small drinking glass. "Taste this. Nereida collected those small green fruits on the way from her village this morning and made this from them."

I tasted it. It was delicious.

Ava handed a glass to Erno as well. "Try this," she said.

He sipped at it as if he was tasting a fine Tokay in an outdoor café in high summer in Budapest. "Excellent."

We sat at the table, the four of us, like we used to at the settlement on Sunday mornings. The truth was it felt good to have them with us. "Erno tells me you have some news about your sisters," I said.

"Yes, finally," Ava replied, reaching forward across the table placing her open hand on top of Helen's and mine.

"She was just telling me this when you came in. It's astounding," Helen said.

"Well?" I prompted her.

"They are in Shanghai!" she said, throwing her hands into the air.

"Shanghai, China?" I said.

"Yes," she continued. "I received a letter from them about a week ago. It took six months to get here."

I was astounded. In the eighteen months we had been here we had heard many stories of escape, but this was unique. "How did they get…?"

"Let me tell you the story," she said with a warm exuberance.

Erno stared at her with the same look of adoration in his eyes that always appeared when she dominated a conversation.

"They were able to go back to Budapest from Vienna and were waiting for me to bring them here. They met a man there who sold them two visas to go to Palestine."

"You know they had no intention of staying in Palestine," Erno added. "Too much dust."

Ava bit her lip and slapped him playfully on the wrist. "They bought exit visas to go to Italy to get the steamer from Trieste to Palestine. When they got to Trieste they went to buy exit visas from Italy and they found out the entry visas for Palestine were fakes."

"They had to get out of Italy or be sent back to Budapest," Erno interjected.

"Are you going to let me tell my story?" Ava said, slapping him on the wrist a bit less playfully than before. "Anyway, there were tickets available on a ship to Shanghai, so they bought them. The situation is so bad in China that they don't check visas, so they paid off the Italian agent to get the exit visas and off they went."

"Why Shanghai?" I said.

"It's as far away from the Germans as one can get. The shipping agent told them a lot of Jews had gone there."

"And they're safe?" I asked.

She sat back in her chair, still smiling. "Safe? What's safe? They're not in Europe."

"She's trying to arrange for them to come here now," Erno said, taking her hand.

"Isn't that unbelievable?" Helen said.

"Yes. This calls for some schnapps," Erno said.

"I've got some rum."

We spent a lovely afternoon together. I saw how good it was for Helen and regretted how lonely she was out here. Perhaps Erno was right after all. Perhaps we should have waited until after the baby came to make the move. As the sun lowered toward the horizon, Ava's mood turned serious and she turned to me. "Erno, do you have the letter?" she said.

I tightened then looked toward Helen. "No letters. I don't want any letters," I said.

Erno pulled a thin envelope from his pocket and placed it on the table. "It came last week, in the pouch from the office in New York. It's from your brother."

I felt my shoulders ease a bit and I reached for the envelope. It was unsealed and unaddressed. I turned it over in my hands, then looked inside and saw two pieces of paper. I took them out. One was a letter from Jack. The other page was on different paper. "This wasn't mailed?" I asked

"No," Erno said.

"Why?"

Erno sat down next to me, putting his arm around my shoulder. "Your brother visited the DORSA office in New York. He saw Dr. Trone. You remember Trone from Italy?"

Trone was DORSA's scout in Europe. He selected the settlers from the hundreds who applied for entry visas for a chance at survival. "Yes, I do. He's in New York now?"

"Yes, there's no work for him in Europe anymore. He was here last week for a visit to see first-hand how we're doing. He brought the mail."

The knot tightened in my stomach. I had seen others receive news like this. "Did you read it?" I asked.

"No, Trone told me what it says. Your brother discussed it with him."

I picked up the letter, the paper damp from the humidity.

Dearest brother,

How can I tell you this? How can I bring you more pain? That day at Ellis Island, I thought my heart would break. It had been so many years since I had seen you, I didn't recognize you. And where was Istvan? I thought he was with you? You were inseparable. Then

I saw in your eyes that light that I remembered from when you were a boy sitting on my lap with our feet in the water of the stream in the hills, Istvan calling to you to follow him into the cave. I blame only myself. I blame myself for listening to all of you. I begged you to come. To come when it was possible. But no one wanted to leave. Business was too good.

They were sent to Poland. All of them. The Red Cross confirmed it. I have enclosed their letter for you to see...

I thought I would vomit. I dropped the letter on the floor and pushed myself back from the table. "I don't want to know what this says." I looked at Helen. Her hands were over her eyes, the tracks of her tears evident on her cheeks.

"Do you want me to read it to you?" Erno said, his voice breaking.

I got up from my chair. "No, no, I don't want to know this," I said. I walked toward the door and looked out over the homestead. Why did I bother to come here? For what? I steadied myself against the doorpost. My legs felt like straw.

"Max, you need to know what it says," Erno said.

I could hear Helen and Ava weeping quietly now. I felt my legs give way and, almost simultaneously, Erno's hands under my arms picking me up. He helped me back to the chair at the table. I took Helen's hand. She placed it on her stomach entwined in her own. "Erno, read it to us, please," she said.

Erno took the first letter and began reading it. I watched, but from a great distance, as if from somewhere else entirely. His voice was far away, it sounded the way Istvan's voice had, echoing in the cave we had secretly explored that day with Jack in the hills above the village when we were boys.

Dear Mr. Rothman,

The International Committee of the Red Cross confirms that members of your family, listed in your letter of May 16, 1942, were deported from Ratko, Slovakia, under a program of resettlement by the government of the Slovak State on April 14, 1942. They were initially sent to a transit camp at Novaky, Slovakia. From Novaky, they were sent to the Government General District in German-occupied

Poland. At the date of this writing their whereabouts are unknown.

I felt the baby move under my hand. "Did you feel that?" I asked Helen.

"Of course," she whispered through her tears. "I'm sorry my darling."

"Sorry?" I said. "Sorry for what?"

"About your family."

"There's nothing to be sorry about," I said.

"Max," Erno said, "they're…"

"They're what?" I shouted, interrupting him. "They've been sent to Poland. They're still alive. Like Fritzy's family. The Red Cross did not say they're dead."

"Max," said Ava, "dear Max. I know how hard this is…"

I wanted to get up from the table and stand in the darkened corner of the room, but my feet were like lead. "Ava, how many months was it that you didn't hear from your sisters?"

"Mischka," Erno said. "This isn't the same. We need to finish reading Jack's letter."

I forced myself up from the chair. "No more, I don't need to hear more. They didn't say they're dead, just that they were deported." I paced around the table, my arms crossed against my chest.

"What are you looking for?" Helen asked.

"My hat. I have things to do and it's getting late."

Erno took me by the arm again. "Please," he said, tears streaming down his face. "Mischka, you're like a brother to me. I have no one else, only Ava and you two. This is breaking my heart. I told Trone I would tell you, that it was better coming from me."

"My mother," I mumbled, "my sisters. I was going to bring them here. She is so old, my mother. So old. How can she survive such a thing?"

I collapsed onto the floor. I felt Erno sink down and put his arm over my shoulder. My face now buried in his chest, the sounds of my own cries drowned out Helen's and Ava's. I pushed him away. "No more," I screamed. "I cannot do this, he is my twin brother. How can I live if he is torn from me?"

I felt Erno lift me up and into the chair again. "Max, you need to know.

You have to know. You have to sit shiva. Here, here is Jack's letter. Please keep reading."

I looked at the letter. Tears — someone's, I wasn't sure whose — had already caused the ink to run on the signature at the bottom. "I'm not sure I can read this," I said to Erno. "Please, you read it for me."

Erno took the letter back with his trembling hands. He sat down at the head of the table. I dried my eyes and took Helen's hand again in mine, both of them wet from tears. "OK, I'm ready, just read it," I said.

Erno sat up straight and continued the letter:

> I wasn't satisfied with this information alone. I went back to their offices several times to find out where in Poland they were sent. They told me nothing more. I called Dr. Trone at the DORSA office in New York. He used his private channels at the Red Cross and after a few days he asked me to come to his office. It was there that he gave me the terrible news. Our mother and our sisters are dead. Anna's husband and children as well. Julian was deported with them but is missing. Of Istvan and Magda there is no trace whatsoever. It's unknown if they were even in Novaky.
>
> I am sorry to tell you this in this way, dear brother, in a letter. If only I could tell you in person, looking at your face. You would know how sorry I am. I tried, I did all I could. You are all I have left, other than my wife and children. I am sorry I couldn't save our mother or our siblings or you. I don't know how I will live with myself.
>
> When you get this letter, you know what to do. Rend your shirt and kaddish for them. Sit low for seven days. For our mother, kaddish for eleven months. Thank God our father didn't live long enough to see this. May God comfort you in their sainted memory. They have died a martyr's death, Kiddush HaShem. Perhaps by some miracle Istvan and Magda are still alive. When this terrible war is over, I promise you I will bring you here, all of you or any of you.
>
> With love, your brother,
> Jack

I rose from the chair, my eyes now dry. I peered out the window of the house toward the sea in the far distance. The room was silent, save for the sounds of the birds in the trees.

"Do you want to come back to the settlement with us?" Ava asked.

"For what?" I said.

"To sit shiva," Erno said.

"Shiva? Istvan isn't dead. You heard what Jack wrote."

"But your mother," Helen said. "And your sisters."

I continued to look out the window. "Shiva," I said. "That's odd coming from you Erno, an atheist."

"Mishka, please," pleaded Helen. "She was your mother. She was a very religious woman."

"And I see where that got her," I shot back. "Shiva? To praise god for seven days by reciting Kaddish, a prayer in praise of god? What kind of god does something like this to an old woman? No, I don't think I will. Jack can sit for them, he is older anyway. He is the Kaddisher. If he still believes."

Ava came up behind me. I felt her lightly touch my hand. "Mishka, I understand, we all understand. But it might be better for a few days at least for you not to be alone here. And it would be better for Helen. She is so far along. She and the baby would be safer back at Sosúa. That's why we came in the truck. Please."

I looked into Ava's eyes, they pleaded with me to be reasonable. I looked at Helen, so worn out from the pregnancy and the heat, slouching in the wooden chair I had crafted. I made a deal with DORSA. Istvan wasn't confirmed dead, I could still bring him over if the farm was functioning. The baby wasn't due for another month. If we went back to Sosúa now we would end up staying for at least a month or until the baby came, and then maybe longer. I couldn't risk everything. "No," I said. "We'll be fine. My child will be born here. This is our future. That letter is our past and the past is gone." I looked back at Helen again. Her silent tears had resumed.

19

Tolya closed the thin red volume on his desk in the living room, stretched and yawned. He was tired and confused by what he just read. He needed a break. He walked to the bedroom and found Karin sitting on the bed with tears running down her cheeks. "What's wrong?" he asked.

"I can't tell you right now, give me a minute."

"Can't tell me what?" he said, sitting down on the edge of the bed next to her. He took a tissue from the box on the night table and handed it to her.

"What's in here?" He picked up the diary at Karin's side.

"Just give me a minute, please," she said, drying her eyes and nose.

"OK."

Karin straightened herself on the bed. She took a deep breath and let out a long shudder, the tears starting again before she calmed herself. "You know," she said, "I've known a lot of Jewish people over the years whose families died in the war, but reading this is different. It's more real because it's not in a book, it's in someone's hand. He wrote this himself. And it was written in my country, in my language. Or at least something resembling my language. I had no idea we had taken refugees." She reached over and took a fresh tissue from the box and wiped her eyes again. "OK, so. Remember he had moved to a farm, the wife was pregnant and he wanted to bring the brother from Europe?"

"Yes," Tolya said, slipping into bed.

Karin opened the book and began translating freeform from the beginning. Tolya listened to the tale of Max and Helen's move to the homestead. Every time Max mentioned Helen's pregnancy, Karin unconsciously put her free hand on her stomach and Tolya's stomach tightened. How was he going to tell her? When was he going to tell her? The diary he'd just completed reading was an account of Helen's pregnancy and Shalom's birth in the early 1950s. It was both troubling and reassuring. Max wasn't exactly elated about the pregnancy, and was at best ambivalent at the prospect of fatherhood. Tolya understood that feeling entirely. His life was good, better than good, without the addition of a child. But once the baby came, Max was elated. Maybe Tolya would feel the same way. Perhaps he should give fatherhood a chance.

Such thoughts were crowded out of Tolya's head when Karin read about Max learning of his family's fate. The similarities between their lives rushed into Tolya so quickly that he choked up. Oleg bounded into his mind. To lose a brother or sister was bad enough, but no one could explain what losing a twin was like. He lost track of what Karin was saying.

"Tolya," she said gently, crying still, touching his forearm, "that's it. That's where I stopped."

Her touch brought him back to reality. "How much more is there?" he asked. He reached over and pushed her hair back from her face.

She showed him the diary. "About half."

He looked over at the clock and saw it was nearly 1 a.m. He could see in her eyes how tired she was. "That's enough for tonight," he said. "I'm going back to the living room to read through more of the English diaries. You go to sleep."

"OK," she said.

He leaned toward her and kissed her gently, turned off the light and left the room, closing the door behind him. He sat down on the black leather couch and propped his feet up on the glass coffee table. He reached into the pile of diaries he had left on the table and took the first one. The date read: September 16, 1963. Tolya laughed to himself. Max had abandoned the old European dating script in favor of the American convention. He'd become a real Yankee Doodle Boy, as Tolya's father used to say. He stared at the first sentence — "I took Steven to his first Yankee's game today." — and realized he couldn't focus. He decided to take a short break and then resume reading. The story Karin had read to him was too intense.

Oleg was stuck in his mind. He struggled to see the features of his face, to hear his voice. That was the hardest. After all these years, he had forgotten the sound of his brother's voice. If only to hear him laugh one more time, to share a joke only they got. Max would understand that.

Moscow
RSFSR
Soviet Union
8 April, 1975
4:30 p.m.

"Tolya," Oleg called from inside the cramped living room of the new apartment they had been assigned after his father's disgrace. It was much smaller than their last one. His parents now slept on a mat in the living room.

"I'm doing my lessons," he called back.

"Aren't you finished yet?"

"No," he mumbled. He hated Oleg for being so much smarter. Oleg could finish his lessons in half the time it took Tolya.

"What's taking you so long? Aren't you the son of the great mathematician Boris Kurchenko?" Oleg shouted from the living room.

"Shut up," Tolya shouted back, "or I'll come in there and show you the son of the great wrestler Boris Kurchenko." He turned back toward the page. The work was even harder now that they had been expelled from school and their father was teaching them mathematics at home. He looked at the page in confusion. He could ask Oleg for help, but didn't want to give him the satisfaction. He felt Oleg's hands over his eyes and the chair give out from under him.

"Oleg Kurchenko, hero of the great Soviet Olympic wrestling team, takes down his younger-brother-by-two-minutes Tolya in one swift move," he shouted as he pulled Tolya off the chair, turned him over and pinned him to the floor.

"Younger by two minutes? Wrong, ninety seconds," Tolya growled as he freed himself from Oleg's hold and flipped him to the floor. Oleg might be smarter and two minutes older, but Tolya was bigger. "And in less than ninety seconds, Tolya Kurchenko takes the superior position as his brother begs for mercy."

"OK, OK. That's enough," their mother yelled from the kitchen. "Have you finished your studies yet?"

At the sound of her voice they ceased the wrestling match. She was not herself these days. She had become short tempered since their father's disgrace. She too was let go from her job when their father had asked for permission to emigrate. Then they had been dismissed from school.

She had taken them to another school — actually a few schools — but none would take them. At one, the headmaster told her they could resume their studies when they got to the Promised Land. He had asked her why the Soviet Union should educate Jews, since they were all spies anyway. Now they were home all day, the three of them. She directed their schoolwork while their father cleaned streets. That was his new job. In the worker's state, everyone worked.

Tolya gave Oleg his hand and pulled him up from the floor.

"Do you need help with the math, Tol?" Oleg asked, brushing himself off.

Tolya hesitated. He hated to admit Oleg could do something he couldn't.

"It's no big deal," Oleg said, touching Tolya's shoulder.

"Yes it is, Oleg," Tolya said. He returned the chair to its upright position in front of the desk. "He'll ask if you helped me."

"So we won't tell him," Oleg answered, leaning over Tolya to get a better view of his work.

"He'll know I'm lying, he always does." Tolya said, pushing Oleg away. "You're in my light."

"I'll lie too," Oleg said.

Tolya turned and looked up toward Oleg. "He'll know you helped me and then he'll make fun of me."

Oleg took a swipe at him, this time boxing. Tolya put up his arm to guard against the punch. He stood up and then knocked Oleg off balance with his foot, a martial arts move he had learned in school just days before they were expelled. Oleg fell against the dresser next to the desk, knocking over the trophies that sat on top of it.

"I told you both to stop that. Please, before you break something," their mother shouted. "I don't want to trouble your father with your bad behavior when he gets back."

They looked at each other and exchanged smiles. Tolya knew what Oleg was thinking. He could do that with Oleg, almost read his mind. It was something he couldn't do with anyone else. He realized he didn't really care what happened to them after that. If they had to leave, go to another city or another country, he didn't care as long as he and Oleg were together.

"See?" Oleg said, getting up. "There are things you do better than me."

Tolya sat down at the desk again and stared at the problem. Oleg stood over him. "Here. Here is your mistake," he said. He corrected one small symbol in Tolya's equation and the answer became clear. "Done," he said, "let's go do something fun."

They stared at the board game their father had brought back from Budapest the previous year. The writing on the board was in English. Their father had translated the words into Russian and written them on tape, which he had placed just below or above the words on the board, so that they would learn the English words. It was called "Risk, The Game of Global Domination." Their father said it was very appropriate for two sons of the Sovetsky Soyuz. He wasn't sure what his father had meant.

"I take France," Oleg said after rolling the dice. He removed Tolya's playing pieces from the board and replaced them with his. Tolya rolled the dice and searched the board for his next move.

"Tol," Oleg said.

"Da," he answered, still perusing the board. Where could he pierce Oleg's forces?

"Tol, stop a minute."

"What, Oleg?" Tolya said picking up his head from the board.

"Where do you think they're going to send us?"

"To Israel."

"No, I don't believe that." Oleg's expression had become very serious.

"What are you talking about?"

"They never let you just leave."

"But papa said we're going to Israel."

192

Oleg hesitated. He averted his eyes from Tolya's. "He said that so we wouldn't be afraid."

"Of what?" Tolya asked.

"Of what might happen to us."

Tolya looked into his brother's eyes. He had never seen fear in them before. Tolya was bigger, but he knew Oleg was tougher. It was Oleg who had bloodied Nicholai Tserverin's nose and split his ear at the swimming pool. And then he told the stupid kulak that if he ever bothered either of them again he'd come to his bedroom in the middle of the night and cut off his foreskin.

"Oleg, nothing is going to happen. Papa said so," Tolya said, attempting to sound convincing. "Remember he said maybe we might have to go live with Baba and Dada in Ukraine for the summer, but that won't be bad."

"Tol, I don't want to go there." Oleg turned toward the wall.

"Oleg, what's wrong?" Tolya asked.

"Tol, if they send us away I don't think we'll ever see them again."

Tolya touched Oleg's shoulder. When Oleg turned toward him, he could see the tears Oleg had been hiding and embraced him. "That's not true, brother. And even if they send us away we'll be together."

Oleg hugged him back. "Promise me you won't tell Papa I was crying."

"As long as you don't tell him you did my homework."

20

Tolya woke on the couch under the woolen afghan his mother had knit for him. "Karin?" he called out. There was no answer. He looked over at the clock on the cable box: 6:33.

"Karin," he called out again. He assumed she was still sleeping. Tolya got up, folded the blanket and laid it over the back of the couch. It looked completely out of place, like an old woman's coat on a young man's body. He walked into the kitchen and opened the fridge. There was enough coffee for one tall glass. He opened the freezer to get some ice. There was none. She never refilled the trays.

Tolya poured the coffee from the pot into a plastic container and put it back in the fridge. He placed the pot in the dishwasher, filled the ice tray and grabbed an apple from the table. As he turned the corner into the hallway, Karin opened the bedroom door.

"Amor," she said and put her arms around his waist. "I'm so tired." She squeezed him and breathed deeply. "You, sir, need a shower."

"Thanks," he said. "Did you sleep?"

"A little. I woke up about 3 and you weren't in bed, so I came out and found you snoring away. I covered you," she said, continuing down the hallway.

Tolya followed her. "Why with that old thing?"

She stopped and turned, her hand on her hip. "Because your mother made it for you."

"Why didn't you wake me?"

"You looked too peaceful and I couldn't sleep anyway, so I decided to finish the diary."

"And?"

"Tolya, it's terrible," she said. "Come into the kitchen, make me an iced coffee and I'll tell you the whole thing."

"There's no ice," he said, following her into the kitchen.

Sosúa
Dominican Republic
18 IX '42
8 p.m.

As I write this now, three months later, my mind is still fuzzy. This is the first time I have had the strength both physically and mentally to recount what happened. I owe it to myself to commit the facts to paper so that with the passage of time the truth does not become distorted in my mind or my heart.

I recall that it was very hot. I heard Helen call out from the bedroom, over the din of summer rain beating down on the roof, for Nereida to close the window. She was getting wet from the spray. She called out again. I didn't answer. But then, I hadn't said much in the three days since Erno and Ava's visit.

"I sent her home," I said finally, standing in the shadows of the doorway to the bedroom.

I could see her shoulders tense up. She asked me why.

"She hasn't been home in three days," I said, crossing the room and sitting down on the edge of the bed.

"Could you close the shutters?"

I caught a glimpse of myself in the mirror next to the bed as I got up. I didn't recognize myself.

Helen had tried to talk to me, to comfort me. I had refused it. She asked me to consider going back to Sosúa until the baby was born. I refused that, too. Ava had begged her to come back with them, for the child's sake. She wouldn't leave me alone.

As I closed the shutter, the sound of the rain receded slightly. I stared at the wall. "It looks like the rains have settled in, at least for a couple of days."

"Max, *drágám*, is there anything to eat?" she asked, fanning herself with an old piece of cardboard.

"I could make you something," I said absently. "I took some eggs from the hens this morning."

"That would be fine," she answered. I watched her as she shifted in the bed, the sheets wet from her sweat and the humidity. Unlike me, I know she will never get used to this climate. She often tells me how she longs to feel the tingle of cold on her skin.

"There's some bread left from what Ava brought," I said, leaving the room without waiting for her response. I pulled a heavy pan from the cupboard and placed it on the stove. The embers heated it quickly. Why had I sent Nereida home? Helen needed her.

The eggs crackled hitting the oil in the pan. I cut two slices of bread from the remainder of the loaf and grabbed a plate. We still had some of Nereida's guava jelly. I spread it on the bread, then took the eggs from the pan and brought Helen her meal, such as it was, and sat down again on the edge of the bed.

"Thank you," Helen said.

"There's nothing to thank me for," I replied, staring off into the darkness.

She looked at me as she ate. I knew her heart was breaking for me and for herself. How would she react on the day she received the same news about her family? It was only a matter of time. She finished the eggs and handed the plate back to me. She tried to touch my cheek but I pulled away.

"Max," she said as I got up from the bed, "we need to talk about this."

"There's nothing to talk about."

"How can you say that?" she replied.

I looked at her, feeling almost as if I were not in my own body. "They're gone. That's it." I turned toward the doorway.

"Maybe not Istvan," she said.

I turned toward her and laughed. "You're right, maybe not Istvan. Certainly not if you hadn't sent him back." I immediately regretted my words. I watched as her breath caught in her throat. What I said was cruel and I knew it, but I couldn't stop myself.

"I didn't make that decision," she said.

I dropped the empty plate and the silverware on the floor. The plate broke into two pieces. I moved to her with one long stride. "Yes you did," I said, my fists clenched.

"No, I did not," she repeated. I saw the tears well up in her eyes. "They said they would go back. They would wait for us to send for them."

"Because you said we didn't have enough money to hide them."

"We didn't," she said through her tears. "Max, please. Don't do this."

"Don't do what?" I said, now standing over her at the bed.

"Don't ruin what we have between us now."

"What do we have between us now?" I shouted. "They would be here with us now. My brother would be here if you hadn't insisted they go back."

I turned and left the room, leaving the broken plate and silverware on the floor. I hated myself for what I'd just done. I had promised myself I wouldn't do this but, once again, I'd broken my promise.

I walked back to the doorway and peered back in. She had one hand under her stomach, cradling the baby. The other wiped the tears from her eyes as she wept silently.

There had been no other choice. I knew the truth. Istvan and Magda knew it too. We didn't have enough money to pay for all of us to go into hiding. Istvan told me they had decided to go back. I blamed Helen all along because she had been the one to point it out. She had gone to Istvan herself to tell him the truth, a truth I refused to accept. We never had enough money for the four of us to escape with.

That night I fell asleep to the sound of Helen crying.

When Nereida began staying the night, sleeping on a pile of straw held together by some old sheets on the floor of the bedroom, I took to sleeping in a hammock in the front room. The bed wasn't big enough for the two of us anyway, with Helen pregnant. I wasn't sure what time it was when I woke to her calling out to me.

A candle flickered on the table in the corner of the bedroom.

"Max," she said over the persistent sound of the rain against the roof.

"I'm in terrible pain."

"Where?" I asked, pulling back the mosquito netting from the bed. The sheets between her legs were wet and stained.

"My lower back," she said. "I think the baby is coming."

"You're not due for another four weeks," I said.

She arched her back and slid her hand underneath to massage the pain away. "The doctor told us this might happen," she said.

I wasn't sure what to do. I felt my legs soften to jelly and grabbed the side of the bed frame to steady myself.

"Which is why we needed Nereida," she said, another pain stabbing at her. "Why did you send her home?" She began to cry again.

"I can handle it," I said. I helped her to move higher up onto the thin pillows. "Move your legs up a bit."

"I'm frightened," she whispered.

"I know. I am too." I sat down on the edge of the bed and took her trembling hand in mine, closing my fingers around hers. "Helen, I'm sorry for what I said."

"I know that, thank you." Another labor pain racked her body, each one frightening her a little more. "I think you should go to the village, get Nereida."

"I don't want to leave you," I said.

"I can't do this without her," she replied.

I ran to the barn through the pouring rain. I was soaked with both rain and sweat. My shirt clung to my body, the wetness seeping through to my skin. I tugged at the shirt, then pulled it over my head completely. Half naked, I flashed an image of the workers in the fields I had seen on the ride into Sosúa from Puerto Plata the day we arrived. Back then I thought they were savages. Now I have become one of them. The truth is I like it.

I saddled the horse as quickly as I could. The ride would be treacherous but faster than by foot. I had little time to waste. I walked the horse to the barn door and mounted him there. "Easy boy," I said, seeking to calm myself as much as the horse. I prayed there would be no thunder or lightning to spook the animal.

The horse was reluctant to leave the barn. Finally, with a little prodding, he moved forward with a snort. The rain pelted us as we made our way down the path, slowly at first, toward the dirt road that consists mostly of truck ruts but functions as the only link between the homesteads, the native villages and the settlement. I listened to the pounding of the rain in the leaves above me, a constant and endless din drowning out the thoughts screaming in my mind. The horse snorted repeatedly as we made our way to the road. I patted him between his ears, reassuring him, quieting him. Then I lifted myself up in the saddle and pressed the horse to a canter. First reluctantly, then with increasing confidence, we picked up a little speed.

I had made this trip many times. I would have to be careful along the last part, where the trail became a bit steep. If the horse slipped in the mud he could break his leg, and then what? I knew how wrong I was. I knew it when I sent Nereida home. Was I so angry that I was willing to jeopardize the life of my wife and my unborn child?

I became one with the horse, moving slightly up and down with each stride. As we reached the end of the path from the farm to the main road, the rain subsided a bit. The clean, fresh scent of the air filled my lungs. I lifted myself a little more in the saddle and bent forward, prodding the horse into a gallop. "Cuidado nene." I said both to the horse and to myself.

I saw the flicker of candles in the window of José and Nereida's house through the trees at the far end of the tiny village. I got off the horse and tied it to a tree nearby.

The door opened. "Quién está allá?" José called out.

"Soy yo, José. Soy Max."

José brought a candle from behind his back, illuminating his face. I felt better seeing him. "Qué pasó?" He asked.

"It's Helen," I answered. "The baby is coming now."

José took my arm and led me into the hut. My eyes adjusted to the dim light. Nereida sat on the bed in the corner of the room, singing softly to her children. She kissed them on their foreheads and turned toward me. "I'm coming with you now. I told you I should stay."

"Thank you, Nereida. I'm a fool."

"No," she said, touching my arm. "You're a good man. El Dios plays with us." I watched her nervously as she grabbed some things off the shelves on the back wall of the hut and threw them into a sack. "José, if I'm not back by midday, come to Max's farm. You'll know what to bring?"

"Sí," he said, the sound of the rain starting up again on the palm fronds that pretended to be a roof. We walked the short distance to my horse. As we reached it, José grabbed my arm, drew me to him and embraced me. "Vaya con dios y buena suerte," he whispered in my ear, then helped me into the saddle. After I was comfortable he helped Nerieda mount the horse behind me. I looked back toward him as we moved away from the little village. He was crossing himself as he mouthed a silent prayer standing in the gentle rain.

"Helen," I called out as we entered the house.

The rain had worsened on our return, leaving both Nereida and me soaked to the bone. "Helen?" I called out again. Still no answer. I turned toward Nereida. "There are dry clothes in Helen's armoire."

"There's no time, Max," she said, rushing past me with the soaking sack she had dragged with her from the village. "I'll be fine. Put up two pots of water," she added, and disappeared into the bedroom.

I replayed the last few days in my head as I placed the pots on the burners and shoved new pieces of dry wood into the bottom of the stove, hoping I didn't smother the embers.

I felt like I had been watching my own life in slow motion since Erno and Ava's visit. I knew the way I'd treated Helen was inexcusable. I blamed her for everything, I always did. But I knew she was right. Istvan had made the decision to go back, not Helen. And she had been right that we didn't have enough money to take them to begin with. And I had spent what we had frivolously and far faster than I should have.

I checked the wood burning in the stove. It had caught and the flame was rising. I covered the pots and went into the bedroom. Helen lay on the bed exactly as I left her. She was awake and in pain. Nereida stood over her, instructing her. I wasn't sure how much Helen understood; her Spanish is not nearly sufficient when she is well and alert.

"Helen, you need to breathe evenly and strongly," Nereida said. "As the pain increases, you need to control the breathing and push."

"I'm in so much pain," Helen mumbled.

I didn't know how much time had passed since the labor had started. I didn't even know what time it was, only that it was the middle of the night. I moved toward the bed and took Helen's hand. "*Drágám*," I said.

She turned to me. Her face was covered with sweat. I wasn't sure if her weak smile was meant for me or was from her attempt to push against the labor pains. She let out a low moan as she arched her back slightly.

"Lift your legs a little higher, hermana. Take a deep breath and push," Nereida said, her hand on Helen's exposed stomach. I translated her instructions into Hungarian. Helen tried to do as she was told, the pain evident on her face.

"No, señora. Breathe like this," Nereida said, demonstrating the quick, shallow breaths she wanted from Helen.

Helen turned to me again. "*Én szeretlek téged*[*]," she said.

I fought back tears. I had brought her to this. "I love you too," I answered, taking her hand again. "I'm sorry I've brought you so much unhappiness." Now I couldn't hold back the tears.

"You haven't," she said.

I watched as the pain returned to her face. She dropped my hand and grabbed the sheet, wrapping the rough fabric around her hand and gritting her teeth.

"Breathe, hermanita, the way I told you and push," whispered Nereida.

I stood up from the chair and took a step backward, away from the bed. What was I thinking when I sent Nereida home?

"Max, por favor, open the shutters. It's too hot in here," Nereida said.

For a moment, Nereida's Spanish didn't register. My mind was still thinking in Hungarian. I had to stop and think. "Sí," I said. After I unhinged the wooden shutters, a gush of warm, wet air rushed in at me. The warm dampness felt cooler than the air in the room.

---

[*] *Én szeretlek téged*: I love you (Hungarian)

"Max," I heard again.

"Sí, Nereida," I said.

"Ven aquí," she said. "I need to show you something." Nereida was standing at the foot of the bed, examining Helen.

My stomach tied itself into a knot. I have birthed many calves in the past eighteen months, but the sight of my wife in labor was something I was unprepared for.

"Por favor," Nereida said, "I have to show you something."

"What's wrong?" Helen asked, gripping the sheet as the next contraction began.

"Nothing, querida. Just breathe and push as I showed you. " Nereida stroked Helen's hand, then whispered to me, "Give me your hand, please."

"Por qué?" I said, willing my muscles to move but not moving.

"Max, something is wrong. I know it," Helen said, this time in Hungarian.

"Nothing's wrong, _drágám_. The baby will be here soon."

Nereida took my hand and placed it inside Helen. I felt the baby just inside her, two tiny feet. I thought my heart would stop. I looked at Nereida, her finger over her lips indicating that I shouldn't speak.

"The head?" I whispered

"Sí, that's what it should be," Nereida said.

Helen's body relaxed again as the contraction ended. "Hermana," Nereida said. "We have to go into the other room to get the water and some other things. We'll be right back."

"Don't leave me alone. Please." Helen was covered in sweat.

"Only for a moment," Nereida said, waving me into the other room.

"You understand?" Nereida continued in a low voice in the front room.

I sat down at the table and looked up at her. "Yes, the baby is breech."

She nodded. "Because the labor came too soon," she said. "He hadn't turned yet."

"What are we going to do?" I asked.

"We're going to bring your baby, gracias a dios," she said, crossing herself. "I'll do my best. She will be in terrible pain."

I touched her hand. "Will the baby live?

"Gracias a dios," she repeated. "Wait here."

"No I'm coming to help you. She needs me."

"No," she repeated. "I need you to stay here. I will call you if I need you." She grabbed the rags she left under the sink and hurried back into the room.

I stood up and walked across the room to the hammock I had been sleeping in for months. I sat on the edge and placed my head in my hands. I pleaded with god not to do this. He had taken my family. He would take Helen's family too, sooner or later. If you exist, I begged silently, don't do this. Let this child live, let Helen live. I looked out into the darkness through the window, toward the sea where the sun would rise. I got up off the hammock and stood by the window, the spray from the rain hitting my face, and said out loud, "If you exist you won't let this happen. If this happens, I'll know you don't exist."

Helen's scream jarred me out of half-sleep. I looked out the window and saw the first break of dawn in the distance. The rain had stopped. I jumped off the hammock and ran into the bedroom. Nereida stood over Helen, a tiny bundle in her arms. She handed it to Helen. Helen's whimpering erupted into weeping.

"What happened?"

Nereida turned her head from left to right slowly, the tears running down her cheeks. "I'm sorry, I did everything I could."

I forced myself to move. My legs were like lead. My heart was pounding. The sound of Helen's crying rang in my ears. I looked down at the tiny face wrapped in old rags in Helen's arms. He looked like my father. The remains of the umbilical chord were still wrapped around his neck. I let out a scream, drowning out the sound of Helen's weeping. I handed the dead child back to Nereida, then looked at Helen. "For what?" I screamed. "For what have I done this? We would have been better off dead." I turned and ran out of the room. As I left the house, I grabbed the shovel resting on the steps to the porch.

Tolya sat speechless in the chair at the dining table. Karin closed the thin, worn green volume and put it down on the table. She leaned back in the chair and rubbed her eyes. "I can't even...," Karin said. "I don't know how the wife went on after this."

She got up from the chair, sat down on Tolya's lap and placed his hand on her stomach. "You've said almost nothing about our baby."

"What do you want me to say?"

"That you're happy, excited, scared..."

Mostly he was anxious. He knew the moment had come. He had to tell her the truth. He took his hand from her stomach. "Truthfully," he said, "I never wanted to be a father."

Karin pressed her hand against the table and lifted herself off his lap. "Did I just hear you say that?"

Tolya reached across to take her hand.

"Don't touch me," she said.

"Karin."

"When were you planning on telling me this? We've lived together six months, we dated for six months before that, and you never told me this?"

Tolya stood up. "I wasn't expecting you to get pregnant."

"Expecting me?" she said, backing away from him. "I think you were there when it happened."

"But you take precautions," he said.

"Oh, I see. So it's my job to make sure."

"It's your diaphragm."

"And how about a condom?"

"Why would I bother if you've got a diaphragm?"

"Because sometimes I'm not planning it. It just happens. That's how it is when you love someone, when you're in love with someone." Karin slumped to the floor. Her body heaved as her tears hit the wood floor.

He walked toward her and touched her arm. "I'm sorry, Karin, please. I do love you."

"Do you want this baby, Tolya?" she asked him, pushing him away.

He stepped back and dropped into the chair, covering his eyes with his hands. "I don't know."

21

Tolya knew something was wrong when he saw Karin enter the station house and head directly for the captain's office. And she wasn't alone. He watched the phone for the next two minutes, which seemed like an eternity. On the fourth ring, just before it went to voicemail, he picked it up.

"Get in here now, Kurchenko," the captain screamed into the phone so loudly that Tolya could hear him through the walls and the closed door.

Tolya slipped the narrow, delicate volume of Redmond's diary into the bottom drawer of his desk under his police department manual, closed the drawer and stood up. This wasn't going to be good.

He walked down the corridor to the captain's office. He could see the captain through the glass partitions speaking directly to the two men in the office with Karin. He caught the captain's glare. It was like fire. Tolya stopped at the door to straighten his shirt, then knocked.

"Enter now," barked the captain.

Karin's back was to him as he entered the room. The captain pointed at the chair next to Karin and said, "Sit there."

Tolya's eyes met Karin's as he sat down next to her. He could see that she was still angry with him.

"Where's your partner, Kurchenko?" the captain asked.

Tolya was not about to tell the captain that Pete was around the corner getting a little mid-morning action from his girlfriend. She'd called just after 9 a.m., badgering him to come over. Pete never said no and Tolya always covered for him. "He's out following up a lead on the Redmond case," Tolya answered, shifting uncomfortably in the hard wooden chair. The captain's eyes were fixed on him. "Um, what's going on, Cap?" he asked.

The captain rose from his chair. "Well, for starters, I think you know Inspector Martinez from Internal Affairs."

Tolya smiled. "Um, yes. Karin, I mean Inspector Martinez and I are acquainted."

"Jesus," Karin mumbled, putting her hand over her eyes and shifting away from Tolya. "He knows about us. I've just explained to him that we're more than friends."

Tolya felt a knot grip his stomach. While there was no rule against it, romantic relationships between fellow officers were frowned upon, especially within the same precinct, let alone between a detective and an inspector in IA. Someone would be transferred.

The captain paced with his arms behind his back in the small space behind his desk. "Tolya, this is Chief Inspector Sullivan, Ms. Martinez's boss." He pointed to the middle-aged man occupying the chair nearest the door. "This other gentleman is Mr. Franco."

Tolya rose and extended his hand. "Don't bother," the captain said, "this isn't a social visit."

Tolya sat back down, the tension in his stomach spreading to his shoulders. He looked over at Karin. Her legs were crossed, her skirt riding up her thighs. He loved those thighs. As he turned back toward the captain, he saw him pull a small, green leather-bound book from his desk and drop it on the table. "Detective Kurchenko," he said. "Can you identify this item for me please?"

"Where did you get that?" Tolya asked.

"It's my fault, Tolya," Karin said, turning toward him and dropping her hands to her sides. "I left it out on my desk this morning and Inspector Sullivan found it there."

"It's Max Redmond's diary, or one of them anyway." He heard Karin groan again and knew he had said too much.

"Where did it come from?" the captain asked as he lowered himself back into his chair.

Tolya looked at Karin before answering.

"They know," she said.

"We, I, took them, it, from Redmond's apartment."

"So let me see if I've got this correct. You, Detective Kurchenko, and your…girlfriend, Inspector Martinez of Internal Affairs, entered a crime scene without authorization and removed potential evidence."

"It's my case…"

"Not anymore, it's not," shouted the captain. "Was Gonzalves with you?"

"No," said Tolya at the same time that Karin said, "I told you we were alone."

"What did you think you were doing?" the captain asked.

"Looking for something to clear Pabon with," Tolya answered.

"You're done. We are charging him. As of this moment you're off this case."

Bachata was playing in the background at the Caridad on 184th Street, the voice of the lead singer crooning about lost love and broken hearts. Tolya looked across the table at Karin. "I'm sorry," he said.

"For what, specifically?" she asked, avoiding his eyes and drumming her fingers on the table. She lifted her coffee to her lips and took a sip.

"For everything I said this morning. And for getting you involved in this mess."

She had a look on her face he was unfamiliar with. "Amor," she said, leaning back into the booth and making direct eye contact with him. "I don't care about this mess, the union will take care of that. But I am very upset about how you feel about our baby."

"It's not that I don't love you." He leaned over the table and tried to take her hand but she withdrew it.

"I don't doubt that you love me, but now I need you to love our baby too."

"Just give me a little time."

"I'm going to give you a lot of time," she said, grabbing her bag and moving out of the booth. "I'm going to stay with my sister for a while."

22

Tolya walked around the living room aimlessly. He didn't know where to put himself. He had finished the small stack of diaries written in English and had found nothing new, nothing that would cast a light on Max's life or his relationship with Shalom anyway. The last diary was dated 1964.

He thought about Karin. He couldn't stop thinking about Karin. He loved her. He knew that and believed she knew that too. He shouldn't have said the things he said.

He had wandered into the kitchen when his cell rang. He rushed back into the living room to get the phone. By the time he reached it, the call had gone to voicemail. Before he could call his voicemail, the doorbell rang. He dropped the phone and headed to the intercom. "Hello, yes?"

"Tol, it's me," said Pete.

Tolya didn't answer, he just buzzed Pete in. A few moments later, Pete's big frame walked out of the elevator and down the hall. Pete stood in front of him for a second, then slapped him in the head. "You big dumb Russian," he said, grabbing him and pulling him into an embrace. Pete made him think of Oleg.

"What the fuck are you doing here?" he said, slapping Pete back. "C'mon in." Pete followed Tolya into the foyer.

"Go in the living room, I'll be right there," Tolya said, "Want a beer?"

"Sure, bring me two."

Tolya was glad Pete had come over uninvited. He grabbed four Coronas and a small plate of lime slices covered with plastic wrap from dinner a couple of nights before. The limes were a little dry around the edges. Before Tolya reached the couch, Pete took two of the bottles, sat down on the club chair and stretched out his legs. "When were you going to tell me about Karin?" he said.

"Which part?" Tolya leaned back on the couch and popped open a beer.

"All of it. I'm your partner, for Christ's fucking sake." Pete pushed a slice of lime into beer bottle. "Shit," he said wiping away the juice that had squirted into his face. "You wanna tell me what happened?"

"I knocked her up," Tolya said.

Pete looked at him, that "fuck you" smile on his face forcing Tolya to laugh despite himself. "OK," he said, "and that's a problem?"

"It is if you don't want kids," Tolya said.

An awkward silence filled the space between them. Pete took a long swig of his beer and leaned forward, his bulk dwarfing the chair. Tolya waited for him to speak. He was glad Pete had come over. He realized how much he needed to talk to someone, to confide in someone.

"You told her that?" Pete asked.

Tolya nodded.

"That's when she left?" Pete said.

"Yeah," Tolya replied, choking up.

"We've talked about this so many times, Tol. What's the problem?" Pete said, waving his hands as he spoke, his thumb over the top of the beer bottle so it wouldn't splash all over the furniture. "What are you so afraid of? You'd be a terrific father. I see you with my kids."

"I've told you before," Tolya said, taking another swig, "I don't want to fuck up another life like was done to me."

"That's a cop out and you know it," Pete said, propping his feet up on the coffee table.

"Maybe," said Tolya, "I don't know. And get your feet off of there."

Pete placed his feet on the floor. "Don't you think you should give this a chance?"

"How?" Tolya said. "Tell her I'm OK with it, happy with it, then in a couple of months decide I don't want this? She's not having an abortion anyway."

"She so religious?" Pete said, raising an eyebrow.

"No, just 35."

Pete took another long swig on the beer. "And you never told her before? You've been living together how long?"

"Six months, and it just never came up." Tolya leaned his head back and stared at the ceiling. "And it was going so good."

"Tol, don't walk away from this so fast. You love her?"

"What do you think?" Tolya said, letting the tears come.

"Oh man," Pete said, shielding his eyes. "I don't wanna see that. What is it with you Russians and the crying?"

"We've got big hearts, beeg Russian hearts." They both laughed.

"Yeah, and no fucking brains."

Their laughter intensified. Tolya sat up and looked over at Pete, who was wiping away tears of laughter. "Who's crying now?" Tolya said.

"Fuck you. And I had to find out about this from the fucking duty officer?"

"She's got some big mouth," Tolya said.

Pete smiled. "It's not just her mouth. How did she know anyway?"

"I'm not sure. I think she's friends with Karin's secretary."

"Where did Karin go?" Pete asked.

"To her sister's place on 173rd Street."

Pete moved to the edge of the chair and put his beer down on the table. "How did you leave it?"

Tolya smiled and wiped his eyes again. "I told her I love her."

"And she said?"

"She said she loves me too, but now I gotta decide if I love our baby."

Pete drained out the rest of his beer and popped open the second. "I wanna tell you something," he said.

"Yeah?" Tolya said.

"I never discussed this with anyone, so don't go repeating this." He tossed the bottle cap in his free hand.

"Who am I calling?" Tolya said. "Page Six?"

"When Glynnis told me she was pregnant the first time, I was scared to death."

Tolya looked up at Pete. "Don't patronize me, please."

Pete reached over and put a hand over Tolya's. "Tol, I'm not. I told you I never told this to anyone. Just listen."

"OK."

"I was so afraid. I didn't know how to be a father. I didn't have a father. My old man ran out on us when I was, what, 6 years old? I didn't want no kids either." He stopped for a moment, looked down at his feet and continued. "But I didn't say shit to anyone 'cause I didn't have anyone to talk to, and no one cared anyway. Then the night Joey was born, I was in the delivery room with Glynnis and they handed that baby to me." He lifted his hands as he spoke, mimicking the action of taking the baby from the nurse. "I fell in love with him like that. I knew I'd do anything for him, forever. I can't explain it, man. You'll see. You look down at that little face and you see yourself."

Tolya rubbed his palms over his eyes, then looked up at Pete. "I just don't know, man," he said. "My old man was a bastard."

"But you're not him," Pete said as he finished his second beer.

"Sometimes I wonder. I look at myself in the mirror and I see him behind my eyes."

"At least you remember him."

"Sometimes I wish I didn't."

"Tol, she's good for you, don't walk away from your own happiness."

"Which is just what my father used to do." Tolya got up from the couch and collected the empty bottles. "Pete, I gotta ask you about something else."

"I'm not supposed to discuss it with you," Pete replied, getting up from the chair.

"Which is why you came over?" Tolya said, heading toward the kitchen.

"No, I came over to see how you are, asshole." Pete followed Tolya into the kitchen.

"Sorry. Tell me anyway."

"Same shit," Pete said. "Levitz pushing for an arrest, Guzmán screaming racism, the captain fighting with the DA over whether we have sufficient evidence."

"And you think?"

"They've got the prints and that's enough. I think they'll issue a warrant for the kid's arrest tomorrow."

Tolya tossed the bottles into the recycling. "Political pressure."

"Plenty," Pete said. He paused a moment, then continued. "Tolya, I gotta ask you a question, man."

"What?"

"What went down with those diaries? Why didn't you tell me about them?"

Tolya put his hand on Pete's shoulder. "I'm sorry man, I don't know."

"Don't you trust me?"

"It wasn't about trust. To start with, I took a couple from the apartment just out of curiosity and I was going to tell you. Then I saw that a couple were in Spanish…"

"I speak Spanish," Pete said.

"I know, but after Karin read the first one and we went back into the old man's place, things started to heat up. I figured it would be better if you didn't know about it, just in case I got caught."

"Well…I guess that makes sense," Pete said. "You got any more left?"

"Yeah, but I don't think you should know about it."

"You're probably right. I gotta get going, brother."

"So, I never mentioned it," Tolya said, walking him to the foyer

"No. And I never asked," Pete replied. "You still think the kid is innocent?"

"Yep."

"And you still think Rothman did it?"

"Yep."

"How you gonna prove it?"

"Not sure yet." Tolya opened the door and hugged Pete. "Thanks, man, for being here."

"What's a brother for?"

Tolya waited outside María's building. The weather had turned colder in the past couple of days. He pulled his heavy sweater up around his neck. His grandmother was always covering their necks when they were boys in Moscow, sure that any draft could infiltrate some imagined spot and cause a deathly flu. She didn't believe in germs, colds came from drafts.

He checked his watch: 7:26. She should be coming around that corner any minute. He knew her schedule from the interrogation. She finished with the old lady on 187th Street at 7. No more Max, the old lady had lucked out and gotten María to cook her dinners.

Tolya watched the passersby. His conversation with Pete was still fresh in his mind. He understood where Pete was coming from. He just wasn't convinced he could do it. He was too much like his father: stubborn, obstinate, proud and foolish — a dangerous combination. He saw María coming up the block with a girl of about 7 and walked toward her. "Buenos tardes, María," he said, attempting the two words of Spanish he had mastered when meeting Karin's family.

"Buenos noches, detective," she responded. "Is already dark, too late for tardes."

"Sorry," he said, reaching out his hand to take one of her packages. "Let me help you."

"Gracias," she said. "This is my granddaughter, also her name is María."

Tolya smiled.

"Detective, how can I help you?" María asked.

"Can we speak for a moment?"

"Niñita, you go upstairs. Tell mamá I be right up and take this," she said, handing the smaller shopping bag to the child. "Sorry, detective, of course we can talk about anything."

"I need your help."

"With what?"

Tolya pulled one of Max's diaries from inside his sweater. "I need you to read this for me. It's in Spanish, it belonged to Señor Max."

María took the small leather book in her hand. She opened it and shook her head. "Detective, I can no help you with this. I no want to get involved. You need to see Señor Enrique. He is Señor Max's friend."

23

The last of the callers had gone. Shalom got up slowly from the shiva stool, stretched his back and rubbed his knees. A few more days and he would burn the stool in the backyard of the building. Whatever his feelings toward his father had been, he was gone now and Shalom had forgiven him. Only HaShem could judge him. "Rachel," he called out.

"Yes," she answered.

"Is Baruch asleep?"

"I just put him in bed."

Shalom followed her voice into the kitchen. He sat down at the table and watched her as she methodically washed the dishes and placed them in the dish rack. Her hair, usually covered by her wig, tumbled freely to her neck. He marveled at her figure. "Why don't you put those in the dishwasher?" he asked.

She turned and smiled. "It's full and it's *fleischik*. These are dairy," she said holding up the plate to show its delicate floral pattern.

"Of course," he said. He hadn't noticed.

Rachel placed the last dish in the dish rack and turned off the water. She sat down next to Shalom and took his hand. "You're tired," she said.

"Yes," he answered. "Too many people. Most of them I hardly know."

"They're showing you how much they respect us."

"You mean how much they respect your father."

Rachel let go of his hand and sat up straight. "Why do you say that?"

"I'm just a quiet *melamed**," Shalom replied. "I also happen to be the son-in-law of the rabbi, and my father was murdered."

"Perhaps our people know and respect you more than you think," Rachel said. She averted her eyes from his. He loved her modesty. "Are you hungry?"

"A little bit," Shalom said.

"I saved you this," Rachel replied, reaching for a plate covered with a large white dinner napkin and revealing a chocolate Danish. "Miriam's sister-in-law brought them from Monsey."

"Thank you." Shalom tore the round pastry in half. "Would you like some?" he said, offering the larger half to Rachel.

"No thank you. It's too late for me to eat and, besides, I've been nibbling all night."

Shalom took a bite of the Danish, savoring the soft, complex dough and the bittersweet chocolate. There were far fewer Jews in Washington Heights than there had been when he was a boy and most of the bakeries had closed. The two that remained brought in their goods every couple of days from larger stores in Teaneck or Monsey and what they brought was often stale. "This is delicious," he said.

"Not as good as your mother's."

"Nobody makes them like she did," he said. "You know, she wrote the recipe down for you. I have it in my desk." Shalom got up from the table and walked into the living room.

"Shalom, don't bother with that now," she called after him.

He checked his pockets for the desk key, but came up empty. He had begun locking the drawers when Baruch was little to keep him out of them. "Rachel," he called out, "I can't find the key to my desk. I had it in my pocket earlier. Have you seen it?"

"No."

He checked his pockets again. Nothing. "I hope I didn't drop it in the trash," he mumbled. He walked down the hallway to the bedroom and checked

---

* *Melamed*: Religious teacher (Hebrew)

the night table and the trash basket. Still nothing.

"What are you doing?" Rachel called out. "Come finish your Danish."

"I'm looking for my desk key," Shalom said, reentering the kitchen. He noticed a plastic Duane Reade shopping bag filled with trash sitting by the door. "I had a bunch of tissues in my pocket that I threw away earlier. Perhaps the key went with them," he said, picking up the bag and rummaging through it.

"You don't do that. Sit down and eat, I'll look," she said taking the bag from his hands. "You're tired. Sit down."

"Rachel, please, let me look," he said, taking the bag back from her. He took several items out of the bag and placed them on the table: an egg carton, a broken coffee grinder, the day's papers, and a pair of gloves. "Aren't those the gloves I bought for you last winter?" he asked.

"Yes," she mumbled, sitting down at the table and placing her hands over her eyes.

"Why are you throwing them out?" he said.

Rachel hesitated for a moment. "I didn't want to tell you, I feel terrible about it. I ruined them."

"What happened?" he asked, examining the dark stain on the fingers and palm of the right glove.

"I went to the butcher and the package leaked, and the stain had set by the time I got home. They were a gift from you and I loved them." She began to tear up. "They were exactly what I wanted."

"My darling, it's only a pair of gloves." Shalom smiled and touched her hand. "I'll get you another, just as soon as shiva is over."

"Thank you." Rachel dried her eyes and took a deep breath to gather herself.

Shalom returned his attention to the bag. He spotted a shiny object settled into some tissues and removed it. "There it is. How clumsy of me." He shoveled the trash back into the bag and left the kitchen.

He returned with a small box filled with old pictures and scraps of paper. He started ruffling through the box, then fell silent. Rachel turned to see him staring at a picture and walked up behind him to get a better look. It was Shalom with Max and Helen at his high school graduation. "Have you forgiven him?" he said to Rachel.

"Have I forgiven who?"

"My father," he said, looking up at her.

Rachel averted her eyes. "Your father is gone, *alav ha'shalom*[*]."

"But have you forgiven him?"

"I'm not sure why you're asking me this question."

"I know how angry you were with him, particularly after that last argument a few weeks ago."

"All I did was ask him to let me kosher the house and buy his food," Rachel said, looking out the darkened window. "He became so angry."

"I know, he shouldn't have said the things he said, not to you."

"He cursed HaShem...and me," she said. Shalom could see the pain in her eyes as she remembered the incident. She had been more upset about his ranting against God than his attack on her.

"Try to understand him, though," Shalom said, reaching out to touch her arm. "He's gone now. He has to face HaShem himself. He had a very difficult life. They lost a child. He lost his entire family. And he blamed himself, especially for Istvan. He didn't mean what he said."

Rachel's back stiffened. She looked directly at Shalom. "Oh, he meant it. There was such hatred in his eyes. I asked him to live like a Jew, to repent before HaShem, and he cursed me." She hesitated for a moment and rubbed her thumb against the inside palm of her other hand. Her anger was palpable. "He lost a child? I am sorry for him, but I was more sorry for your mother. What he put her through. If he hadn't lived like an *apikoros*, this might not have happened to Baruch."

Shalom felt that remark like a knife in his stomach. "Rachel, we've been over this so many times. We've been to how many doctors and professionals over how many years? You can't possibly believe that."

"I do believe that," Rachel said, rising from the table. "HaShem punished him by punishing us. Baruch was normal, brilliant even, then this." She pointed toward the books stacked on the little table under the window. The pile grew every year, and if she removed one book another would soon appear, all with titles like "Living with Autism" or "The Path from Autism," always that word, that curse in front of her eyes.

[*] *Alav ha'shalom*: May he rest in peace (Hebrew)

"How can you say that?" Shalom said. "It's how he was born, not a punishment."

"Then tell me why he started to improve, finally, last spring when your father asked you for that copy of *Pirkei Avot* and started reading it."

Shalom did remember. What Rachel didn't know was that his father had agreed to read a portion of the classic work on Jewish beliefs after a several long, soul-searching discussions with Shalom. His father certainly knew he was at the end of his life. Shalom wanted him to make peace with HaShem. Being an intellectual, his father had wanted to reacquaint himself with the materials he had studied as a young man in Europe before he engaged in any philosophical argument with Shalom. "You believe Baruch was improving because my father was reading *Pirkei Avot?*"

"No. I believe HaShem was helping Baruch because your father was considering *ba'al t'shuvah*."

Shalom looked into Rachel's eyes for a long moment. His love for her, and his pity for her endless guilt over Baruch, far outweighed the anger and disappointment he felt every time she walked this irrational path. "Rachel, he wasn't reading *Pirkei Avot* to repent," he said. "He was reading it to refute my arguments that he should consider some personal peace with HaShem. Baruch got better because we sent him to that school."

24

Tolya stood outside the apartment door at 730 Ft. Washington Ave., fidgeting nervously. He hesitated before knocking. He felt inside his trench coat pocket again for the diaries, then rapped on the door. After a moment, he heard footsteps and a voice in heavily accented English.

"May I help you?" a small, attractive woman said as the door opened.

He straightened himself. "Yes," he answered. "I'm here to see Señor Enrique Hierron."

The woman looked Tolya up and down a few times before answering. "This way." She started down the hallway, then turned back. "And please, take off your shoes and leave them by the door."

Tolya did as she asked, then followed her down the hall into the living room. In the far corner sat a very old man in a wheelchair. He appeared at first to be asleep, but he lifted his head and smiled as Tolya entered the room. Tolya was caught off guard by his smile, which brought his face to life and made him look almost young.

"How nice to meet you detective," Enrique said. "Please forgive me for not rising to greet you."

Tolya couldn't quite place the old man's accent. It was unlike any he had ever heard. "No need for apologies. May I sit down?" he said.

"Yes, please. But sit here, near me," the old man said, gesturing toward the end of the couch nearest him. "My hearing is not so good anymore."

"Of course," Tolya said, taking a seat at the end of the couch.

"You're a big boy."

"Yes," Tolya said, shifting himself on the couch to find a position comfortable for his legs.

"Where are you from?" Enrique asked him in Russian.

"Excuse me?" Tolya said in English.

"Moskva? Leningrad?"

"You speak Russian?" Tolya said in English.

"Da, a little, along with eight other languages" Enrique smiled. "My parents were Communists."

"Moscow," Tolya said.

"May I offer you some coffee or tea?" Enrique said.

"No, nothing."

"Please, I insist." The old man leaned forward a little. The sunlight coming through the blinds fell on his face. His skin was nearly translucent, the tiny blue veins more noticeable under the strong light.

"What will you be having?" Tolya asked.

"Tea," replied Señor Enrique.

Tolya smiled. "I'll take tea then as well."

"Anisa," the old man called out. "Lleva nos dos te."

"Sí Señor," the woman called back from the kitchen.

"Do you prefer milk or lemon?" Señor Enrique asked.

"Lemon," Tolya said.

"Y limón," the old man called out.

"Lo oí," she responded from behind the kitchen door.

The old man turned back toward Tolya. "María called me about you."

"Yes. She suggested you might be able to help me. Should I call you Señor Hierron?

"No, Enrique is fine."

Tolya leaned toward the old man. "I am, was, the lead detective on the murder investigation for Max Redmond."

"I know."

Tolya was a little surprised. "I've been removed from the case."

"I see," said Enrique.

The maid brought the tray with two tall glasses in silver holders and placed it on the coffee table and left the room. There was a large pitcher of hot water on the tray along with sugar cubes, lemon and cherry preserves. On a separate plate were small chocolate covered pastries.

"Gracias Anisa," Señor Enrique called out. He turned to Tolya. "We Mitteleuropeans never tire of our little cakes."

"I thought you were Dominican?" said Tolya.

The old man smiled then chuckled. "I lived there for many years, that's where I met Max. Would you assist me please?" Enrique pointed to the tea set.

"Of course." Tolya reached over and poured hot water into the glasses. The tea bags and spoons were already in them. "My grandparents took their tea in glasses like this."

"Old habits," Enrique said with a small laugh.

"Lemon?" Tolya said.

"No, preserves actually," Enrique replied. "Would you mind passing them?"

"Of course," Tolya said stretching over the coffee table to hand the cherry preserves to Enrique. "Where are you from originally?" Tolya asked.

The old man brought the glass to his mouth and took a sip. "Budapest." He closed his eyes for a second and smiled slightly. "Max was my dear friend."

"How long did you know him?"

"Seventy years."

"That's a long time," Tolya said before breaking off a bit of pastry with the fork then putting it in his mouth. The sweet, gooey chocolate icing reminded him of the pastries his mother made when he was a small boy in Moscow.

"It's a lifetime." Señor Enrique lifted the glass slowly to his lips, his hands shaking slightly. "May I call you Tolya?"

"Of course."

"How was it you were removed from his case? Is it alright to ask you that?"

Tolya put his tea down on the serving tray and fumbled in his pockets for several of Max's diaries. "Because of these," he said, handing them to Enrique.

The old man took the volumes and turned them over in his hands. "Max's diaries." He laughed again, only this time a deeper, more personal laugh. "I told him these would come back to haunt him some day."

Tolya sat back on the couch, feeling the tension in his shoulders ease a bit. He sensed the old man could be an ally. "I shouldn't have taken them," he admitted. "The department doesn't know I have these. I don't read Spanish. María said you could translate them for me."

"Why are you interested in the thoughts of a dead man from so many years ago?"

"Because I believe something in these diaries will lead me to figure out who killed him. And I want to know what happened to them in Sosúa."

Enrique looked directly at him. "You don't believe Carlos beat him up, then?"

"No,"

"Neither do I."

Tolya sat forward on the couch. "Why?"

Enrique thumbed through one of the diaries. "Carlos loved Max and Max loved Carlos. Understand detective, that boy quickly became a conduit for Max. He connected Max back to a part of his life he had buried for decades. You see Max, more than any of us, any of the settlers in Sosúa, had become Dominican. He loved that country down to the depths of his very soul. The boy brought the best part of his life back to a very old man."

"That explains a lot about their relationship." Tolya took another bite of his pastry. "These are excellent by the way."

"Thank you." He looked at Tolya and hesitated for a moment. "It's all very complicated. Could I trouble you to give me one of those pastries please?"

"Por supuesto," Tolya said, placing a pastry on Enrique's plate and handing the plate back to him.

Enrique took a forkful of cake and savored it for a moment. "You speak a little Spanish?"

"Not much, a few words. I have...I had a Dominican girlfriend."

Enrique smiled. "Like Max," he said. "He loved the Dominican women.

That was part of the problem." Enrique hesitated for a moment. "You said 'had' very quickly after 'have.'"

"We split up yesterday."

"Ay, to be young."

"I'm not so young."

"You're very young, you just don't know it."

Tolya hesitated for a moment, not sure how to respond. "Enrique..."

"First of all," the old man interrupted him, "if we are going to spend some time together, call me what Max used to call me. There's no one else left to call me that anymore. It would make me feel young. Well, younger, anyway."

"What should I call you?"

"Call me Erno."

Sosúa
Dominican Republic
1 III '43
8:50 p.m.

A gentle breeze filtered through the recently installed screens into the dining room. I closed my eyes, relishing the feeling of the breeze against my skin.

"Max," Erno said, tapping my arm. "Are you coming with us into Puerto Plata this afternoon for the parade?"

"I don't know," I replied, stretching my arms over my head.

"You speak better Spanish than any of us," Fritzy said. He didn't look up at me, just continued to review the ledger on his clipboard. "We could use the help."

I leaned my chair back against the wall and sipped my coffee. Although it wasn't yet 9 a.m., I was tired. I haven't completely regained my strength since the malaria. I still become exhausted every few hours and need a nap. I thought the trip into Puerto Plata might be too difficult. I looked at both of them. "Truthfully, I don't know if I'm up to it."

"Think about it," Fritzy said, getting up from the table. "We're leaving at noon. I have to go to the office now and finish the monthly production reports. New York is getting difficult about the pace of our work."

"Tell them it's the tropics," Erno said.

"They don't care," Fritzy replied, waving at us as he left the mess hall.

Erno shifted to the seat next to me. "Little brother," he said, "you can't mourn forever. You need to get out, be with people."

"It's not that," I lied. "I just don't feel like myself. I have no strength. I still can't work. And besides, what would I tell Helen?"

He leaned back in his chair and rubbed his brow. "Why do you have to tell her anything?"

"Because we all know the main reason we're marching in the parade is so the younger men have the chance to meet some young women at the fiesta afterward."

He smiled at me and hesitated before continuing. "But the two of you aren't living together anymore. Max, I haven't pressed you on this. Is it something you want to talk about? Are you OK with Helen seeing Fritzy? You certainly don't betray yourself when he's around."

"What right do I have to be OK with it or not after what I put her through? I'm the cause of it. Was I there for her? Did I put her welfare first? I have no malice toward her. If she's happy with him I wish her well." I sipped my coffee again. I knew he was right but my own emotions wouldn't let me move on. "But we're still married."

"Say you're the chaperone," Erno said.

I looked him in the eye. "And Ava doesn't mind that you're going?"

"Why should she mind? I organized it."

I knew why she should mind. "Let me think about it." I got up from the table to end the discussion.

"OK, but be at the gate at noon," Erno said. "I have to go get the pick-up trucks ready."

I sat in the back of the pick-up truck under the shade of a tarp as we bumped our way over the dirt path that passed for a road to Puerto Plata. It was Dominican Independence Day. Why not celebrate? José was slumped beside me, sleeping. Four of the younger settlers sat across from me, also sleeping. I didn't understand how they were able to sleep with the truck ratcheting back and forth.

I looked out over the countryside toward the hills where my homestead sits. Perhaps Erno was right. It was time to stop mourning. I just didn't know how. I couldn't get the image of my dead son out of my head. Tiny, lifeless, covered with blood and Helen's silent tears.

I took all my rage out on her. She was right to leave me and return to Sosúa. I was a fool to have stayed at the homestead. I'd be dead if it wasn't for José and Nereida. When they came to check on me, they found me disoriented and burning up with a fever. José road back to Sosúa with me tethered to him and barely conscious.

José stirred next to me when the truck hit a bump. He opened his eyes, sat up and looked around. "Not too much farther," he said. "We should be there within an hour. How are you feeling, Max?"

"Better."

I hadn't been to Puerto Plata in over a year. Nothing had changed. The low wood buildings, their formerly vibrant colors fading, were all in need of repair. The streets were crowded with people strolling slowly toward the plaza in the middle of town for the Independence Day celebration.

"Erno," I shouted from the back of the truck, "where are we unloading?"

"Behind the town hall," he shouted back from the driver's cab. We made a right turn off the main road onto a side street choked with stalls that sold everything from long, brown, gnarled yuca roots to cast-iron pots and first-communion dresses. The air smelled of limes, cilantro, smoke and garbage.

I inhaled deeply, a feeling of lightness filling me for the first time since I received the letter from Jack. I am different here, more at peace surrounded by the Dominican world. Tranquilo. I belong here. It doesn't make a difference to me if it's the beach or the slums. It feels like home. The Spanish language, coming at me in shouts from every direction, sounds like music.

"Max," José said, "de qué te ríes?"

I said nothing, aware of the smile on my face.

"It's the first time I've see you smile in many months."

At the end of the market street Erno made a left into a makeshift parking lot. The two other trucks carrying the rest of the settlers and their instruments followed into the lot. The young men shouted to one another between the trucks to unload the instruments and assemble the banners.

"Will they ever learn Spanish?" José asked me as we jumped over the side of the truck.

"Probably never," I said. They don't really need to. Living separately from the Dominicans, as they do in the settlement, the lingua franca is still German. Even now, three years later, a huge argument erupted at a recent community meeting over what language of instruction will be used at the newly built school. Our agreement with the government requires that our children be educated in Spanish. The settlers think otherwise.

"The mayor is very excited about our band marching in the parade," Erno said, walking around the truck and helping José and me with the large poles on which the banner would be stretched.

"Really, why?" I said, leaning the poles against the side of the truck. "They're terrible."

José and Erno laughed, dropping the last of the poles on the ground. "They're not terrible, just a little tinny," said Erno. "And besides, the alcalde says El Jefe keeps asking him about whether the young men from the settlement come into town."

As always, at the mention of Raphael Trujillo's self-chosen moniker, José looked in both directions and spat.

"Cuidado, José," Erno and I said almost simultaneously.

"Por qué?" said José. "No one is listening."

"You never know who's listening," I said. "And why does El Jefe want our young men visiting town anyway?"

"Ah Max," said Erno. "Remember why Trujillo invited us here to begin with. He massacred 20,000 Haitians along the border in 1938. Roosevelt was furious with him. He wanted to show the world and Roosevelt how tolerant he is. Hence his offer at Evian. But he had his own agenda. The reason we have so many single men at the settlement is because Trujillo wants us to marry with the local women. Lighten the population, such as it is."

"Then why do we live under travel restrictions?" I said, lifting the banner from the truck handing one end to José to unfurl it.

"Because he is insane and a bigot," José said.

"José," I said, again catching Erno's eye. "Careful."

Erno took the first of the posts and held it up at a 45-degree angle for José to slip the corner of the banner over it. "He is a rapist," José whispered. "He travels the country looking for young girls. If he finds one he likes, he tells the alcalde to bring her to him for a private dinner. If the family refuses, he finds an excuse to arrest the father and take their land, their house, whatever they have."

"José," said Erno, stopping for a moment, "I've heard this before but…"

José moved closer to Erno and placed a hand on his shoulder. "No, Enrique, it's true," he said quietly. We leaned in to hear him clearly. "I saw this myself, the daughter of the family that lived next door to us when we lived here in the city."

"You're sure about this?" Erno said. "How old were you when this happened?"

"I was 18 years old, señor. He came to Puerto Plata for a fancy dinner, a cotillion, and he spotted her. The next day he asked for her. She was 14 years old."

"What did the father do?" I asked.

"He said no. The secret police came. The next night she went to his room at the mayor's home. Two days later she killed herself. The next week the father killed himself."

Despite the warm temperatures, a chill passed through me, and it wasn't the malaria. "This Trujillo, he is no better than the Nazis we ran away from."

"But at least he doesn't hate the Jews," Erno said, fidgeting with the cloth and the pole.

"Yet," I said.

Erno took a deep breath, his brow furrowed. "Whatever may have happened, we need to finish this up."

José slid the other end of the banner over the wooden pole I was holding. "I believe you," I whispered to José.

"Let's talk about something else," Erno added.

We lifted the banner upright and unfurled it. It read, "Dominican Republic Settlement Association Salutes Generalissimo Raphael Trujillo, El Jefe." I was sick to my stomach.

I walked through the plaza with José. Despite the lingering effects of the malaria, I felt better than I had in months. The temperature dropped as the sun set. I began humming to the music I heard off in the distance as we walked through the plaza.

"Max," José said. He had mischief in his eyes.

"Sí?" I replied.

"I want to take you someplace." He grabbed my arm and pulled me into a small street to our left. I followed him, picking up my pace to keep up with him. It was difficult, as my breathing was still shallow from the malaria. As we snaked through the alleys, the streets became darker, lit only by whatever light escaped the shacks that lined them. The damp night air felt good on my skin. José turned toward me. "Just a little farther," he said.

Music got louder as we approached a cinderblock building almost hidden by the trunk of a large tree down an alley on the left. The rhythm of the music filled me, my body moving with the beat even before we entered the building. I could feel the music in my bones as the door opened.

Through the haze at the opposite end of the room, I saw a band — more like a small orchestra. In the darkness, a mass of bodies moved to the seductive rhythm. The heat generated by dancing bodies escaped through the open door as we stood there.

"José," said the big man at the door, embracing him. "Comó se va amigo. No te veo pa' mucho tiempo. A donde tú fuiste?" I listened carefully. Although the conversation was rapid and music blared in the background, I understood everything.

José hugged the big man back. "Ocupado," he answered.

The big man flashed a broad smile at José. "Con qué?"

"¡Trabajo!"

"Entonces. Ya, tú tienes dinero?"

I envied the easy manner between them. Europeans are never so casual as to ask someone, no matter how well they knew them, if they had money. But here, no one seems to mind.

"No, mucho trabajo, pero poco dinero."

"Igualmente," the big man said, both of them laughing. José turned to me. "Por favor," he said, "this is my friend, Fernando. This is Max, mi amigo de alma."

"Él habla español?" the big man asked.

"Sí," I answered.

José placed his hand on my shoulder and guided me into the hall. The air was thick with the humid heat of the dancers. Weak lamps against the walls and candles on the tables cast a dim light over the room, the only other light coming from the spotlights focused on the band. Against the right wall was a long bar with people packed against it. Two men stood behind it selling bottles of Presidente. Around the edges of the dance floor were empty chairs and tables covered with empty bottles. Most of the customers were on the dance floor. The men held the women close, much closer than even married couples allowed themselves to be in any dancehall I had visited in Prague, Budapest or Vienna before the war.

"You want a beer?" José asked, his hand grasping my arm and pulling me across the room toward the bar. I felt the sweat begin to drip from my temples.

"Sí, a beer would be perfect."

"Dos cervezas," José shouted at the bartender.

The dark-skinned, muscled, shirtless man behind the bar popped the caps off two bottles and handed them to José. "Algo más?" he asked.

José turned toward me again and smiled, then turned back toward the bartender. "Sí, dos ron."

The bartender disappeared for a second under the bar. He reappeared with two small shot glasses, both full. He handed them to José. José handed one to me. "Salud, hermano," he said and tossed the shot down his throat.

"Igualmente," I replied, doing the same, a tear forming in my eyes as I thought about the word "brother." The burn from the homemade liquor hid my emotions. José has been like a brother to me these past three years —

since shortly after my arrival, really — helping me, teaching me how to adjust to life here. He stayed with me for four days at the settlement after rescuing me from my own stupidity while I lay in the infirmary, delirious from fever.

"You like the music?" José shouted over it.

"Sí," I said. "What is it?"

"Merengue, easy for dancing."

"I can see that," I said, surveying the room.

"Do they have places like this where you come from?" José asked, moving next to me.

"We have dance halls, but not like this. Men and women don't get this close in public."

José laughed. "I see that at the settlement. You never touch each other."

"No we don't."

"But you would like to," José said, clinking the neck of his bottle against mine twice, once on each side.

"Yes, I would."

Both of us were laughing now. José turned to me again, as if to say something, then stopped. "José, were you going to ask me something?" I said.

José hesitated again. "I was, pero…"

"No, please. Go ahead."

José took another swig of his beer. "You and Helen are not together. You told me she's with Fritzy now and you're OK with that. Are you ready to meet someone?"

"Yes," I said. "Por qué?"

"I could tell."

"How?"

"By the way you were looking around in town today and just now."

"Was I that obvious?"

"Yes."

I could feel the beat quicken as the band picked up the pace. My hips began to sway with the beat.

"I think you would like to dance," José said.

"I don't know how."

"We can fix that," José said. He pointed to a woman of medium height on the dance floor. Her body had the roundness common to Dominican women. In Europe she would be considered too heavy for her size, especially in what she was wearing: a low-cut, red sleeveless dress with lace trimming. She danced with another woman, their hips gyrating as she raised her hands to slowly turn her partner.

"She's my cousin. Her name is Anabela," José said, waving his hands to catch her attention. The music was too loud and the room too dark. "Follow me," he said, grabbing my arm again and leading me onto the dance floor. We squeezed through the crowd. The air was even thicker and heavier than it was by the bar.

I breathed in the scent of the room — a combination of beer and sweat — which, along with the music, awakened something inside me. José tapped her on the shoulder from behind. She turned, threw her arms up in the air and embraced him. José took her hand and put it in mine. "Teach him."

The caramel color of her skin darkened and reddened around her lips, which framed the most perfect, even set of white teeth I had ever seen. Her eyes were dark, set deeply above her high, delicate cheekbones. She was more than alluring. She was beautiful. She took my right hand and placed it on her left hip, all the while moving to the music. She placed her right hand in my left and raised it over our heads, placing her free hand on my hip. Ever so gently, she pushed my hip with her hand to force me to move with the music. She didn't have to push too hard. The rhythm came naturally to me, like I was born to it. I could feel it. My feet began to move with my hips.

"Qué bueno," she whispered into my ear.

I breathed in her scent when she leaned into me, a drop of sweat passing from her cheek to mine. My senses were in overload. The music filled not only my ears, but also my body. Her presence filled my vision and my soul. We were drenched in our sweat. I closed my eyes for a moment and felt her hand in mine as she spun. She finished the spin closer to me, our bodies grazing each other. She stayed that way, with her back to me bent slightly forward, for what seemed like forever. Our hips swayed in unison.

"Facil," she said as she turned back to face me, still dancing. "El merengue."

"Sí," I replied. "Qué rico."

The music stopped and the crowd screamed for more as the band left the stage for a break. "My name is Anabela Pabon," she said, extending her hand to me.

I took her hand and gently kissed it. "Encantado."

25

The room was dark and warm, despite the cool evening. A haze of hookah smoke hung in front of the lighted mirror behind the bar. Tolya hated the smell of smoke. It reminded him of those last days in Russia. He leaned in to hear Pete over the music blaring from speakers in corner of the room.

"Her last name was Pabon?" Pete said. He sipped at his beer with one hand and rubbed his forehead with the other. "It's a pretty common name. And how many generations later? That would be a huge coincidence."

"Stranger shit has happened," Tolya said.

"You think the son knows anything about this?" Pete said. He nearly emptied the bottle in a swig.

"If he did, he might understand why Max was so attached to Carlos," Tolya replied. "Did they get the arrest warrant?"

"I'm expecting it tomorrow. They have the kid's prints on the prayer book and the video of him with the fenced goods. They don't need anything else. And the political pressure is over the top."

Tolya turned away from the glaring mirror. "I'm certain it's the son. I think he had enough of the old man. I'm going to interview him again."

Pete straightened up and leaned back on his heels, smiling broadly. "Yeah, big shot? How you gonna do that? Did you forget you were suspended?" He slugged the remainder of his beer and slammed it down on the bar. "Want another?"

"Sure." Tolya smiled. "Yeah, I was suspended, but that don't mean I can't make a shiva call."

Tolya stood in front of Rothman's door listening to the sound of mumbled prayers coming from inside. He waited for the chanting to stop before trying the handle and finding it open. As he entered the apartment, two women turned and looked at him. He recognized one as Rothman's wife. She turned and left the room. The other approached him, wiping her hands on her apron.

"Can I help you?" she said.

"I came to pay my respects to Mr. Rothman," Tolya said, taking a step farther into the apartment.

"Your respects?" the woman said. "I'm surprised. I didn't think you respected anything. Honestly, I'm not sure you're welcome here."

"Are you asking me to leave?" Tolya said, aware that the crowd in the living room had become silent.

"HaShem forgive me, I think I am," she replied.

Tolya caught sight of someone coming from the living room.

"Miriam, please ask the detective to come in," Shalom said.

"If that's what you want," she said, backing out of the foyer. "Please, come in then."

Tolya walked up to Shalom and offered his hand. "My condolences, Mr. Rothman."

"Thank you, detective. Perhaps you could wait here a moment while we finish our prayers."

"No problem," Tolya said. Shalom walked back into the living room, the crowd parting for him. The men resumed mumbling for a few moments, then only Shalom's voice rang out. The men responded to each phrase with a heavily accented "amen." Tolya recognized the prayer as the mourner's kaddish. He had stumbled over it himself with the help of the rent-a-rabbi who had officiated over his father's funeral — a jumble of traditional Jewish practices, Russian customs and American showmanship.

Tolya surveyed the apartment. He felt claustrophobic. Unlike his spartan abode, there was clutter everywhere; books, religious objects, piles of newspapers, more books, stacks of old mail and items (some of which were books) lined every hall and hallway. Books everywhere. Books stacked helter-skelter in bookcases and on the floor. He was all in favor of books, but this was a little much.

The men finished their prayers and whispered in Yiddish as they filed past Shalom and out the door. As the crowd cleared, Tolya entered the living room. Shalom was seated on a low wooden stool, his knees approaching his chin. "Again, my condolences," he said.

"Thank you, detective. Please sit down."

Tolya sat opposite Shalom in a worn gray club chair. There were lace doilies over the arms of the chair. "You know, detective," said a voice from behind him, "we have an offering of condolence that is traditional from one Jew to another."

Tolya turned to see Shalom's father-in-law enter the living room.

"*Abba*, I don't think that will be necessary," said Shalom.

The rabbi stopped directly in front of Tolya, pointing his big stomach at Tolya's face. "I thought the detective might be interested, seeing that he's Jewish."

Tolya looked up at the rabbi. He considered the remark odd, as that certainly wasn't what the rabbi thought that day in his study when Tolya was 12 years old.

"Detective, this is my father-in-law, Rabbi Schoenweiss," Shalom said.

"We've met before," Tolya said, rising from the chair and extending his hand to the rabbi.

"Really?" the rabbi said, keeping his hands at his side. "I don't recall. When and where?"

"It was many years ago, in your study, with my parents." Tolya withdrew his hand.

"My apologies, detective. My memory is not so good anymore," the rabbi said, lowering his large frame onto the couch. Tolya backed into the club chair again facing Shalom.

"Mr. Rothman..." Tolya said after a long moment.

"Please, detective, call me Shalom."

"Yes, Shalom, and please call me Tolya." He made himself comfortable in the chair. It was deep and soft. "I'm sorry we got off to such a bad start."

"So am I," Shalom said, shifting uncomfortably on the shiva stool. "Do you live in the neighborhood?"

"Yes. Just a couple of blocks away. I've lived here since coming to this country."

"When did you come?" Shalom asked. He began to reach for a glass of water on the coffee table, but stopped. "Would you like something to drink?"

"Actually, I would. 1977. From Moscow."

"Rachel," Shalom called out, "the detective would like something to drink." He took a sip of his water and placed it on the floor. "That's a long time, which is why you have no accent."

At moments like this, he had to pay attention to every syllable that escaped his mouth. "It comes out at the most inopportune times."

"A small price for a great gift," said Shalom.

"I'm not sure what you mean."

Shalom placed his long arms around his knees. "The opportunity to live in this country."

"True," replied Tolya, "and so my father believed."

"I'm sure he is a fascinating man," Shalom said.

Before Tolya could respond, he heard Rachel from behind. "What can I get you?" He turned to face her and she averted her eyes.

"Water with a little ice would be fine," Tolya said. "He was, let's just say, an interesting character."

"Is your father alive?" Shalom asked.

Tolya looked at the rabbi. He was asleep; his head slumped against his chest, his beard pushing up around his mouth and nose. "No," Tolya said to Shalom. "He...actually both my parents are dead."

"*Alav ha'shalom*," said the rabbi, his head popping up suddenly. Rachel came back into the room and placed the water next to Tolya. She turned and left as stealthily as she had entered.

"Thank you," Tolya called after her.

"I'm sorry for you," said Shalom. "It's a terrible feeling, being an orphan."

Tolya sipped his water. "You get used to it."

"Like everything," replied Shalom.

They both turned to see Baruch enter the living room. He was tall and thin like his father. His face was without expression. He took a book from the desk by the bookshelves, walked across the room and sat on the floor next to Shalom. Shalom placed his hand on his son's head, bent over and kissed him. Baruch didn't respond. He simply opened the book — a collection of photographs of everyday life in Israel — and stared at the pictures, running his hand over each page in exactly the same motion before turning it. Baruch swayed as he did this, in the same manner of Orthodox men when they pray.

"Do you have children?" Shalom asked.

"No. Not yet."

"Children are a great blessing," Shalom said, beaming down at his son. Baruch continued his ritual stroking of each page, all the while swaying slightly in silence.

"To tell you the truth, I'm not sure I want any," Tolya said, surprising himself with his candor to a man he hardly knew and didn't trust.

"That's for HaShem to decide," the rabbi commented, rising from the couch. "If you'll excuse me, I have to be going."

Tolya began to get up from the chair to offer his hand again, but the rabbi walked quickly toward the foyer without offering his.

When the rabbi was sufficiently out of earshot, Shalom said, "Please forgive my father-in-law. He's very old-fashioned. He also suffers from the disease of advancing age. He thinks he can say whatever he likes whenever he likes."

"Yes, that's quite evident," Tolya replied. They both chuckled. He searched Shalom's face, looking for any kind of expression that might betray what Tolya thought he already knew.

"If I'm not being too forward, why is it you don't want children?" Shalom asked.

"That's a very personal question," Tolya said.

"I hope I haven't offended you."

"No, that's OK. I just don't think I'd be a good parent. My father was a terrible parent and I am very much like him."

"Parenting is like anything else," Shalom said, looking toward Baruch. "We don't know how we'll do at it until we try."

"I don't know that I'm willing to take that chance with someone else's life."

"I see." Shalom leaned back against the wall and put his hands behind his head.

Tolya watched Shalom fidget. He didn't know how he could sit like that all day. "Was your father a good parent?"

Shalom smiled and hesitated for a moment. "Yes, I think, yes he was. Why do you ask?"

"Just curious," Tolya said.

"Sure you're not interrogating me again, detective?" Shalom replied, a broad grin on his face. It was the first time Tolya had seen Shalom smile and it changed his demeanor entirely.

"No, not at all," Tolya lied. Though he wasn't quite sure who was interrogating whom at this point. He had Shalom relaxed, disarmed, in a position where he might trust him enough to open up a little. "I asked because you and your father seemed to live in such different worlds."

"We didn't always," Shalom replied, stretching his legs out a bit under the coffee table. "I didn't become religious until I was in college. We were actually quite close until then. After that we drifted apart. He could never accept my faith."

"Why is that?"

Shalom frowned and shook his head. "Because he had none. He wasn't much of a believer to begin with. But after the war, he had no use for faith. He'd lost too much."

"I can kind of understand that. He was a survivor, wasn't he?"

"A refugee actually," Shalom said. "I'm curious, Tolya, how it is that you know that? We never discussed it."

Tolya smiled and lifted an eyebrow. "I am a detective, Shalom."

"Yes, of course."

"The maid told me he had escaped Europe and gone to the Dominican Republic," Tolya replied. He felt like he had Shalom a little off-kilter.

"Yes, my parents did live there," Shalom said. He picked up the water again from the floor and took a sip, then caressed Baruch on the back of the head and mumbled something to him in Yiddish. "What kind of relationship did you have with your father?"

"A very tempestuous one," Tolya said, again surprised with his own honesty. He felt a twinge in his stomach, the way he always did when he talked about his father. "As boys in Russia, my brother and I…"

"Ah, you have a brother," Shalom said, interrupting him.

"Had a brother, a twin. He died in Russia."

"I'm sorry," said Shalom. "You know my father was a twin. I'm named after my uncle."

"No, I didn't know," Tolya lied. "We were afraid of our father. He was larger than life, both physically and in terms of his personality. Here, he became difficult. Morose and self-centered. He refused to speak to me after I chose the police academy over Princeton."

Shalom sat up on the stool. "Princeton, that's quite impressive. I myself went to Brandies before I studied in Yeshiva." Shalom reached for a bowl on the coffee table and took a handful of nuts. "Would you like some detective?"

"Thank you," said Tolya, reaching across the table for the bowl. "It just wasn't for me."

"Did you try to reconcile with him?" Shalom asked.

"Not hard enough, and when I did he never made it easy."

"I understand that," said Shalom, easing back against the wall again. "I had the same experience."

A silence descended between them as they chewed on the nuts. Tolya felt more comfortable with Shalom. "You tried though?"

"Many times," said Shalom.

Tolya popped a few more nuts into his mouth and chewed. "My one regret is that I didn't get to the hospital in time to see him before he died," he said.

"It was sudden?" asked Shalom.

"Yes, a heart attack. And though he didn't speak to me for, I don't remember how long it was, my name and the precinct phone number were found in his wallet. I got the call while I was on a case. By the time I got to the hospital, he was gone."

"I know the feeling," he said. "It's a terrible shock. Like last week when you pulled me out of the Simchat Torah celebration. At first it doesn't make any sense."

Tolya looked in his hand and picked out the Brazil nuts first. "To tell you the truth, Shalom, that's why I was so surprised when you said you couldn't… didn't want to go to the hospital immediately. I would have given anything…"

"Thank you for telling me that, detective…" Shalom said.

"Tolya, please."

"Tolya, now I understand a little better your reaction."

"My apologies."

Shalom hesitated a moment. "May I say something quite personal, Tolya?"

"Sure," Tolya replied. "Haven't you already?"

Shalom smiled. "Perhaps your reticence about fatherhood has more to do with your actions as a son than his as a parent."

"Possible," Tolya said. "Do you feel that way?"

"No, perhaps because as a parent I learned that my father made mistakes, but that despite those mistakes he still loved me. That in fact he may have made those mistakes because of how much he loved me."

Tolya smiled. "Life is too short to make enemies of those we love," he said.

"My father used to say that," Shalom said.

"I know, the Dominican kid told me."

Shalom laughed. "Ah, Carlos Pabon. I assumed our conversation would get around to that, sooner or later."

"That's not why I came to see you," Tolya said.

"I certainly hope not."

Tolya sat up in the chair. "Shalom, do you really believe that boy killed your father?"

"Detective, I don't know who killed my father." Tolya watched as Shalom's face became dead serious. "Right now, all the evidence points to Carlos Pabon."

"True," said Tolya. "But I asked you what you believe."

Shalom leaned in toward Tolya. He lowered his voice. "My friends, my family, Levitz, they all have tried to convince me Pabon did it. I studied pre-law at Brandeis and I studied Talmudic law for three decades, and what I know is that the evidence is there."

"So then you believe he killed your father?"

"As a Jew I can't...I won't see a man convicted of a crime he didn't commit. No, I'm not convinced. If you think someone else is responsible, find that person. I want justice for my father, despite our differences."

26

Shalom stared at the ceiling. Rachel's breathing was slow and steady like a ticking clock. Occasionally she would moan or twitch her leg slightly. He wondered what she was dreaming about. Sleep wouldn't come for him. He said a short prayer asking HaShem to calm him and bring him rest. It didn't come.

He got out of the bed and left the room, closing the door behind him. Perhaps a few pages of Talmud would calm him. He turned on the small light over his desk and opened the large book, running his fingers over the gilded edges of the pages. The paper had an almost feathery feel. He turned to the tractate Nezikin that deals with laws pertaining to witnesses and began reading. He became consumed with the ancient words, as he always did.

After some time, Shalom looked at the clock: 12:30. The morning minyan would be here at 6. Perhaps he should give in and take one of those pills the doctor had given him.

He got up from the desk and walked toward the kitchen. Halfway down the hallway, he stopped and walked to the foyer. He hesitated before turning on the light. When his eyes adjusted he reached down into the bag Rachel had placed by the door destined for the garbage and took out the gray wool gloves tucked inside.

Tolya tossed and turned in his king-size bed. There was a time when he couldn't sleep with anyone. Now he couldn't sleep alone. Karin had only been gone two nights, but it felt like a lifetime.

He turned again and looked at the clock: 12:30. He thought about calling her, picked up his cell and stared at it. What would he say at this point? He knew what Karin wanted to hear. But she wouldn't believe that he had gotten there in twenty-four hours. Maybe Pete was right: He needed to give it a try. Maybe Rothman was right: He needed to trust himself. Funny how he was thinking of Rothman, the last person he would have expected to take advice from on anything, let alone his personal life.

What the hell. He called her. His heart raced as he waited for an answer. After five rings it went to voicemail. He hung up.

He lay back on the pillow staring up at the shadows on the ceiling and reached his left arm out to where Karin would be, the phone still in his right hand. He felt the phone vibrate as the screen lit up. It was a text from Karin: "Good night amor."

He texted back, "I can't sleep."

After a moment, the phone vibrated and lit up again: "I know, I luv u."

"I luv u 2. Can we talk?" He pressed send.

"No not tonite," her message read.

"When?" he texted back.

The phone went dark again. Finally it vibrated. He looked at the screen: "When we've both had a little time to think."

His big Russian heart broke just a little.

Shalom sat in the darkened living room on the low shiva stool holding the gloves in his hands. He was sick to his stomach. How could he even consider such a thing? Rachel was the best, most gentle person he'd ever known. Dedicated, caring, a woman of valor. She would never hurt his father, or anyone for that matter. He hated himself for doubting her.

He got up from the shiva stool and walked back to the foyer. The clock on his desk read: 1:30. He tucked the gloves back into the bag without turning on the light and went back to bed, ashamed of himself.

Tolya lay in bed unable to sleep. His mind drifted back over the conversation he'd had with Rothman, still believing Rothman was hiding something. He was too calm, this Rothman. He stood the most to gain from the old man's death: whatever money the old man had and the peace of mind of no longer being responsible for him.

Finally, sleep seemed to come. Tolya closed his eyes and eased back into the pillows. The feeling of aloneness was familiar, more familiar than he cared to remember. The whistle of the wind outside the window and the emptiness of the room reminded him of those days just before Oleg died.

Outside Archangelsk
Soviet Siberia
Near the Arctic Circle
10 February, 1976
1 p.m.

Tolya looked out of the train window. He was blinded by the whiteness. The snow was everywhere, settled into deep drifts of frozen dunes.

It had been more than a year since this nightmare had started. Their father was sentenced to twelve years hard labor in a gulag outside Archangelsk. Their mother sent them to live with her parents in Ukraine while she looked for a new home near the gulag.

Tolya was actually happy in Kiev. His grandmother cooked for them every night. She made the things he loved, piroshki and blini and borscht with sour cream. Their grandfather walked them to school each morning in his jacket from the Great Patriotic War. The medals helped ward off the taunts of the other children and their parents, taunting meant more to curry favor with the local party apparatchiks than to torture them for their father's crime of personal honesty. After school he would take them to the sport center to play or to the woods to forage for mushrooms. Ah, what his grandmother could do with those mushrooms.

Oleg wasn't so happy. He missed their parents. Tolya could hear him crying at night under the covers of his narrow bed when he thought Tolya had fallen asleep. This surprised him. Oleg was always the tough one. Tolya missed his mother and father a little, but Oleg was inconsolable. He was convinced he'd never see them again.

Tolya nudged Oleg as the train pulled into the station. "Oleg, we're here. Get up."

Oleg slowly opened his eyes and then closed them quickly. "It's so bright."

"I know," Tolya said. He looked at Oleg. His face had changed over the past few months. They used to look almost exactly alike, except Oleg always a little bit tougher than him and his smile was a little more mischievous. Now Tolya was little tougher and Oleg didn't smile anymore.

"Do you see her?" Oleg asked, peering out of the window.

Tolya scanned the scene before him. There were too many people standing on the platform, all of them dressed in almost indistinguishable clothing — wrapped in heavy, full-length winter coats, faces wrapped in scarves, hats pulled down on their heads — to guard them from the unforgiving cold.

"No, not yet," he said. "But we'd better get dressed. We won't have a lot of time to get off."

"Do you have the bags, Oleg?" Tolya asked, adjusting his scarf.

"No, not yet. Come help me with them," Oleg said.

Tolya turned to find Oleg struggling with the suitcases. "Oleg, slow down," he said. Tolya saw that Oleg had misbuttoned his coat like a small child. "What have you done with your coat?" he asked.

"I don't care," Oleg said. "I can't wait to see her." It was the first time Tolya had seen his brother smile since they left Moscow.

Tolya didn't recognize his mother's voice at first. It was deeper, raspier and somehow weaker than he remembered. Then he saw her eyes through slits between the scarves and the hat. He remembered her eyes: a clear, cool, powdery green, like the Ukrainian hayfields in May.

"Tolya, Oleg," she called out, waving at them.

They dropped their suitcases in the snow and ran to her, embracing her tightly and feeling her body beneath the heavy winter coats to make certain she was really there. Tolya looked up and saw the tears nearly freezing as they fell from her eyes. Oleg began to weep and fell to his knees as she touched his face, slipping a hand under his scarf and kissing him with a million tiny kisses. She did the same to Tolya. Her presence swept through him like a strong spring wind clearing a musty house.

"Mama," Tolya said, picking up Oleg by the underarms out of the knee-deep snow.

The snow never stopped coming. The winds howled all night. Their mother had found them a school and a small apartment a few blocks from it. She had taken a job at a canning factory near the docks. They processed fish that had been caught and stored before the ice locked in the harbor. She worked six days a week. She smelled of fish seven days a week.

Twice a month she would take them to see their father in the gulag. She would pay the guard to bring him to the gate. They could touch him through the fence. Once, he took his glove off his hand to touch their faces. Tolya saw his blackened nails and his bony fingers. It was hard to tell through the heavy, torn scarves he wrapped around his face, but he looked very thin.

When they returned home his mother would sit by the window in the gray apartment smoking silently. She would stare out into the darkness. When she finished what cigarettes she had, she would empty the butts of any tobacco that hadn't been burned and roll them into more cigarettes. When that ritual was finished, she would sigh and go to bed in the small alcove off the main room behind a worn curtain.

Tolya lay in bed listening to Oleg's breathing. The sound of the wind and the shutter tapping against the window kept him awake. Oleg had been a little better when they first arrived. He was calmer, happy to be with their mother. The new school wasn't so bad. It was much easier than their school in Moscow and certainly easier than his father's endless mathematics lessons.

No one knew them or why they were here, so there was no taunting from the other children. Besides, there were many people in Arkhangelsk who were on internal exile.

Oleg got sick. It started as a cold. Then he got fever. It got so bad one night he had a seizure. His mother sent Tolya to the hospital to fetch a doctor. They sent a nurse. Together the three of them had to carry Oleg back to the hospital through the snowdrifts. Oleg was in the hospital for a week, in a creaking bed in a large room full of coughing people. The doctor said he had pneumonia and that the seizure was from the high fever. He didn't think it would happen again. He had given Oleg strong medicine, but that medicine emptied out their ration card for the rest of the year and it was only February. If any of them got sick again, his mother would have to pay for the medicine.

Tolya could hear the rattle in Oleg's breathing every time he took a breath. With each rattle, Tolya shuddered. He had promised his father he would be strong. He didn't know how much longer he could keep that promise.

Tolya felt his mother's hand on his forehead.

"Tolya, my darling, wake up. It's time to get ready for school."

He pulled the heavy wool blanket over his head, the texture of the fabric rough against his cheek. "Nyet, mama, I didn't sleep. Let Oleg wash first."

"Of course you slept, my darling," she whispered in his ear, her breath warm and moist. "I just woke you. Your brother needs more sleep, he's been so sick."

Tolya let out a sigh. The room was cold. He could see his breath. He pulled himself up out of the cot and walked the few feet to the sink in what passed for a kitchen. He reached under the sink and took out a slop pail and walked behind the flimsy curtain to the alcove where his mother slept. He relieved himself into the pail. He would dispose of that later on his way out to school. He walked back over to the sink and turned the tap. A thin stream of icy cold water came out. This was the one thing he would never get used to, the sting of the icy cold water against his face. He tried to remember what running hot water felt like every morning. Then he heard his mother begin to weep.

He turned to see her perched on the edge of Oleg's bed. "Mama, what's wrong?" he said, drying his face with the thin towel she had left by the sink for him.

She said nothing. Tolya walked the few feet across the room. She took Tolya's hand and put it against Oleg's forehead. "He's burning up," she said.

As his mother touched Oleg's cheek, he opened his eyes. Tolya wasn't sure Oleg knew where he was. When he opened his mouth, he drooled a small trickle of blood onto the pillow.

"Mrs. Kurchenko, please sit down," the doctor said.

Tolya watched as if from outside his body as his mother lowered herself into the wooden chair in front of the doctor's desk. She held her half-smoked, still-smoldering cigarette in her shaking hand. Tolya sensed the doctor was waiting for her to say something, but she remained silent.

After what seemed like an eternity, Tolya said, "What is wrong with my brother?" The doctor lifted his bald head to look at Tolya standing behind his mother. Her head and shoulders drooped. A barely audible sob escaped her lips as cigarette ash fell to the floor. The doctor's face was fat, with small features pushed together into its center.

"Your brother has tuberculosis," he said as nonchalantly as if he had said, "Your brother has a cold." Tolya stepped forward and put his hands on his mother's shoulders. Her sobs grew worse.

The doctor continued as if she weren't there. "He is quite far along. I'm afraid, though, you've used up your ration for medication."

Tolya's mind was in chaos. He was 11 years old. How could he answer? He walked around the chair and bent in front of his mother. "Mama, talk to him please."

She continued to weep, a thin layer of tears covering her face. He realized how her face had changed in the past year. In Moscow she had been young and beautiful, her skin the color and texture of a peach, her blond hair radiant. Now, her face was pale and drawn with deep lines, her hair dull and shot with gray.

The doctor continued flipping through the file and making notes as he spoke to them. "He's at a critical point. His lungs are filling with fluid. If we don't administer medication, he'll soon die."

Tolya felt like he had been punched in the gut. Die? Oleg, die? "Mama, please talk to him," he said again.

She raised her head. The tears had stopped. She placed her hand on To-lya's shoulder and pushed him aside. She dropped the remainder of the cigarette on the floor and stamped it out with her boot. The doctor looked down at her foot as she did this, then toward her face as she got up from the chair and approached his desk. She stood up straight and looked at the doctor, pushing back her hair from her face. "I was pretty once, doctor," she said.

The doctor rose from his chair. His tiny mouth smirked, causing the fat around his chin to bunch up. He surveyed her as she arched her back and leaned against his desk, engrossed in an act so desperate even the doctor couldn't take advantage of it.

"I'm sure you were, Mrs. Kurchenko. Frankly, you still are. But I'm sorry. I can't help you in that respect. If you want your son to be treated, you'll need to find the money for the medicine. Your ration card is empty."

She fell to her knees. "Please doctor," she pleaded. "My father was a hero of the Soviet Union."

"But your husband is a traitor."

Tolya came up from behind her again. He placed his arms under her, lifting her from the floor the way he had lifted Oleg out of the snow the day they'd arrived. "Mama, we need to go," he whispered in her ear.

She began to cry again. "Yes, we need to go," she said. "I need to go see my son."

27

Tolya breathed in the cold morning as he walked briskly down Bennett Avenue. The chill of the autumn air reminded him of Moscow. He pulled his gloves on a little tighter. Though he couldn't go to the station, he had gotten up anyway. He didn't want to sit around the house thinking, so he pulled on some sweats and set out for the gym on 181st Street. Perhaps a workout and some mangú con tres golpes at the Dominican restaurant would clear his head before his meeting with Erno.

As he passed the intersection of 187th Street, he gazed to the right. He saw Rothman's wife leave their building. She moved at the same frenetic pace she always did, as if she was late for whatever she needed to do next. He stopped and watched her. She walked to the corner of Overlook Terrace and placed a large Duane Reade shopping bag into the trash basket on the corner.

He thought about jogging up and giving her a ticket. Placing personal trash into a public receptacle was patently against the law. Thanks Mayor Bloomberg. Every building had garbage disposal facilities and every resident had to use them. Then he realized he couldn't give her a ticket. He didn't have any to write and, besides, he'd been suspended. He watched her push the bag down into the bin a little, look both ways and continue on in the same manner as she arrived — speedily, diligently and with stealth — toward the steps up to

Ft. Washington Avenue.

She was hiding something. Why wouldn't she just put it into the trash in the back of the building? Perhaps she didn't want to take the time to go out back before she left. No, she didn't seem that lazy.

Tolya walked toward the trash bin at a measured pace, his hands in the pockets of his heavy sweatshirt and his head slightly down. When he reached the bin he looked up and down Overlook Terrace and behind him down 187th Street. Two men in suits were approaching from behind him on 187th Street heading toward the subway at 184th Street. He waited on the corner for them to pass before pulling the Duane Read bag out of the bin and walked up Over-look to a bench across the street. He sat down on the bench and gingerly inspected the items in the bag. A couple of old newspapers, an egg carton, a broken coffee grinder, some old rags that looked like they had been dishtowels in a former life, and a pair of gloves. The gloves were neatly tucked away in the side of the bag behind the newspapers. He turned the gloves over in his hands and saw the darkened area on the right glove. He pulled his cell out of his sweatshirt pocket and called Pete. The phone rang twice before Pete picked up.

"Yes, Detective Kurchenko?"

"I'm sitting on a bench just north of the 187th steps on Overlook. Come here now, I have something for you."

Tolya wiped his feet nervously on the welcome mat outside Erno's apart-ment before tapping on the door. As he raised his hand to knock, Erno's maid opened the door to take out the trash. She jumped back, startled. "Ay señor," she said. "Why didn't you knock?"

"I was just about to," he said.

"All right then, please come in. El señor is in the living room waiting for you. Please leave your shoes here. You want coffee when I get back?"

"Yes," he said, brushing by her. He leaned against the wall of the foyer and slipped off his sneakers. On his way through the foyer Tolya noticed a photograph on the wall. He stopped to look at it. It was the same beautiful beach as in the photo Pete had found in Max's apartment. There were three men in the picture. They stood with their arms over one another's shoulders, smiling in the brilliant sunlight.

"Detective," Erno called out to him. "What's taking you so long? It's quite a short journey from the front door to where I am seated."

"I'm looking at one of your old photographs."

"Bring it with you, please. And, if you don't mind, would you bring me my pipe and tobacco as well. They're sitting on the writing desk at the end of the hall."

"Of course," Tolya answered. He was surprised that Erno still smoked at his age. But then, he'd survived just about everything else. He carefully slipped the photo off its hook and took it with him.

"How are you today, detective?" Erno said as Tolya entered the living room.

"Please Erno, call me Tolya," Tolya said as he handed the pipe and tobacco to Erno.

"Alright then, Tolya." He put the pipe in his mouth and opened the bag of tobacco. "Let me see the photo that's so caught your interest."

"That's Max in the picture with you?" he said, handing the frame to Erno.

Erno held the photo up to the light streaming in through the windows. "Yes, yes it is. It was taken just before Max moved out to his homestead."

"Who's the other guy?"

"Fritzy."

"That's Fritzy? You all look very happy there."

"We were, at that moment. Things got very complicated later on." Erno reached for the thin volume next to him on the end table. He clutched the diary in his hand, the boniness of his fingers accentuated by the worn green linen material stretched over the cover of the book. "Reading this has brought back a lot of memories, some of them very sad. You know with time we forget things. Our prospective changes."

"That, unfortunately, hasn't been my experience," Tolya said, making himself as comfortable as he could on the couch. "I remember every detail of every day as if it just happened. That can be a curse."

"Yes it can, unless we learn a bit of forgiveness. That was Max's biggest problem. He would say he forgave something but he never forgot that it happened, in the minutest detail."

Anisa came into the living room with the tea service. The pot was filled with strong coffee, the aroma of which filled the room. On a plate next to the coffee pot was a pile of croissants.

"Funny you should say that," Tolya said. "It runs against the most significant thing Carlos said to us."

"What did the boy say?"

"He said that Max told him, 'Life is too short to make enemies of those we love.'" Tolya watched a smile appear around Erno's lips again. It brought light and youth to his face, as it had the day before. He looked like the man in the photo now: young and full of life. "Why are you smiling, Erno?"

"Because Max would say that. He was wise enough to acknowledge his own shortcomings."

El Batey
Dominican Republic
26 II '44
9 a.m.

I watched entranced as the sunlight moved in millimeters across the skin of her leg, the light changing its color from caramel to coffee with cream. I loved the way her skin felt soft like velvet. I was tempted to touch her, but didn't want to wake her. I moved closer under the thin sheet, my skin grazing hers. She stirred, took my hand and entwined her fingers in it, then moved my hand to her breast. I took her large, soft nipple between my fingers and tweaked it gently. She let out a low moan, so I moved closer. I felt myself harden and then felt her hand guide me into her. We became like one being. I lost myself in the moment. Every time I made love to her, it was like the first time. It took me to another place, a place I'd never imagined.

She slid off me and turned gently, pushing me down on my back against the pillows. She straddled me.

"Ay," she said. "Qué rico. Despacio, mi amor. Slowly. I want you forever like this."

I pulled her face down to mine and kissed her hard, my tongue in her mouth, her lips soft against mine, her teeth biting me ever so slightly. "No mueve querida. Don't move," I whispered in her ear. Her hair brushed against my cheeks as I held her hips and moved slowly, deliberately, in and out of her.

"Quiero mover," she said.

"No, esperas, no mueves," I answered.

My movements quickened. She began to move as well. At the moment of climax I looked into her eyes and saw happiness, both hers and mine. She collapsed on top of me, both of us soaked with sweat. Making love to Helen was never like this.

I moved to the village in September. I had no reason to stay at Sosúa. After meeting Anabela I became obsessed with seeing her. Despite my separation from Helen, a relationship like this with a native woman, and one so much younger, is frowned upon. While they are supposedly building a new way of life here, the community is still pretty much controlled by its Mitteleuropean values. In the heat of August I packed up a few things —

what did I really need anyway? — and moved from Sosúa to the native village down the road to live with Anabela.

I rarely visit Sosúa now. Why would I need to? I am happy here in the jungle, near the beach. If I never hear German again, it will be fine. And Hungarian brings back too many memories.

We moved into a two-room casita behind José's house where his parents once lived. His father died a few years earlier and his mother stays with them now, helping to tend to the endless stream of children running in and out of the house.

I can't keep the children straight, even after six months, who belongs to whom. It doesn't really matter. They're raised as one family regardless of their bloodlines. Soon, one of those children will be mine. Anabela is three months along. Apart from her breasts swelling a little, she isn't showing. But you can see it in her face, in the smile that crosses her lips every time she gently touches her stomach when she thinks no one is looking.

I am happy, ecstatic, at the prospect of being a father. But then the image of my dead son comes into my mind and sends a chill through me. Nereida was afraid my thoughts would bring bad luck to the baby. She took me to the bruja, the local witch, to rid me of my demons. I love her for caring, but it did no good. I'll never forget what happened and how much of it was my own fault. I told her my devils were gone. Now I keep them to myself.

I saw José approaching the casita through the open front door. "Buen día, pana," I called out to him.

"Igual," José called back. He brushed off his feet at the door and entered. I took his hand and embraced him. "Nereida sent this over," he said, handing me a clay bowl with a thin towel on top.

"Mangú," I said, pulling back the cloth.

"She made too much and she doesn't want to waste it. She said it's good for Anabela, for the baby."

"Gracias."

"Would you like a coffee?" Anabela asked, entering from the bedroom. She walked to José and kissed him, then sat down on my lap.

"Sí, if you have some," José said.

"I was about to make some," she said, leaning over to kiss me. "Mi marido cannot start the day without it."

She rose from my lap, but I pulled her back down to me. "That can wait a moment," I said. I kissed her again, deeply, passionately, more intimately than I should have in front of José. Out of the corner of my eye I could see José smile. When he sensed that I was aware of his response he averted his eyes and cleared his throat. "It's a beautiful day," he said.

Anabela's lips parted from mine. She smiled and caressed my cheek. "What's this?" she said, reaching for the covered bowl.

"Mangú, from Nereida," José and I both said.

"Dios mío," she said. "She takes good care of me."

José reached across the table and touched Anabela's hand. "Because for her you are like a daughter and that baby is her grandchild," he said.

I watched her every move as she rose from my lap and walked across the small kitchen to put on the coffee. She calms and excites me at the same time.

"Are you coming with us tomorrow to Puerto Plata?" José said, breaking into my thoughts.

"Of course," I answered, my eyes still glued to Anabela as she moved slowly over the wood floor. "It's our anniversary. She's very excited about it."

"I've got the same dress ready," Anabela said.

"But this year you have to be careful, not too much dancing," José chuckled. "Nereida will be watching."

Anabela turned and put her hand on her hip. "Ay, she's like a mother hen," she said. She moved her hand from her hip to her stomach. "I will be careful." She smiled, then poured the coffee into two small cups and brought them to the table. "Señores, sus cafés."

"Gracias querida," I said, taking her hand and kissing it.

"I have much to do," she said, leaving us at the table.

I turned my attention to José. He seemed hesitant as he sipped his coffee. "What's bothering you, hermano?" I asked.

"Erno was here again yesterday," he replied.

A tinge of sadness passed through me. "What did you tell him?"

"That you were in the fields."

I said nothing.

José looked me directly in my eyes. He sighed heavily. "Why won't you see him, pana?" he asked.

I drummed my fingers on the table for a moment before answering. It was very complicated. "He'll just try to convince me to come back to Sosúa."

José leaned back in the rough wooden chair. He crossed his arms against his chest and smiled. "You're a morenito now," he said. "Erno knows that. He's a good man. He just wants to see you. He's your friend."

I know that he is right, but I also know that every time I see Erno, or anyone from the settlement, it all comes rushing back: the baby, Istvan, Helen, every mistake I made. Here I am free to be whoever I want. I turned as Anabela came back into the room.

"What time tomorrow are we leaving for Puerto Plata?" she asked.

"After siesta," José said.

I got up from the table. "Give me a minute to get my hat, José. Let's go pick some mangoes."

The evening breeze picked up the strands of Anabela's hair, blowing them back gently into my face. We stood silently on the ramparts of the old fort overlooking the sea a half hour's walk up the coast from the village. The sun set in the distance over the mountains toward La Isabella, where Columbus landed in Paradise. I wrapped my arms around Anabela's waist, then buried my face in her hair, kissing the back of her neck and breathing in her scent. I too had crossed the Atlantic to discover paradise.

"Qué lindo," Anabela whispered, looking out toward the horizon. "What a beautiful color."

"Sí," I said, nibbling at her cheek. My hands massaged her stomach carefully. "What a beautiful color, every inch of you."

She slapped my hands gently, laughed and kissed me.

"You make me happy," I said.

"Igual," she said. "We should get home. We have a busy day tomorrow."

"No, just a little longer." I pulled her closer to me, the warm breeze caressing us as the waves lapped gently at the shore below. "I want you here forever," I said, her beautiful face inches from mine.

She kissed me again, this time with passion then whispered in my ear, "You have me always, amor."

A. J. SIDRANSKY

El Batey
Dominican Republic
6 VI '44
9 p.m.

We received the news today. The Allied forces have landed in Normandy. Perhaps finally, after all these years, the war is about to end. I have not written in this journal for many months, since before those terrible days in February. My life will never be the same. My memories of what happened over those few days are breaking my heart. Perhaps if I write about them I can come to some peace.

The evening was cool and dry, as the weather is in February. José stood waiting at the steps of the town hall in his best white shirt, freshly laundered, with his hat in his hand. I watched him from a distance. As we neared him, Nereida appeared with their children. Josecito, 12, was dressed like his father. He looked like a miniature copy of him.

Their daughter Camilia, 15, looked almost like a grown woman. Nereida had made her a dress for the cotillion. Its turquoise folds revealed her young body. The excitement in her face was palpable. She'd be married soon enough. I waved and called out to José, but the noise from the crowd was too loud. We were next to them before José turned and saw us.

"Querida," Anabela said, embracing Camilia. "Mírate, you are a grown woman. How beautiful you are."

"Thank you," Camilia said, lifting the sides of the dress slightly and curtsying. "How was your walk?"

"Romántico," Anabela said, taking my hand in hers. "Are you excited?"

"Sí, this is all she's talked about for days," said Nereida as she fidgeted with Camilia's hair.

"And no dancing with any boys unless they ask me first," José said.

Camilia stamped one foot against the pavement, making a face that betrayed her as the girl she was, not the woman she appeared to be. "Papá, por favor."

"You heard him," Nereida said. Then she touched Camilia's shoulder and whispered, "Don't worry, I'll take care of him. You just dance with whoever you want."

272

"Shall we?" I said, pointing toward the broad stairs leading to the covered portico of the town hall.

"Vamanos," José ordered.

I heard the band inside playing a rumba, its soft, swaying rhythm floating on the breeze. It was still early. I knew the pace of the music would pick up as the evening progressed. Before long, the room would fill up and the beat of the meringue would take over. The lights would dim and it would seem as if the walls were swaying with the bodies and the music.

There would be no Musica de Amargues though. El Jefe disliked it. I had come to love the sound of it, always sad, always a man singing about a broken heart. The men in our village played these heartfelt improvisations at night in the clearing between the houses. They gathered around a fire sipping homemade rum from the still I built, while the children ran around in the darkness. It was the sound of my new life and, despite the sadness of its words, its notes fill me with happiness.

"Máximo," José said as we ascended the steps. "You need to be very careful tonight."

"Por qué?" I asked.

"I heard from Carlos that El Jefe is in Puerto Plata and is expected to attend this cotillion. You can't be here. Fade into the walls."

I stopped halfway up the steps, other people brushing past me toward the fiesta. "José, first of all, who would notice me?" I said. "My Spanish is as Dominican as yours."

José laughed and took my arm. "Except how many fair-haired Dominicans do you see? Hermano, you may speak like us and live like us, but you don't look like us. And if the police found out you were here, they could — no, they would — arrest you."

"For what?"

José threw his hands in the air then slapped the side of my head playfully. "Coño, for the ransom and you know that. The refugees are under curfew. They would hold you till the settlement paid a fine and then they'd be watching you. You'd have to move back to Sosúa."

I knew he was right, but continued anyway. "And what makes you think El Jefe would attend this cotillion. This party is for the poor to keep them pacified. He'll go to the party at the governor's mansion with the landowners."

"Carlos works with the police," he said. "When he tells me something, I believe it. Be careful." He turned and took a step up toward the veranda.

I placed my hand on his arm and stopped him. "You're afraid for Camilia," I said.

I could see the emotion in his deep black eyes. They always betrayed him. "Sí, I begged Nereida to leave her at the village, but she'd made that dress and I promised her."

José sat down on the steps. I sat down next to him. "I would never let anything happen to that child," I said.

José stared out into the thickening crowd ascending the steps. "He's a rapist and he's the president. He can do what he wants," he said. "Ten cuidado."

"Igual," I said, then we rose and continued our way to the party.

"Look how happy she is," Anabela said, pointing to Camilia.

I turned Anabela on the dance floor and smiled as I looked across the room. Camilla was standing by the far wall, her hands in front of her, her back and head straight, her smile illuminating her face. José stood no more than ten feet away, watching her like a hawk. The young man she was talking to looked to be a little older, though I doubt a razor had yet crossed his cheeks. He was tall and thin and smiled as broadly at Camilia.

I thought back to gatherings that my parents had taken us to back home to meet potential wives. It was different from this, very different. There was no dancing at all and the music was subdued. The fathers would disappear into an adjacent room to discuss business and size one another up, the mothers and the matchmakers would supervise the young people. It was there

I first met Helen. It was also at one of those meetings that both Istvan and I met Magda. I had looked at Magda the same way this boy looked at Camilia, but so had Istvan. I loved my brother too much to have gotten in between them though, and that's what my father had wanted anyway. Our father bargained for Magda for Istvan, and Istvan had fallen in love with her the first moment he saw her. But so had I.

The music stopped suddenly, dragging me back from my thoughts. A shrill whistle sounded as the police chief stepped up to the stage where the band had been playing only a moment earlier.

"Atención," he called out through the microphone. "Ladies and Gentleman, I have the great pleasure on this most happy day for our nation, the day of our independence, to announce to you that our leader, El Jefe, Generalissimo Raphael Trujillo, the savior of the nation, the beloved of his people, is outside this room at this very moment."

The room broke into applause, the men whistling and the women shouting for El Jefe.

"He has come to grace us on this special evening with his presence. Ladies and gentlemen, please make way for and welcome, El Jefe."

At the mention of the Generalissimo's name, a squad of uniformed soldiers entered the ballroom, each carrying a rifle. They pushed the people back from the dance floor to make room for Trujillo to enter. The applause became even louder. Anabela grabbed my arm and pulled me back toward the wall where José was standing with Nereida and Camilia.

"Stand well behind José," she said. "And for god sake, if he comes by us and speaks to us, slip behind someone or something. If he sees you he may ask questions."

El Jefe entered the room. He was shorter than I had imagined. His military uniform was covered with medals. He carried his plumed hat in his hand. The chief of police bowed deeply to him and accompanied him to the stage. I laughed to myself. Trujillo reminded me of Mussolini, a caricature of himself, dressed up like a spoiled child in the uniform of his father's regiment, adults running before and after him, making sure he was content so as not to incur his childish wrath. Why did these people put up with this?

I knew the answer only too well. They didn't really care. Politics made their lives neither better nor worse. It mattered little to them who sat in the

Presidential Palace. They would still have to get up every day to milk the cows and feed the chickens and coax what little they could from the poor tropical soil. They wished only to be left in peace to enjoy one another and a little rum now and then.

Trujillo spoke briefly. I was too busy staring at Anabela to pay attention to what he was saying. He descended from the stage and slowly toured the room, followed by his entourage: a man of the people among his people. His people, meanwhile, played their role. He offered his hand and they kissed it. He asked them inane questions and they answered, never looking him in the face, but staring downward at their feet and thanking him profusely for all that he had done for the nation.

He stopped before José. I was about five feet behind them and struggled to hear the conversation. Trujillo stared lecherously at Camilia, at one point taking his right hand and tilting her chin up to get a better look.

The color drained from José's face. Anabela moved up next to Camilia and put her arm around her, explaining to El Jefe that this was her first cotillion and how grateful she was to him for providing this celebration to the people.

Trujillo looked at Anabela, his eyes aflame. I inched closer, struggling to hear the exchange. "And you are her mother?" he said.

"No, no," Anabela said, averting her eyes from El Jefe, "her cousin. But I have cared for her since she was born."

Trujillo crossed his arms and leered at Camilia again. "A beautiful flower, like her name," he said, then abruptly turned and walked on.

José grabbed both Anabela and Camilia and moved back into the crowd toward me. "Keep them here," he said. "I'm going to find Nereida and Josecito, then we need to get out of here. Fast. As soon as he's gone." As José turned to look for Nereida, two men in uniform came toward him through the crowd. Fear crossed his face.

"Señor," one of the men said.

"Sí," José answered lowering his eyes to the floor.

"El Jefe was very impressed with the young woman…"

"Por favor," José said, his voice nearly cracking.

"He has requested that you bring her to his suite at the governor's mansion tomorrow afternoon at 4 for tea."

"Señores, please," José stammered as the band returned to the stage and the music started. "She's only 15 years old."

"No señor, not the girl. The young woman, there in the red dress," the soldier said, pointing at Anabela.

I felt my body nearly explode.

"She has to leave," shouted José. He picked up the wood chair he had been sitting on and slammed it into the floor. The little house shook from the force of it. "We all have to leave. There is no choice here."

"She's not leaving, no one's leaving," I shouted. "Where on earth would we go?"

"You're going back to Sosúa," José said, pointing a finger at me.

"No I'm not." I grabbed the chair he had slammed into the floor, turned it around and sat down. "I'm not going anywhere."

"Coño," he shouted. "I've already sent word to Erno about what's happened. You don't understand. If she doesn't show up at the governor's mansion at 4, they will send men to get her." He held up one finger. "She'll be given one more day. If she doesn't show up they'll come and get her. And if she refuses to go they'll take her or kill her and the rest of us too."

"I'm not leaving her and I won't leave you. I made that mistake once I will never make it again. We'll go someplace together."

"Where?" José implored. He walked around the table and put his hands on my shoulders. "I'm sorry Max, where will you go? You can't travel freely. The police would pick you up and then you're finished. And if they catch the two of you out here together…"

"I've been a refugee before," I interrupted him. "I've been hunted before.

You think I'm afraid of these guys?"

"I think these guys don't care if you're afraid of them," José said. "We need a plan."

We sat silently in the clearing between the houses. It was eerily quiet. Where the sound of children playing and women calling after them normally filled the air, there was only silence. We sent the other families who shared our small patio into the fields to wait until we had settled the matter with the president's henchmen. Nereida was in her house, she had refused to leave. Anabela was with her, also refusing to leave.

I would explain to them that she was pregnant, that the president hadn't known, that he wouldn't want a pregnant woman. If I had to I would kill them, then Anabela and I would disappear. I would never be apart from her. We would go to Samaná. It was even more remote than here. José had a cousin there. We would hide there until Trujillo had forgotten about us.

In the distance I heard the sound of an engine stop and then footsteps through the leaves on the forest floor. Six armed men in uniforms approached. I recognized the leader of the group from the day before. He walked toward us slowly, a cigarette dangling from his lips. He stopped about twenty feet from where we were sitting and called out to us: "Buenos tardes."

We said nothing. The soldiers came nearer. José and I picked up the machetes we had placed behind us and put them on the ground before us.

The lieutenant laughed and tossed his rifle in the air, catching it with one hand. "Hombres, por favor. What are you thinking?" The five other soldiers came up behind him. "Is the young lady here? El Jefe found her fascinating. He only wants the opportunity to enjoy a quiet tea with her and learn more about the life of his people."

I got up from the ground taking the machete in my right hand. José followed my lead. "Lieutenant, please. May we talk about this?"

"Señor, we really have nothing to talk about. You can't decline an invitation from the leader of the republic."

I stepped forward again. The five guards behind the captain raised their rifles. José came up behind me. "Máximo," he said, "don't move."

I put my machete down beside me. "Lieutenant, please, can we talk?"

"Lower your guns," the lieutenant said to his men. He walked toward me. "What is it you would like to talk about, señor?"

"She's pregnant."

The lieutenant smiled, looking me up and down. "And I suppose you're the father. Are you married to her?"

"Yes, it's my child," I said.

"I asked if she is your wife. You have a strange accent, señor," the lieutenant said. "You are not Dominican, from the look of you."

The five guards laughed. The lieutenant continued, pacing slightly from side to side. "You know your people were allowed to settle in Sosúa, but you are not permitted open movement as you aren't citizens. We could just take you back to the settlement."

I took in a deep breath to calm myself. "Lieutenant, do you have children?" I said.

"My life is not your concern," he said, puffing out his chest and taking a step toward me. "It's your life that should concern you at the moment."

I sensed José moving closer to me on my right and slipped my left hand to the dagger hidden in the fold of my pants.

"Señor, I have no more time for this," the lieutenant said. "It's a slow trip back to Puerto Plata. Where is the girl?"

"Teniente, I am asking you to go, now," I said, puffing out my chest and taking a step toward him. I felt my heart in my mouth, my dry tongue making it difficult for me to speak.

"Give us the girl and we'll go. She'll be back in the morning," the lieutenant said, crossing his arms. "Do it for your new country, gringo."

I drew the dagger and lunged forward. The lieutenant grabbed my wrist and turned me, throwing me to the ground. I could see José out of the corner of my eye reaching for the machete he had placed on the ground. The lieutenant called out to his guards. Three surrounded José, their guns drawn.

"Drop the machete now," one of them shouted at José, "or I'll shoot you." The other two grabbed me and held me down on the ground, smashing my hand repeatedly until I dropped the dagger.

"Stand him up," shouted the lieutenant.

They dragged me to my feet. The lieutenant dropped his gun and swung his fist directly into my jaw. I'm not sure whether I heard the crack of the bone or felt the pain first. The punch would have knocked me off my feet if the two soldiers hadn't been holding me up.

"Where is the girl?" shouted the lieutenant again.

"Here I am," screamed Anabela, standing in the front door of the casita.

"No," I screamed through the pain. "Run to the settlement, Erno will help you."

"No, no more running, no more hiding," she screamed. "You want me?" She banged her palm against her chest. "Take me."

"You two, take her," the lieutenant screamed at two of the men surrounding José.

They dropped their guns and ran toward her. As the first one reached her, she pulled a long sharpened stick from behind her and plunged it into his chest. He dropped to the ground in front of her, a puddle of blood seeping out of him. The second man stopped short in his tracks.

"Take her," screamed the lieutenant.

The second guard hesitated for a moment, then moved forward. As he neared Anabela, Nereida came running through the door with a cast iron pot. She heaved it over her head, tossing the liquid inside at the head of the soldier. He screamed as the nearly boiling oil covered him.

"Die," Nereida shouted at him. She turned toward the lieutenant. "Take that back to El Jefe."

The lieutenant raised his gun in silence. In the moment before he shot her, Nereida smiled at him, crossed her arms and raised her chin in a last gesture of defiance. The gunshot rang through my head. I watched as Nereida's body first stiffened, then crumbled and collapsed next to Anabela. Anabela knelt next to her and cradled her head in her arms, the blood from her chest staining Anabela's yellow dress.

José's screams were in my ears now. Out of one eye I saw his body strain against his captors. "Nereida, mi amor. I told you to go to the forest."

"She was your wife?" the lieutenant said, taking large strides to where his men were restraining José.

José said nothing. The lieutenant walked closer to him and hesitated a moment before punching him hard in the stomach and then in the chest. José fell to his knees, unable to catch his breath. I wanted to scream something to him but no sound came out of my mouth.

The lieutenant reached into his back pocket and pulled out a pistol. "Your wife and that bitch have already cost me two men," he said. He pointed the pistol at José at nearly point-blank range and pulled the trigger. The top of José's head flew off backwards with the force of the bullet. My knees gave way.

I watched as Anabela rose and ran toward José's body. The two men who had been guarding José let his body drop and grabbed her. She screamed. Her face contorted so that I could no longer recognize her. She grabbed her stomach as they grabbed her and held her down on the ground.

"I should take you myself, right here, you bitch," the lieutenant shouted standing over her, "but El Jefe wants you and I value my life." He turned toward me. "Maldito Judío, a bullet is too valuable for you. Pick him up, get him on his feet."

The lieutenant came at me and punched me hard in the stomach, then in the face, over and over again. I had never imagined such pain existed. My mind begged to slip into unconsciousness but my heart wouldn't let me. I stared at Anabela. She stared back at me, our eyes meeting. I pleaded for her forgiveness in words that never left my mouth. I knew her reply, "Te amo mi amor, por siempre."

I knew it was over, that I would soon be dead. I wanted her to be the last thing I saw. Instead the last thing I saw was the lieutenant picking up a large stone and hurling it at my head.

"And that's how I found him the next morning," Erno said to Tolya. "He was near death. José and Nereida were dead. The rest of the villagers hadn't returned, out of fear. They came to us at the settlement late that night. José and Max told them that they would come to them in the forest when it was over. They never came, so they fled to us."

"And the girl? Anabela?" Tolya asked.

"Never seen again. In those days that wasn't unusual. People disappeared all the time. The soldiers probably took her back to Trujillo, had her cleaned up, he had his way with her. Or they did the job for him if she was too badly damaged. No one will ever know. He raped thousands of young women."

"Cruelty," was all Tolya could manage. He took a sip of coffee. "So how did Max end up here with Helen?"

"We brought him back to the settlement. He nearly died a few times. It took more than a year for him to heal up. When the war was over, Fritzy learned of his family's fate. He and Robert, his brother, committed suicide together."

"Max's diaries mention their brother and sister being sent to Poland," Tolya said.

"How do you know that?" Erno asked.

"From the journals Karin translated for me."

"Of, course," Erno hesitated a moment. "Then you know that I was the one who brought Max the news of his family."

"Yes."

Erno drifted off for a moment. He cleared his throat. Tolya could see the pain in his eyes. The sixty years that had passed had not lessened that pain. "He was my best friend you know," Erno said. "The settlers in Sosúa left behind about 300 families in Europe. We had to do this almost 300 times. Can you imagine what that was like? Each time was as bad as the one before. That moment when your friend, your neighbor, your spouse or you yourself had to face the truth."

"I can't imagine."

"Because even now it's unimaginable." Erno let out a long slow sigh.

"So Max got back together with Helen?" Tolya asked.

"Yes," said Erno.

"That's kind of surprising after everything that happened."

"Not really. Despite what happened between them, they had each other and a common past. Max loved Anabela so deeply that he was incapable of starting any new relationship. He broke off his contact with the native community in El Batey. Remember, it wasn't just Anabela he lost. He lost José as well. He kept to himself.

"Then Fritzy killed himself and Max tried to comfort Helen. She was overwhelmed. About a month later, she got her letter. Her twelve brothers and sisters were confirmed dead along with her mother and father. One nephew had survived and went to Palestine. He confirmed the information the Red Cross had supplied. They all died in Auschwitz during one deportation in 1944. He was there. He had been selected for work, for life.

"She was suicidal. Ava begged Max to move back in with Helen to keep an eye on her. About a year later, Max's brother Jack was able to obtain visas for them to come to the U.S. They had no one else and, though Max loved the island, the pain of every memory was too much for him to stay."

"And you?" Tolya asked.

"We stayed about ten more years. The community shrank every year, till it was pretty much just the younger men who had married local women. Ava and I didn't fit in to their world." He smiled that smile that made him look young again. "So Max helped us come here. To try to start again…again."

28

"Good work, Kurchenko," the captain said, leaning back in his chair. "Welcome back."

"Thank you captain."

"I called Levitz," the captain replied.

"Why?" asked Pete.

"To short-circuit the drama." The captain handed the file to Tolya.

Tolya thumbed through the file absently. "What time we doing this, Cap?" he asked.

"The shiva is over this morning. We'll be there around 11. Make sure you've got everything we need, and no cameras."

Tolya stood with the captain and Pete just north of the corner of Bennett Avenue and 187th Street. They watched Shalom walk up the street, followed by his father-in-law and Levitz.

"Explain this to us again, please," Pete said.

"It's an old custom," Tolya said. "In Europe, when the shiva period ended they would walk around the house three times. Here, they walk around the block."

"Did you do that?" Pete asked.

"Nah." Tolya smirked. "I'm a modern Soviet man. No superstitions for me."

"They've turned the corner," said the captain. "Let's give them about ten minutes."

"I wish we could give them more than that. I don't want to do this," said Tolya.

Pete and the captain both looked at Tolya. "Boy, what a difference a couple of days off make," said the captain.

Tolya knocked loudly on the door of Rothman's apartment.

"One moment," a voice called from inside.

"Levitz," the captain said. "You know, once I told him what we'd uncovered, his whole attitude changed. He went from attack mode to helpful."

The door opened. Tolya looked directly into Levitz's eyes and saw only sadness. "Please come in detectives, captain," Levitz said, moving out of the entry foyer.

"Have you told Rothman yet?" the captain asked Levitz.

"His father-in-law is telling him now."

Tolya exchanged glances with Pete. "I don't envy him," he said.

"Where is Mrs. Rothman?" Pete asked.

"With her mother in the bedroom," Levitz answered.

"And Baruch?" asked Tolya.

"Here," said Levitz.

Tolya, Pete and the captain followed Levitz down the long hallway to the living room past the stacks of books. Shalom sat silently on the edge of the couch with his hands clasped together. His face was gray, the edge of his beard wet with tears. Baruch sat at Shalom's feet looking at the same book of photographs as the last time Tolya was here. The rabbi sat next to him, swaying back and forth and weeping. Shalom rose from the couch and extended his hand to Tolya.

"Please, Shalom, don't get up," Tolya said, his voice cracking. When he looked at the boy sitting there, a wave of sadness passed over him. Who won here, really? So he'd solved the case, he'd figured it out. Mostly it was dumb luck and this family was destroyed. He knew he was thinking more like a parent now and less like a child.

"No, I insist," Shalom said. "I asked you to do something for me detective and you did. Now I need to face the truth, if it is the truth."

"I'm sorry Shalom," Tolya said.

The captain turned to Levitz. "What have you told her?" he asked.

Levitz looked at Shalom, then at the rabbi, then back to the captain, everyone standing now, no one knowing exactly where to turn or look. "That you have new evidence and want to speak with all of us together."

"Could you bring her in here please?" the captain said.

"Of course," Levitz said, then walked toward the bedroom.

Shalom turned to Tolya. "Detective, I want to speak to Rachel before you arrest her. I want to hear the truth from her."

Tolya looked at Pete and the captain, both of them nodding in agreement. "OK Shalom, you go first. But understand we have to take her into custody."

"I understand," Shalom said, his tears flowing freely now.

When Levitz returned with Rachel, Tolya watched Shalom's face as he took Rachel's hand. He thought of his mother and the expression in her eyes every time she looked at his father through the chain-link fence, standing in the knee-deep snow in the depth of a Siberian winter. It was that same look.

No matter what he did or said, she never stopped loving him. He realized that there was nothing Karin could ever do to make him love her less.

Rachel sat down on the couch next to where Baruch was sitting on the floor. "Papa, why are you crying?" she asked. The rabbi remained silent.

Shalom sat down next to her. "My love, the detectives think they have found the person responsible for my father's death and they wanted to speak to us about it."

"But we know who did it," Rachel said, rubbing her hands on her apron, "that boy, that awful boy."

Shalom took her hand, turning toward her slightly on the couch. "No Rachel, you know that's not true."

Rachel pulled her hands back slowly from Shalom's and clasped them on her lap. "Of course he did this. Who else would have?"

The rabbi's weeping became more audible. "Mendele, why are you crying?" Rachel's mother asked, sitting beside him.

Shalom reached for Rachel's face and caressed her cheek gently. "Rachel, you know how much I love you."

"Yes, but why are you saying that?" She pulled back a little, her tiny frame folding in on itself.

"Because I have to ask you a question." He touched her cheek again.

"Shalom, you're frightening me," Rachel said.

"I'm sorry, my darling. Rachel, did you visit my father that afternoon before he was attacked?"

"I told you, no. I hadn't seen him in a few days."

Shalom looked down at the floor before continuing. "Rachel, why would you not tell me the truth?"

"I am," she said.

"Mrs. Rothman," interrupted the captain. "I'm afraid we have evidence to the contrary."

Rachel turned toward the captain and opened her mouth. Instead of words, she began to dry heave, her tiny body jackknifing twice. Shalom grabbed her to steady her.

"What are you talking about?" her mother shouted, jumping up from the couch. She quickly took the few steps across the living room and instinctively placed herself between her daughter and the captain.

"We have a surveillance tape from the rear of the convenience store behind the building Max Rothman lived in that shows your daughter entering and exiting the building at 5 p.m. and 5:38 p.m. on the day of the attack," Pete said.

"That proves nothing," shouted Rachel's mother. "Perhaps she forgot, she's so busy all the time," she said, turning toward Shalom. "You think she has an easy time caring for Baruch and keeping the house and helping us? To say nothing of her responsibility for your father."

"Mama, please," said Shalom through his tears. "There's more you don't understand." He got on his knees in front of Rachel. "My darling, please tell me what happened. I won't be angry, please, I just want to understand."

"Nothing happened, nothing," Rachel mumbled, looking away from him. "Nothing."

Tolya couldn't stand it any longer. The scene was excruciating. "Mrs. Rothman," he said, "I'm sorry, but then how do you explain this?" He threw the evidence bag containing her bloodied gloves onto the coffee table.

"Where did you…?" Rachel screamed. Jarred by the sudden noise, Baruch jumped up and started screaming. Shalom rose quickly from his knees and moved around Rachel to Baruch, taking him gently around the shoulders and steadying him. He walked him over to the other corner of the room and sat him at the desk. He returned to Rachel to calm her. "Rachel, please sit down. It's time for the truth. My father's blood is on your gloves."

Rachel crumpled into the corner of the couch. Her mother began to hyperventilate. Rachel looked at Baruch sitting across the room, oblivious to what was going on around him, and waved her hand in his direction. "It was all his fault. That's why Baruch is like this."

"Excuse me?" Tolya said.

Shalom looked at Tolya but didn't answer him. Instead he sat next to his wife on the couch. "Rachel, you know that's not true."

"Yes, yes it is," she said. "HaShem was punishing your father through us."

"Punishing him?" Pete whispered to Tolya.

"*Meine tochter**,*" the rabbi said, moving toward Rachel, tears covering his face. "How I've failed you. I'm so sorry."

---

* *Meine tochter*: My daughter (Yiddish)

"No papa, you never failed me," she said, reaching up and touching his face. "You told me, you taught me, HaShem is like our parents. When we fulfill his desires, he rewards us. When we disregard him, he turns away from us and punishes us."

"But he hasn't punished us," Shalom said, taking her hands in his again.

"Yes he has, he did this to Baruch," she said, withdrawing her hands and pointing at Baruch.

"No he didn't," said Shalom. "He blessed us with Baruch." He dried his eyes and tried to calm her, taking her arms and putting them at her side.

"He was a brilliant child," she said. "Look what happened."

"And why do you think he punished you, my child?" asked the rabbi.

"Because Max was spared, but he turned away from HaShem," she said, looking up at her father. "What happened to Baruch was our fault. HaShem chose to punish us all. It was our responsibility to bring Max back to HaShem. We didn't do enough."

A silence descended on the room. Tolya watched as Shalom and the rabbi looked at each other. Shalom stood up straight as the old man slumped onto the couch next to Rachel. "I told you she believed this and you dismissed me."

"I'm sorry, *mein zindel*," he said and began to cry again. "How could this happen to us?"

"I know you are," Shalom said. "Leave her to me. Go to *Ima*, please, and help her." Shalom then turned back to Rachel. "Darling, please tell me what happened."

Rachel looked at him, her eyes searching his face for comfort. "Will I go to jail?"

"I don't know, but HaShem respects and commands the truth. Please Rachel."

Rachel sat back on the couch. With her hands on her lap and her eyes cast off somewhere else, she began. "I went to see him. I let myself in from the back with my key."

"Where was my father?"

"He was sitting up in the bed."

"Why did you go to see him?"

Rachel whimpered a little and then sighed. "It was Simchat Torah. I wanted to beg him one last time to become *ba'al t'shuvah*. He laughed at me again. I told him how Baruch had been improving since you and he had begun studying parshot together, and that was proof that Baruch was like this because of him, and that if he made t'shuva Baruch would continue to improve. He laughed at me, told me I was a stupid, superstitious woman, that I should step into the modern world and stop blaming him."

As Rachel took a breath, the rabbi put his arm around his weeping wife. "Why didn't we see this?" she asked him through her tears.

Rachel wiped her eyes and sat up straight against the high-backed couch. "He told me that you weren't studying together, that he was simply pointing out to you where you were wrong in your analysis of the scripture." Rachel paused for a moment. Her face became agitated. "I begged him to return, to do something, to keep kosher, that I would come and cook for him. He told me he'd rather starve, to leave him in peace. I begged him to at least read some psalms. I saw your mother's prayer book on the dresser. I brought it to him and begged him. I put it in his hands and he threw it on the floor."

Rachel stopped again. She bent down, reenacting what had happened. "I picked up the book. I was so angry. It was so heavy. I looked at him. He shouted at me again to take my superstitions and leave him." Her voice was rising now. Her hands were in the air in front of her face. "I asked him, 'How could you throw HaShem's word on the floor?' And he laughed. 'HaShem's word?' he said. 'Those words were written by men to control other men. Men just like your father and his father before him.'

"I don't know why," she said as she lifted her arms over her head into the air. "I lifted the book and I hit him with it. How dare he insult HaShem so?"

"How many times did you hit him?" Tolya asked, moving toward Rachel from the back of the room.

Rachel looked up at him, her eyes vacant now. "I don't recall."

"Detective, please read Mrs. Rothman her rights," said the captain.

"You have the right to remain silent..." Tolya began, the sound of his own voice incomprehensible to him at that moment. He watched as Rachel laid her head on Shalom's shoulder. When he finished, Shalom silently helped Rachel from the couch and handed her over to Pete. Tolya looked over toward Shalom and, for the first time, felt sorry for him.

Pete took the handcuffs from his pocket. Shalom reached out to stop him.

"Pete," said Tolya. "I don't think that will be necessary."

"Thank you detective," said Shalom.

"Will you be accompanying your wife to the precinct?" Tolya asked.

"Yes," Shalom said. "*Abba*, can you and *Ima* stay here with Baruch for a little while?"

The rabbi nodded his head. "Of course," the rabbi answered through his weeping.

"Let me get our coats," Shalom said, walking toward the stairs to the hallway. He stopped briefly by his desk where Baruch was sitting, bent down and kissed him on the top of his head. "You're a blessing Baruch, just like your name," he said, then touched Baruch's cheek as he stepped away from him. Baruch stopped studying the book of pictures for a moment and looked up at Shalom.

Tolya thought he detected the slightest smile around Baruch's mouth. It was then he realized that the miracle of birth was not just that a baby was born, but also that a father was born with him, that the bond was immediate and everlasting. Tolya waited a moment, then followed Shalom into the hallway. He placed a hand on Shalom's shoulder. "I'm sorry," he said.

"You needn't be," Shalom said. "You only led us to the truth. You know detective, the Hebrew word for truth, *Emet*, is also one of the ways we refer to HaShem ."

"What will you do now?" Tolya asked.

"What I've always done: love my wife and my son."

29

Tolya watched the front door of the restaurant from the booth at the back. Karin had called him when she heard about the arrest. It had taken a bit of convincing to get her to meet him for dinner. He looked at his watch. He saw her through the window and smiled to himself. Every time he looked at her he felt it in his stomach. He stood up and waved as she entered the restaurant. As she dodged the tightly packed tables, her dark hair fell in front of her face, hiding her smile just a little. She came around the table to him and kissed him lightly on the lips. The scent of her lifted him.

"Congratulations, detective," she said and sat down across from him. He reached out his hand and entwined his fingers in hers. "Honestly, I've missed you."

"Gracias, igual," he said. He took her other hand in his.

She pulled back from him. "Not so fast."

"Why?" he asked, trying to take her hand again.

"Because it's too soon," she said, moving away from him.

"Karin, I love you."

"I know that, but..."

"No, I love you and the...our baby."

She looked up at him and smiled. "I think you're just saying that. A few days ago you didn't want this child."

"A lot has happened in a few days."

She hesitated and looked out the window at the traffic rambling down Broadway. "You can't turn around that fast."

"I want to tell you something," he said, reaching out and touching her shoulder. "Something I've never told anyone."

"A little dramatic, don't you think, amor?"

"No, I'm serious." He could hear his accent thickening. "I want to tell you how Oleg died."

"I know how he died, you told me. Tuberculosis."

"I didn't tell you the whole thing."

Archangelsk
Soviet Union
Feb 26, 1977
Noon

They stood outside the gate of the gulag for what seemed like hours. The snow and wind swirled around them, the world a blinding white two-dimensional image. Finally, he saw a bent over creature in rags trudging through the snow toward them. The figure was thinner and more ragged than the last time they had seen him.

When his father arrived at the fence, Tolya looked into his face. His eyes were sunken into his head, his beard was full and what skin you could see had a yellowish tinge to it. This man wasn't his father. It was someone who had stolen his father's body and destroyed it.

"Did you bring me bread?" the mouth under the sunken eyes asked them.

"Nyet, my love, we had none to bring," his mother said, taking the glove off her hand to touch his hand through the fence.

"I didn't expect to see you till next week," the skeleton said. "Where is Oleg?"

"I have something to tell you," she said. Her voice had become monotone in the three days since the doctor had given them the truth about Oleg. "Oleg is very sick."

His father's eyes remained vacant. He waited for her to continue.

"He has tuberculosis," she said, dropping to her knees. The sound of her weeping began anew. Tolya's father remained silent.

"He's in the hospital," she said, her voice cracking. "He needs medicine. My ration is used up. Boris, you have to do something. Maybe you could bribe the guards. He is going to die." Her weeping grew worse with each sentence and her body heaved with each plea.

His father held her hand through the fence, the blackened tips of his fingers resting gently on hers. "There is nothing to be done," he said as if he were talking about a broken vase.

"Boris, please." She looked up into his eyes.

He smiled. "He is our ticket out," his father said, bending down and moving closer to her face, the mist of his breath frozen around the hairs of his unkempt beard. "When he dies you will contact the World Conference on Soviet Jewry through Ivan Kislov and tell them what has happened. They will move us to the top of the list."

His mother collapsed into the snow. She banged her fist against the white powder. The only audible sound was her wailing as she begged him. "Please Boris please, do something. Help me save him."

He withdrew his hand from her shoulder with a jerk. He stood straight and said, "We cannot save him. We must save ourselves. I am too important to the movement to stay in this camp. They need me in Israel to continue my research."

Tolya couldn't believe what he heard. He felt the vomit rocket out of him. What little he had eaten in the past day now lay on the snow as so much yellow mucus. He looked at this man who would sacrifice his son for his own freedom and hated him. Yet, in his gut, he was somehow relieved. He knew Oleg was already gone. If his father was right, they would leave this evil place.

"Now you know," Tolya said, noticing the tracks of the tears that had slipped down Karin's face.

"I'm sorry," she said. "I know how much Oleg meant to you."

He stared at the table, unable to look Karin in the eye. "My father was a bastard and I was afraid I'd be like him."

"You're not him, amor," Karin said, reaching across the table for Tolya's hand. "And you were a child, there's nothing you could have done to save him."

"I realize that now," he said. He looked into Karin's face. "I want this baby too. I want our baby with you."

Karin walked around the table and sat down next to Tolya. "Are you sure?"

"Yes I am." He kissed her gently on the lips.

"If it's a boy, would you like to name him Oleg?" Karin asked.

"No," said Tolya. "I think I want to name him Max."

Washington Heights
NYC
22 February, 2006
1 p.m.

Epilogue

"I'm happy to hear this news from you, Tolya," said Erno. "This is my one great regret, you know."

"That you never had children?" Tolya replied between bites of his sandwich.

"Yes. When is the baby coming?"

"It's a long way off, about four months."

"I hope I live that long," Erno said.

"It's a boy. Perhaps you'll come to the bris?"

"Well," Erno said, putting down his sandwich and smiling. "Another surprise."

"I'm trying to rid myself of all my demons," Tolya said. "You know Erno, I had an unusual upbringing for a Jew…or a half-Jew, or whatever it is I am."

"What do you mean?"

"Well, as a kid in the Soviet Union we didn't know anything about being Jewish. We were Communists and Russians. Then when my father asked to emigrate we were suddenly targeted, cut off like lepers."

"I know that feeling well."

"Then we came here and I was so confused. My parents wanted me to have some connection. We went to a rabbi, who it turns out was Rachel Rothman's father, and he told us as far as he was concerned I wasn't a Jew because my mother's mother was a gentile."

"We spend a lot of time defining one another in these terms, unfortunately."

"Sadly yes. But over the past few months, especially learning your stories, you and Max and Sosúa, I've come to feel a connection I never did before. I think there's something important in it, both as a Jew and as a human being, and I want my son to have a connection to it."

"I'm glad about that," Erno said. "Keep thinking that way and you'll be a terrific father." Erno looked off toward the window frosted by last night's snow flurries, momentarily far, far away. "Our story was both joyous and sad, you know. We were refugees in paradise, only I don't think we knew it at the time. We were too busy surviving." He picked up the sandwich from the plate on his lap and took a bite. He savored it. "And making cheese and salami. We made very good salami at Sosúa."

"So you've told me," Tolya said, taking a bite from his sandwich as well.

"I still love a good salami," Erno said.

"Me too." They both laughed. "Erno what was it you wanted to see me about."

Erno downed the crust of his lunch and looked at Tolya. "We never finished Max's diaries."

"I thought we had."

Erno lifted the small gray volume from the table beside him. "We never discussed this one. As it turns out, I never knew any of this and it was written in Hungarian. It explains a lot."

Tolya leaned forward. "Tell me…"

Genoa
Italy
1 V '40
9 a.m.

Istvan and I sat huddled over the radio in the master bedroom of the suite, the curtains drawn over the doors leading to the balcony. Helen and Magda were in the salon waiting for us. The broadcast was in Italian. Neither of us spoke it well enough to understand exactly what was being said, though the reality of the Axis attack on France was clear enough. The real war had started.

"What are we going to do?" Istvan asked.

"I don't know yet. We have to see what Mussolini does. It might make it easier to cross over into France if Italy is occupying it. Then we just have to get to Spain."

"That's not what I was asking Mischka," Istvan said. I saw the fear on his face. "You heard the edicts. All non-Italian Jews must leave the country at once. Where are we going to go?"

I got up from the chair and paced for several minutes before answering. "No place, yet. They have to give us some time."

"The edict was clear," Istvan replied. "It said immediately, or be interred in a camp."

"That's better than deportation," I said.

He put one hand on my shoulder. "In the end they'll deport us anyway. You know that."

"What are they saying?" Magda called from the other room.

"What do you want to tell them?" Istvan asked me in a low voice.

"Nothing yet," I whispered. I felt my stomach turn. Where had I led us?

301

The room was so dark with the curtains drawn. I longed for a little sunlight. I went to open the curtains but Helen stopped me.

"The concierge said to keep all the draperies drawn," she said.

I paced in the small space between the bed and the bureau. "Helen, please. What you're asking is impossible. I can't send them back."

She sat at the edge of the bed. "Mischka, we have no choice, we're almost out of money," she said, holding a pile of bills in her hand.

"That's not possible." I stopped pacing.

She rose from her perch. "But it is," she said. "We've been here in this suite for months." She gestured around the room, some of the bills falling to the floor. She sat down on the bed again with her back to me. "You've been living like a lord. Fancy dinners, gambling. I told you we didn't have the money to bring them to begin with but you insisted…"

I walked around the bed to face her. "How could I leave them? He's my twin brother."

"The same way we left everyone else," she said. "I left my sisters, my mother, my nieces and nephews."

"It's not the same," I said, waving my hand at her.

"It isn't Istvan you won't leave, it's Magda."

"Helen, please don't start that again."

She crossed her arms. "I see the way you look at her, the same way you've always looked at her. You're in love with her and you can't bear to leave her behind. And she's your brother's wife." Even in the semi-darkness I could see the anger in her face and tears well up in her eyes.

I came up to her to confront her. "That's what's behind this?" I said, lowering my voice so as not to be heard through the door. "It's not the money. You think I'm in love with her, that I'll leave you for her? Ask yourself this question: Would I do that to my brother?"

She turned away. She was right. I was in love with Magda. I had been since the first time I'd seen her. Our father had decided she was a better match for Istvan, and so it was. Istvan had married Magda and I was matched with Helen. Helen's father provided a dowry big enough to support all of us. When I asked my father why it hadn't been the other way around, he said because I had the more level head for business. Istvan wouldn't be able to handle the pressures. He was too much of a dreamer. Perhaps my father was wrong to think of me as any different.

"You'll take Magda into hiding with you and Istvan and I will go to the camp to wait this out," I said, slipping into the deep velvet chair and covering my eyes with my hands.

"That won't work," said Helen. "We don't have enough money to pay the woman to hide both of us and provide us with food from the black market. And she only has one bed. Besides, what would the two of us do if both of you were deported back to Slovakia and we were still in hiding?"

"We won't be deported," I shouted.

"You don't know that," she snapped at me. "And don't dare shout at me."

I looked up at her standing over me. "I won't send them back," I said.

"You have to tell them," she said.

"I can't." I felt the knot in my stomach tighten.

"Then I will." She turned and walked out of the room. I heard the front door of the suite slam shut.

I tapped gently on the door of the second bedroom.

"Yes, who is it?" Magda called out.

"Mishka," I answered.

The door opened slowly. Magda stood half hidden behind it. She smiled up at me weakly. I marveled at how delicate her features were, the complete opposite of Helen's.

"Istvan went out," she said. "He said he needed some air to think."

"May I come in?" I asked.

"Of course," Magda said, opening the door. I looked around and over my shoulder as I entered.

Magda stood by the window, her slight willowy frame outlined by the brilliant spring sunshine streaming into the room. She had opened the curtains, despite the hotel's instructions to the contrary. "What are we going to do, Mischka?" she said.

I moved across the room to her and touched her arm. How soft her skin was.

"Magda, run away with me now," I said.

She stared at me. "Max what are you saying?" she said, then pulled back. "Is this a joke? Nothing is funny at a time like this."

"No," I said sinking to my knees. "It's not a joke. I mean it. I love you. I'm in love with you and have been since the first moment I saw you. We could escape, the two of us. I have the key to the safe. I'll take the money and the jewelry and we'll disappear right now."

She recoiled from me. "I'm your brother's wife," she said. "Your twin brother. How could you even suggest such a thing? And besides, I love Istvan. I adore him, I would never leave him for anyone, even for my life."

I stood up. I thought I might vomit. I turned away from her at first, then back toward her. I reached out to her again, but she pulled away. She walked to the other side of the bed, putting it between us.

"I'm sorry Magda, I don't know what came over me," I said, my heart broken in too many pieces. I turned away from her in shame. What had I just done? "Please forgive me," I begged her. "Please don't tell Istvan what I said."

I felt her eyes burning into the back of my neck. "I won't tell Istvan and I will keep up a charade in front of him," she said. "I would never hurt him like that. Never speak to me in private again. Please leave, now."

I walked through the door and closed it behind me, then fell to my knees and wept.

I stood on the platform of the main railway station in the center of Genoa, facing Istvan. "Don't go, please," I said.

"We have to," he replied. "You know that. There is no choice, there's no money. We'll be OK. You'll send for us when you get to wherever you end up. We'll be together soon." He squeezed my arm gently. "Besides, Magda is tired. She can't do this anymore. The running away is too much for her. She misses her parents and her brothers."

I felt my chest tighten. I put my hand on Istvan's shoulder and pulled him close. Istvan wrapped his arms around me tightly. I started to cry. "I can't let you go," I said through the tears. "You're like my heart. You've been there always, no matter what, at every moment."

"You'll be fine," Istvan said, continuing to embrace me. "So will we. It's only for a little while. Get to someplace, find us a home and then send for us."

I could feel Istvan's tears on my cheek. "Promise me I'll be with you always in your heart," I said through my tears.

"You will be, and I with you, always."

The sound of the conductor calling the train broke our solitude. I looked up at the window. Magda was waving at us as the train prepared to depart.

"Istvan," I said, "I have something to tell you, something to confess. I did a terrible thing."

Istvan smiled at me and pulled me close to him again. "No, don't, brother. I know. And I forgive you. I've always known, from the first night we met her."

I began to weep again. "Is that why you're going?"

"No, and you know that. There's no other way." The train whistle blasted its three-minute warning.

"Swear to me that you forgive me," I said, dropping to my knees.

Istvan extended his hands to me and pulled me up to him. He smiled. "Of course I do."

"You're not angry?" I asked, looking deep into his eyes. He was a million miles away from the horror we were facing.

"No, my dearest brother, how could I be?" he said. "Life is too short to make enemies of those we love."

A.J. Sidransky is a longtime resident of Washington Heights, New York. He travels frequently to the Dominican Republic. He has written several articles and short stories. This is his debut novel.

Made in the USA
Lexington, KY
20 February 2015